The Uncertain Heart

Heart Series, Book One
Rebecca's Story

*In loving memory of Mildred Taylor,
formerly of The Woodlands, Texas,
now resting in the arms of Jesus.
We shared the belief Georgette Heyer set the
gold standard for Regency era novels.*

Acknowledgements

Some people are irreplaceable in my life.

Foremost is my husband, James T. Ellis. He has been my unfailing support in too many ways to count throughout our fifty-four plus years of marriage and especially during those times when my mind was so busy with characters vying for my attention that I didn't hear him.

No one produces a book without considerable help from others. I'm fortunate to have known and worked with people who willingly listened to me as I droned on about my stories.

Dawn Aldridge Poore (author of Regency mystery and romance series (https://www.amazon.com›Dawn-Aldridge-Poore) and my niece, who chooses to be anonymous, did major jobs nitpicking my Regency novels.

Elgin and Melissa Cook gave expert assistance on the cover picture. https://www.amazon.com/Call-Last-Frontier-Twenty-Year-Adventure-ebook/dp/B09K2WWJ8F?ref_=ast_author_mpb

Randolph Shaffner shared his publishing expertise in the publication of this book.

My endless appreciation to all.

Books by Peggy Lovelace Ellis

Regency
Heart Series
The Uncertain Heart, Book One

Short Stories
Silver Shadows, Stories of Life in a Small Town

Anthologies
Challenges on the Home Front, World War II
(Second Edition)
A Beautiful Life and Other Stories
Lest the Colors Fade

The Uncertain Heart

Heart Series, Book One
Rebecca's Story

Peggy Lovelace Ellis

Faraway Publishing

Copyright © Peggy Lovelace Ellis
All rights reserved

No part of this book may be used, reproduced, or transmitted in any form or by any means, electronic or mechanical, including photo-copying, recording, or by any information storage or retrieval system, excepting brief quotes used in connection with reviews, without the express written permission of the writer, except where permitted by law.

Peggy Lovelace Ellis
76 Wagon Trail
Black Mountain, NC 28711-2565
https://www.peggyellis.com

First Edition

2023

Printed and bound in the United States of America
Published by Faraway Publishing
125 Spring View Drive
Black Mountain, NC 28711

ISBN: 978-0-9710130-6-3

The Uncertain Heart
Heart Series, Book One
By Peggy Lovelace Ellis

1. Historical Romance; 2. Regency Romance; 3. Regency Morals and Manners; 4. The Regency *ton*; 5. Napoleonic Wars; 6. Wellington; 7. Regency Nobility; 8. George III; 9. The Prince Regent; 10. Regency Vernacular; 11. Child Labor

An Overview of the Heart Series

In 1774, three ten-year-old girls living in Somerset, England, made a decision which had a far-reaching effect on their lives.

Bright sunshine had found its way through the barred windows of the nursery at Shelburne Park, reflecting on the tousled curls of the three young misses sitting on the window seat.

Becca, the fair-haired pampered daughter of the earl who owned this estate, held sway over her two visitors, Louise the raven-haired only child of a duke, and Marie the auburn-haired offspring of a vicar.

Suddenly, Becca bounced to her feet and whirled around the room. "I have the most wonderful idea! When we grow up, we will each have a daughter and give her all three of our names. They will be best friends just as we are."

"Will the names not be confusing? I mean, with mother and daughter having the same name?"

"No, Marie. We will give our daughters our own names as their third name."

Becca continued without waiting for another question. "My daughter will be Marie Louise Rebecca. Your daughter will be the Louise Rebecca Marie, and Louise's daughter will be Rebecca Marie Louise."

After some squabbling over the best order of their names, both Marie and Louise capitulated to Becca's insistence.

Years passed, as years will do. These three girls became young ladies and entered adulthood still the best of friends.

Table of Contents

Prologue   (1)
Chapter   1—Those Haunting Blue Eyes   (3)
Chapter   2—Chance Meetings   (19)
Chapter   3—Shelburne Shares His Frustrations   (29)
Chapter   4—An Earl Comes to Tea   (41)
Chapter   5—Vanishing in Green Park   (53)
Chapter   6—Surprising Encounters   (65)
Chapter   7—Friends?   (83)
Chapter   8—Tribulations of Separation   (97)
Chapter   9—Unwelcome Attention   (111)
Chapter 10—Military Intrusion   (123)
Chapter 11—Uncertain Tempers   (139)
Chapter 12—An Unexpected Visitor   (155)
Chapter 13—Shelburne Intervenes   (167)
Chapter 14—Happy, Yet Unhappy   (183)
Chapter 15—Reunion   (203)
Chapter 16—Country Pursuits   (215)
Chapter 17—Vigilance Relaxed   (231)
Chapter 18—The Military Intervenes   (245)
Chapter 19—Caught!   (257)
Chapter 20—The Countess Comes Calling   (269)

Prologue

An Orphanage in Hampshire, England, 1800

"Girls, a new friend has come to live with us, is that not exciting?"

An assortment of little girls looked up from their play and stared at a tiny slip of a child with a finger in her mouth, her black hair a mass of curls. Tears stood in her blue eyes.

"Yes, Mrs. Dysart." Their reply came in concert as they gathered around the newcomer. Some children could barely walk. The eldest girl, who appeared to be about ten years old, appointed herself the leader as she shepherded the younger children in front of her, tightly clasping the hands of two toddlers. When one stumbled, she patiently helped her back on her feet.

"This is Rebecca Black, who is six years old. Her mama has gone to heaven to live with Jesus, so Rebecca has come to live with us." Mrs. Dysart glanced at the older girls. "We will all let her play with our toys, will we not?"

"Yes, Mrs. Dysart!"

A chubby child wearing her auburn hair in braids walked closer. "Rebecca is one of my names. Do you have others?"

Rebecca opened her quivering lips. "My name is Rebecca Marie Louise."

The other child's hazel eyes grew wide. "Oh! Those are all my names, only in a different order. My name is Louise Rebecca Marie. Am I not right, Mrs. Dysart?"

"Yes, Louise, those are certainly your names. This is an interesting coincidence. Louise is the same age as you, Rebecca, so you have two things in common already."

Louise took the newcomer by the hand. "We have the same names, so we will be special friends. Come see our picture books now. We have lots. Can you read? I can teach you. We will be bestest friends for always!"

Chapter 1

Those Haunting Blue Eyes

London 1812

Placing his high-crowned beaver at its usual jaunty angle, Edward John Carlisle Cecil, Tenth Earl of Shelburne, paused outside Hatchard's Book Store. There, he perused a passing female strolling by on Piccadilly. There was a hint of long limbs as her skirts swayed which gave him a glimpse of slender ankles. Shelburne lifted his gaze to her face and met her astonishing blue eyes. The clatter of carriages and the boisterous shouts of friends greeting friends receded. The earl ignored the crowd shoving past him. Nothing existed at that moment except those eyes, dark blue and filled with shadows. He stared until delicate color flooded her face, and she turned away. He watched her until she and her companion passed from his view around a corner.

"I say, Shelburne, are you listening to me?" Sir Vincent Morrison tapped him on the arm.

"Did you see her?" Shelburne demanded. "She looks familiar, but I can't place her."

"Which one? Seems to me you have quite a choice." Affecting a languid air, the dandy raised his quizzing glass and surveyed the street. "I wouldn't mind getting acquainted with the one wearing the pink bonnet with three plumes. Fetching, is it not?"

"No, no, not her," Shelburne protested. "The one who turned the corner. She's tall for a female, raven hair and those eyes that look like they were put in with smudgy fingers."

"I don't believe I ever heard you wax poetical. Next thing we know you'll write an ode to her orbs."

"*Moi* write poetry?" he joked. "Perish the thought. Oh well, let's forget her. I thought I might get into a game at Watier's. Are you interested?"

Vincent agreed, although he admitted he didn't know why he subjected himself to so much abuse. "I always lose to you. It's deuced unfair you should be so lucky at both love and cards."

Shelburne gave him a light buffet on the shoulder and they continued their way toward the club most favored by gentlemen of the *ton*.

Stepping through the hallowed portals of Watier's, Shelburne's first sight was of Beau Brummell reclining in a leather chair, legs stretched before him, wafting a bumper of brandy beneath his nose.

The beau placed the glass on the table at his elbow then lifted his quizzing glass to one sleepy eye. He acknowledged Shelburne's presence with a languid wave, then stared in horror at the sight following the earl into the room. "I say, Shelburne, what is that with you, my dear boy? Send the thing away."

Shelburne stood aside controlling his twitching lips. The leading light of fashion, the arbiter of correct dress for gentlemen, stared at Vincent, who bristled at the insult.

"I take leave to inform you, Brummell, my attire is the height of fashion."

An expression of revulsion settled on the beau's pale face. "Fuchsia small clothes? Puce coat? It pains me to tell you this, Morrison, yet in the interest of my continued good health, I must. That color combination is nauseating. You may expect me to cast up my accounts at any moment."

Shelburne intervened before Sir Vincent could fly into a pelter. "We came to get into a game. Care to join us?"

"Macao?" Brummell's eyes lit up.

"Suits me." Shelburne knew that Brummell found Macao irresistible even though he seldom won.

Calling for a new deck of cards, they found an empty table. Shelburne grinned at the beau's obvious pleasure in winning the first game. However, a grimace replaced the grin when Brummell continued to win.

Vincent chortled. "Shelburne, I must say I never thought to see the day when you would run out of luck with the cards."

"They are against me today," Shelburne admitted and shoved them aside. He met Brummell's smug glance as the latter flicked open his snuffbox and lifted a pinch of snuff to his nostrils. A cascade of lace fell away revealing a pampered hand and wrist.

"No matter how much I practice, I cannot get the hang of taking snuff as you do." Vincent admired the beau's one-handed manipulation of a snuffbox. "No one partakes of snuff as well as you."

"Shall we get back to the cards?" The earl's brittle words interrupted Morrison's envious words.

"Why? You will only lose more of your blunt to Brummell." Morrison chortled again. "I've heard it said unlucky at cards, lucky in love. Perhaps your ill luck in cards will make you even luckier in love. Appears you will need all the luck you can muster with this new chit."

Shelburne knew his losing streak had nothing to do with luck. Try though he did, he was unable to concentrate on anything other than the female in question. Unsettling to say the least. No female had ever commanded his attention for any length of time, in particular a stranger he saw on the street. She should have disappeared into oblivion before he reached Watier's.

"Found a new *chère-amie*, have you, Shelburne?" The beau lifted his eyebrows inviting elucidation but was disappointed.

Shelburne pushed his chair away from the table. "You must recall Morrison has a vivid imagination," he replied, and with a bow, excused himself.

Strolling down the street, Shelburne's thoughts returned to a pair of haunting blue eyes. He wondered at the invisible cord which bound them. No, surely their closeness in those few seconds must be his imagination because no eyes could affect him so deeply. He ought to know. The much-in-demand Earl of Shelburne had been familiar with many eyes ever since his days at Eton.

Not hers. That thought still drummed in Shelburne's skull hours later when he sprawled in a massive leather chair, his booted feet resting on a stool, in his study. Flames curled around wood in the fireplace, sending sparks against the screen.

Shelburne knew beyond doubt he had seen her before. He searched his memory, bringing her entire face forward—the generous mouth, the straight nose, the rounded chin, eyes like no other. Those eyes had frowned at him at some time in the past.

This unknown young woman was lovely, quite out of the ordinary, even setting aside those haunting eyes. If he had not seen them, his life would have continued its mundane course of wine, cards, and females. Shelburne had seen them, though, and his life forever changed in that instant.

For some time after the incident in front of the book store, Rebecca Black's thoughts were all for the gentleman with incredible green eyes. They reminded her of the emerald necklace worn by the Duchess of Dorchester, patron of the orphanage where Rebecca lived from age six. She could not believe how the man had affected her. And to think, she had allowed herself to return his stare in such a brazen manner. Properly brought up females did not behave in such a way, she scolded herself. Matron had emphasized proper decorum to the girls times without number. Rebecca's thoughts slid back to her years in the orphanage where the matron had guided her natural exuberance into proper behavior.

Rebecca had all but forgotten her companion until the exasperated woman demanded, "Whatever is the rush? We were enjoying a leisurely stroll like rational human beings when you started imitating a horse at Epsom Downs."

"Now, Amelia, what do you know about horses at Epsom Downs?" Rebecca gave her a teasing smile but shortened her steps. "I beg your pardon. My mind was on other things and I failed to notice how fast I was walking."

"Other things! 'Pon rep, child, I have eyes in my head. That gentleman with the green eyes made you take off at a gallop." Mrs. Peters chuckled as she slipped her arm through Rebecca's. "You can't gammon me."

Rebecca bit her lip. "No such thing. I hardly noticed him. Besides, the rudesby should not have stared at me in such a way."

"Oh ho, Miss, hardly noticed him, did you? I never heard such a clanker. If you hardly noticed him, how did you know he was staring? Just tell me that if you can."

Thankfully, Rebecca was not obliged to answer, because how could she account for the heat in her face? They reached the house in Harley Street where she and her childhood friend, Louise Tracy, lived in a set of rooms with their companion, Amelia Peters.

[7]

Beyond doubt, two respectable girls, who had not yet reached their majority, could not live without a chaperone even in these enlightened times. She smiled at the doorman who ushered them into the large square hall.

"Good afternoon, Mrs. Peters, Miss Black. Miss Tracy sent a message she will return a little later than usual but will be here in time for dinner."

"Thank you, Mr. Jamison." Rebecca smiled and continued toward the broad, carpeted stairs leading to their rooms on the first floor.

Rebecca sifted her fingers through a bowl of rose potpourri setting on a cherry wood table in their small entrance hall. She had gathered the petals at the orphanage and felt a momentary loss because she was not there. Shaking off her thoughts, Rebecca motioned her companion into the drawing room where they spent most of their time. She pulled the bell rope, then sank onto a sofa with silk upholstery reflecting the apple green of the drapes and the darker green of the wing-backed chair Amelia occupied.

Waiting for the tea tray, Rebecca asked, "Do you like the dark blue fabric we saw at the drapery shop? I am unable to decide whether the white dots make the gown too frivolous for an employed female."

"Not at all, and with your nimble fingers, you can set the stitches in no time. 'Pon rep, never have I seen such a selection of fabric. One must be able to purchase every type of dress goods there instead of trotting all over town."

"I could spend all my wages there and overload my armoire," Rebecca confessed.

The duchess had encouraged her to develop her talent for figures, then had persuaded Mr. Wright, the orphanage man of business, to offer Rebecca a position in his London office. He did so even though public employment for a female was unheard of in 1812 polite society. Rebecca occupied a cupboard-sized room and few people knew she was there. Those who did looked askance at a female who poached on masculine preserves. She shook out her skirts as she rose to her feet. "However, I must use my funds in a more prudent manner."

"The duchess is most generous, though, in supplying us with a home as well as a cook and a footman," Amelia reminded her.

The widowed Duchess of Dorchester had no children of her own and lavished her affection on others. She also supported the girls' orphanage she established near her home in Hampshire upon the death of her only child, a daughter, some forty years earlier.

"To be sure she is, as well as in employing you as our companion," Rebecca added with a fond smile. "Louise and I are fortunate that she found you and that you are willing to accommodate us. Otherwise, I would have to find employment in an academy as a teacher or in a private residence as a companion. I don't relish the thought of giving up my freedom, which either of those occupations would entail."

As Amelia struggled to her feet, Rebecca pressed her shoulder. "No, my dear, you stay here and relax after that footrace I led you. I'll return the tea tray to the kitchen and offer my help to Mrs. Morton."

A short while later the hall door opened, then closed with a bang.

"Rebecca, Amelia, where are you?" Louise Tracy called when she burst into the drawing room. "I have two new pupils. Is that not stupendous? I must say, teaching merchants' daughters how to play the piano is a very lucrative livelihood. I'm truly grateful for the duchess's letter of recommendation."

With her laughter bubbling before her, Rebecca hurried from the kitchen. "We can see your day has been an eventful one. You must tell us every little detail over dinner."

Over baked chicken and asparagus salad, Mrs. Peters suggested Rebecca tell Louise about the dashing, green-eyed gentleman on Hatchard's steps. "He stared at her until we turned the corner."

"Amelia, how can you possibly know what he did?" Rebecca demanded.

"I looked back at him," she said with simple logic. "How else?"

"Oh, yes, do tell me," Louise implored. "Contrary to my hopeful expectations in Hampshire, I have yet to meet any dashing gentlemen. I'm glad to hear they do exist in London."

Sipping lemonade, Rebecca ignored Amelia's grin and tried to dampen Louise's natural curiosity. "I just glimpsed him in front of the book store as we walked by. Amelia is exaggerating the incident. I doubt I will see him again."

"Yes, you will," Louise assured her. "A meeting is just a matter of being in the right place at the right time. After all, you saw him this time."

"And you didn't plan or expect to see him, did you?" Amelia added her mite of encouragement. "So, we'll just be on the lookout for him every time we set foot out the door."

"Or you could place an item in the *Times*. Wanted: one emerald-eyed gentleman."

"Just think how many responses you might have to choose from," Amelia told her with a grin. "A regular parade would come to our door."

Rebecca joined their nonsense. "Or I might place a sketch of him in the shop windows with a notation: Do you know this gentleman?"

"Oh, I have a better idea!" Louise told her with a twinkle. "You could put the message on a placard and parade back and forth in front of the gentlemen's clubs,"

"Girls, girls," Amelia called them to order. "'Tis fun to speculate, but I saw a glint in the gentleman's eye that was not gentlemanly, so beware of him should you meet him again."

Later in her bedchamber, Rebecca donned her night robe and brushed her hair the requisite hundred strokes, still thinking of the handsome gentleman she had seen earlier. They had seemed closely attuned as their gazes held for those few seconds. She lay sleepless in bed for what seemed like hours, staring at the ceiling before she managed to push away thoughts of him and drift into sleep.

Shelburne was no longer a bored nobleman, coasting through life as only a young, wealthy English aristocrat can. Instead, he set his footsteps toward identifying the owner of those haunting eyes. Nothing swayed him from his goal—her identity. The stack of invitations heaped on his desk would be the quickest way to find her. He laughed aloud at the thought of how surprised the Society hostesses would be when the most sought-after bachelor of the *ton* attended the social functions he usually avoided like the plague. He knew he would avoid them again at some point in the future, but not now. Now he had reason to brave even the most persistent matchmaking mama.

The evening after his chance encounter with the blue-eyed girl, Shelburne caused a minor riot when he strolled into Almack's Assembly Rooms soon after the doors opened. Lady Jersey and Princess Esterhazy, two of the toplofty patronesses of these exclusive assembly rooms, exchanged glances at the sight of this almost reclusive man. Lady Jersey glided in his direction, an eager smile lighting her face.

"Shelburne, you unsociable creature, to what do we owe the pleasure of your company? 'Tis all of five years since you set foot in this place."

He raised her gloved hand to his lips, and then murmured, "Sarah, you must know I came to see you. Does not everyone?"

Lady Jersey tapped his arm with her painted chicken skin fan, and smiled at his audacity. "La, Shelburne, you do have a way about you. Since you've honored us with your presence, you can be sure we intend to keep you here the entire evening. Everyone is stunned to see the *ton*'s most eligible bachelor at the Marriage Mart. Which young miss shall I introduce first?"

The room had gone silent after the buzz upon his arrival. He sensed stares directed at him but, with his usual aplomb, ignored them. "No need, Sarah. I see my sister just over there." Shelburne bowed as he left her and strolled in the direction of a petite matron whose fair hair had begun to fade, but whose cornflower blue eyes were as bright as ever. His only sibling, he had looked up to her from early childhood as she, ten years his senior, had guided his footsteps, kept his secrets, and made sure his hands were scrubbed for tea so his nurse wouldn't scold him.

"Becca, my dear, I trust I see you well?"

She twinkled at him and mimicked his drawl. "Tolerable, my dear, tolerable. What moved you to enter these portals after declaring you would never do so again? Not once but several times, need I remind you?"

He quirked one eyebrow at her and turned to the young miss standing beside her. His glance passed over the requisite white muslin gown adorned with a blue sash fastened at the high waist, its streamers almost reaching the floor. His niece bore a close resemblance to her mother at the same age. "Your gown is fetching, my child."

"I'm not a child," Marie reminded him. "Uncle Edward, I did not expect to see you here of all places. This makes the evening perfect. I will be the envy of every female here if you lead me in a dance. Say you will." She had to tilt her face upward to look into his amused eyes.

"I must say no one looks as well in dress finery as do you, Uncle Edward." Marie laughed at his frown and rushed into speech before he could give her one of his famous set downs. "You will come to my ball next week, will you not? 'Twill be the veriest squeeze, I assure you."

"Calm yourself, child." Shelburne turned to his sister. "Are you sure this chit is ready to be in polite company, Becca? Couldn't have been more than a sennight since I hauled the little hoyden out of some scrape or other, and not for the first time either."

Becca gave her daughter an indulgent smile and turned a mock frown toward her brother. "Don't be a dunce, Shelburne. You know very well how old Marie is. We would have brought her out last year had we not still been in black gloves."

The reminder of his father's death sent a stab of pain into Shelburne's heart. He missed the old gentleman more each day as he dealt with the estate matters which he had hoped to avoid for many years. The ninth earl had met an early end when thrown from a horse he was trying to break to bridle. He was an estimable man in most ways, but he had refused to admit this activity was best left to younger men. Now his only son gave Becca a reassuring smile knowing how much she missed their father, who had doted on her.

Becca slipped her arm through his and watched him scan the room. "Do you seek someone special? Do tell me who has attracted your attention enough for you to break your resolve."

"Why do you think someone has?"

"I know your aversion to girls barely out of the schoolroom."

Her brother ignored her and turned instead to his niece. "Come, Marie, we'll join this set. And be warned, should you step on my toes, I will send you back to the schoolroom."

"I will be happy to help you find a wife, Uncle Edward, if you have come to Almack's to seek one," his niece announced as they moved down the line.

Shelburne stared after her as the dance took her away from him. Help him find a wife indeed, as if he would need help when the time came for him to become a tenant for life. Shelburne had reached the age of eight and twenty without succumbing to the wiles of the matchmaking mamas. Furthermore, he intended to resist them for several more years, being content with the delights of his bachelor life, as he assured anyone impertinent enough to ask. He had decided early in his career on the Town that five and thirty would be soon enough to step into parson's mousetrap. When the steps brought Marie back to his side, he tried to depress her pretension with a frown.

"Any number of my friends would love to fill the void in your life," she assured him, her face lit with a sunny smile. "Your mirror will tell you that you're too handsome by half, and you must have noticed how all the females swoon over you. Still, because you need help choosing one, I'm at your service. I know every eligible *parti* better than do you."

"Alas, your best efforts would be in vain, my dear. I do thank you for the offer. You're quite thoughtful. However, please understand, there is no void in my life and matrimony does not interest me in the least."

"Marriage will be my fate in life regardless of my wishes," she said, despair coloring her voice.

When the steps again brought them together, Shelburne pursued the matter, happy to turn her attention from him. He didn't recall ever hearing such a wistful tone from her. He gentled his voice as he had done when she was still in leading strings. "What would you like to do instead, little one?"

"My heart is divided," Marie confessed with a sigh. "Sometimes I want to be just like Mama, married to the man I love."

"And at other times?" Shelburne couldn't imagine what other aspiration a young miss reared in Society would harbor. All females seemed only interested in hunting husbands. Why else would they come to this place known for weak lemonade and stale cakes?

"Travel," she answered. "I would like to see Spain or perhaps Italy. Even the Americas."

Shelburne had thought he knew his niece inside and out, but this surprised him. When they met again in the dance, he said, "You could do both. Marry and travel, I mean."

"How could I do both?"

"You could marry a diplomat. Or a missionary to Africa," he teased. Marie could be fun, but that was hardly a prerequisite for either of his suggestions. He had yet to see one iota of seriousness in her.

"Do you think a female as frivolous as I could do such a thing?" A giggle escaped her as the dance separated them again.

"Could, would, or should?" he asked on her return.

She twinkled in answer. "Any or all."

Shelburne laughed. "Perhaps you can discover a way to travel without endangering either of those two professions."

"And I could if that French monster would behave."

"Careful, brat, frowns leave lines." She dimpled at him as he escorted her back to her mother. There, he stood a few minutes scanning the room once more, then departed for another ball, and yet another.

Shelburne didn't see the one face he sought and carefully avoided making eye contact with anyone. In the following days, he caused many hearts to flutter at various balls, routs, and musicales. He rode in the park every afternoon at the fashionable hour, and scanned faces around him but to no avail. Finally, on one such ride, his friends took him to task.

"Shelburne, you're neglecting us beyond bearing. We haven't seen you in the clubs for at least a sennight. Have you lost your fortune on 'Change?" Morrison's worried query brought shouts of derision.

Vincent ignored their laughter as he took in the earl's appearance. The green superfine coat from Weston was the perfect accompaniment for the lighter green waistcoat and the simply tied snowy cravat. "I must say you don't look like you have dipped too deep, still if you would wear some rings and watch fobs, you'd catch an heiress on the instant."

"When I outrun the constable, Morrison, I'll hang on your sleeve," Shelburne threatened.

"That would require a much larger allowance than m'father gives me." Vincent's worried frown eased midst the following laughter.

"I must say it's indecent for one person to be as wealthy as you, Shelburne. The very least you could do is to give us the opportunity to win some of your blunt at the card tables." This loud complaint came from a rotund young man clad in a bright blue coat over a waistcoat of red and white striped satin, and trousers in a nauseating shade of butter yellow.

In truth, Shelburne realized haunting blue eyes kept his mind occupied to the extent gambling with his friends didn't occur to him. He shaded his eyes from the sight before him and peeked through his spread fingers. "Has your luck changed, Hamilton? I had not realized congratulations were in order."

One voice rose above the others' hoots. "I agree with him, though, Shelburne. You have neglected us of late. Where are you keeping yourself these days?"

Shelburne glanced at Lord Rushton who slouched in the saddle, reins held loosely in one hand, a sharp gleam showing through his narrowed eyelids. Aside from his dislike of the earl, Shelburne possessed a profound aversion to discussing his private business. He shrugged off the question. "My secretary keeps me busy. Horror of horrors, the fellow thinks I should make speeches in the House."

Their laughter died down, and the group disbursed in various directions. Shelburne made his way home, his glance constantly on the move searching for a pair of haunting blue eyes.

"Uncle Edward, you came! Now my ball will be perfect, even if no one else asks me to dance."

The ballroom at Haverford House glittered with hundreds of candles. Flowers in every hue imaginable graced the small tables scattered along the walls, interspersed with several gilt chairs and small sofas. Placement of tall, green potted plants created small nooks for private tête-à-têtes, albeit not too private for respectability.

Shelburne saw none of the splendor. Absently, he patted Marie's shoulder even as he scanned the crowded room, searching for those blue eyes. Marie had been correct. Her ball was, indeed, the veriest squeeze. He'd planned to arrive early, and watch for his quarry. Now he must maneuver his way through this crowd and hope he didn't miss her.

The earl's intentions were all for naught. She didn't come. Shelburne did his duty by dancing with some of the young misses lining the walls and found partners for others. He had his ear assaulted by the booming voice of a crony of his father who regaled him with the previous earl's derring-do on the hunting field. Then Shelburne delivered plates of food to dowagers who sat like lumps at small tables in the dining room.

When the last guest left as the clock chimed two, Shelburne hadn't been so tired after a pitched battle in Spain.

"Uncle Edward, you're a Trojan!" Marie exclaimed. "I expect you realize all those old biddies have fallen head over heels in love with you."

"Brat, referring to your grandmother's friends as old biddies is not seemly."

"I know. You won't tattle on me, though."

Shelburne rumpled her curls as he had done throughout her childhood. He had been her confidante from the time she first escaped the nursery to climb trees, little hoyden which she was. He let her excited chatter roll off him until the butler announced his carriage then pulled himself out of the comfortable chair and left, her chatter following him.

Chapter 2

Chance Meetings

Nearly a week had passed since Rebecca saw the green-eyed gentleman. When his face intruded into her thoughts, which happened far too often for her peace of mind, she pushed his vision aside. Those green eyes intruded too often, especially during her work hours as the days passed.

"Mr. Wright said I need not go to his office today," Rebecca pushed away her now empty breakfast plate. "I cannot decide what to do first. I feel frivolous with so much free time."

"My first lesson today is in the afternoon, so we can go shopping. What better way to spend this beautiful morning?" Louise flashed a mocking grin. "Of course, I could give my bedchamber a thorough turnout, but helping you enjoy your day must be the duty of your bestest friend."

Rebecca joined her laughter, knowing of old the other's dislike of all things domestic. "Yes, we will forget housework for once, my bestest friend. Amelia, can we tempt you to come with us?"

"I need to return some books to the circulating library this morning," Amelia told them. "Otherwise, I have no plans for the day. A shopping expedition would be most enjoyable."

At Hatchard's, they browsed among the shelves, choosing one book each after considerable debate on the merits of each. Turning away from the counter, Rebecca collided with an older gentleman, who was dressed in the fashion of the previous century and was none too steady on his feet. Teetering back and forth, he clutched her shoulders for balance.

"Oh, sir, do please forgive me!" Rebecca tried in vain to avoid wine fumes emanating from the puffy red face too close to her own.

Slurred words greeted her efforts. "No, no, m'dear. My fault." Still clutching her shoulders, he repeated, "My fault entirely. I must beg your pardon." Attempting to bow, he bumped her head, and again begged her pardon.

"That is quite all right, sir. I failed to pay attention." Her face hot with embarrassment, Rebecca tried to move away.

Refusing to release his clutch on the helpless girl, the inebriated gentleman peered into her face and exclaimed, "Louise! I haven't seen you in an age."

By dint of sheer effort, Rebecca managed to free her shoulders. "Sir, you mistake me for a different person. My name is not Louise. Please permit me to pass."

He ignored her plea. "Of course, you're Louise. I could not be mistaken. You were the most beautiful gel at your court appearance. Even Farmer George thought so. That was back in ninety-two, before he went mad."

Rebecca gasped and stared into the bleary eyes peering at her. She knew many people referred to the king as Farmer George in a derogatory manner, but in public? Such disrespect toward a reigning monarch must be treasonable, or something. However, the gentleman's audacity was not the important part of his words. Court appearance? Looked enough like this person named Louise to cause a mistaken identity? Who? Before she could quiz him, a voice behind her entered the conversation.

"Ma'am, is this man insulting you?" With those words, a slender young gentleman propelled the older man out the door, waving off Rebecca's thanks.

Rebecca turned to her companions. "Let us go before we attract more attention."

"That was a nice young man," Amelia commented.

"His name is Toby Williams, the brother of one of my students," Louise announced. "I got a glimpse of him once when he visited his family. I suppose he has rooms someplace."

"A small world indeed," Amelia said.

"Did you notice what the gentleman said about a court appearance?" Louise clasped Rebecca's arm. "Could he have known your mother? His words imply you look like this person, whoever she is."

"The gentleman was in his cups, so I doubt we can place any stock in his words." Rebecca turned to Amelia. "Shall we admit we only came out so we could admire ladies' fashions? Let us continue our walk."

"True, so we will."

Strolling along the walkway, admiring the walking costumes of the other ladies, they stopped when a masculine voice exclaimed, "I've found you! At last, I've found you!"

A vision dressed in a bottle green jacket and buckskins sat astride a black horse that nudged passersby out of his path. Glittering green eyes stared at Rebecca, who felt heat rising above her modest décolletage.

The vision swung down from his mount, looping the reins around one arm as he bowed and doffed his hat in their direction. "Please excuse my forwardness, ladies. However, ever since I saw this lady some days ago, I've tried to figure out where I've seen her. We are acquainted, are we not?"

Rebecca met his expectant gaze while her heart danced against her rib cage. His precisely cut attire showed his athletic build to perfection, while his tanned complexion signified his love for outdoor life. Calling him handsome didn't do him justice. Rebecca had never seen a man who equaled him among the gentlemen who frequented Mr. Wright's office. Before she could gather her wits, Louise gasped, drawing his attention.

The gentleman glanced at her, and then looked closer. "Oh, I say, I know you too. Surely, I do."

Amelia chortled. "'Pon rep! Saying such a thing to one filly is bad enough, but saying it to two is beyond anything. And them standing together, too, mind you. Whatever next?"

"I beg your pardon, ladies." The gentleman tore his gaze from Louise's face and turned to Amelia. "I don't mean to be rude. I know these two young ladies although I am unable to remember right off where I've seen them."

Rebecca stood in silence, unable to remove her gaze from his face. Her quickened breathing must have reminded Amelia of her own position because she stretched to her full five feet, tilted her face upward, and stared him straight in the eyes. "Young man, your manners leave a great deal to be desired. Please permit us to pass."

"Oh, but, Ma'am . . ."

The three ladies passed him by and continued down the street. Mrs. Peter's next words floated on the slight breeze. "Handsome creature. 'Tis a shame he has a queer kick in his gallop."

"Rebecca, is he the dashing green-eyed man you saw the other day?" Louise asked in a low voice. "He's apparently been looking everywhere for you. Is that not stupendous?"

"Then we must live in different worlds, Louise. Otherwise, he would have seen me before now. I'm not a recluse after all." With determination, Rebecca pretended indifference and changed the subject.

"Where did you hear that word? You use stupendous indiscriminately."

Louise laughed. "Oh, stupendous is the current favorite word among the schoolroom set. I failed to realize I had picked up their habit."

"Habits are easy to acquire and difficult to break, you must remember," Rebecca teased in a singsong voice reminiscent of Matron at the orphanage.

Amelia said, "Girls, 'tis such a warm day I'll treat us to ices, at Gunter's Confectionary before we return home."

"Stupendous!" Louise's face glowed with her enthusiasm. "I could eat ices every day, and someday I will."

"Here is Gunter's now, and we have time for a quick ice before you begin your teaching duties."

The ladies seated themselves at a small table where they ordered their favorite strawberry ices, a rare indulgence. While they chatted quietly, Rebecca became aware of an uncomfortable sensation, the feeling someone stared at her. Glancing to her left, she gave a small gasp. The familiar pair of emerald eyes gazed at her from the next table. She was unable to break the invisible tie between them. He had followed her, that much was obvious even to a nodcock, but she didn't see how anything positive could come of his perseverance.

Rebecca's gasp called Mrs. Peter's attention to her. Following Rebecca's gaze, Amelia stiffened, a frown crossing her face. Gathering her gloves and reticule, she said, "Come, girls, we've dallied longer than we should."

When Rebecca didn't move, Amelia touched her arm. "My dear, we must go."

Blinking, Rebecca turned to her companions, heat rising in her face. "Yes, we must go."

Rebecca cast one last look at the green-eyed gentleman. Would they meet again?

With a sigh, Shelburne watched the ladies leave the confectionary telling himself maybe the girl with the haunting eyes would inquire around town about him. Gossip mongering being all the rage, he would learn if she did. Then the earl almost groaned aloud when realization struck him as he walked out the door. She could not ask about him because she didn't know his name. Dash it all, why did he not have the presence of mind to introduce himself?

Shelburne had followed the three ladies to the confectionary hoping to find someone to introduce them. He had risked his mount in the hands of a filthy street urchin to follow the ladies inside but to no avail. Embarrassed at being bested by a pint-sized chaperone, and irritated for not identifying himself, Shelburne decided he would simply forget the young lady. Forget those blue eyes that gazed into his time after time even when the owner was not present. Full of resolution, Shelburne turned toward his town house in Grosvenor Square. The attraction wouldn't last, he assured himself. They never had and there was no reason to believe they ever would.

Rebecca was quiet during their walk home, her thoughts occupied with her reaction to his green eyes which mesmerized her. With his chiseled features and side-whiskers, he was even more handsome than she had first thought him. Next to those eyes, Shelburne's voice and crooked smile appealed to her the most. The cheerfulness transformed what might be an austere countenance into boyish charm. The deep melodious voice lived up to the rest of him, sending shivers down her spine at the memory. She would like to hear him speak again, preferably soon, she admitted to herself. And often.

Rebecca soon regained her customary calm countenance although her thoughts were in a whirl. She considered herself a contented person, seldom voicing her thoughts about her ancestry. That evening, however, she broached the subject with Louise as they sat over their needlework. Mrs. Peters had retired early to her bedchamber, causing the girls to converse in low voices. Windows opened a couple of inches allowed a small breeze that alleviated some of the early summer heat without too much noise and dust entering the room. After living their entire lives in the country, they'd found these aspects of city life difficult.

Rebecca confessed. "I don't expect to find a family who will claim me. Still, knowing who my ancestors are would be nice."

"I truly sympathize, Rebecca," Louise assured her. "However, I admit that I am a fatalistic type of person. If something is meant to be, it will be."

"I know that too. My impatience drives me into forgetting all too often."

"I was always the impatient one," Louise reminded her. "The only times I can recall when you were impatient was in waiting for the roses to bloom. From the moment you discovered the rose garden, you believed the bushes should be full of blooms year-round."

Rebecca nodded at Louise's recollection. The orphanage rose garden had been her special place.

There, she could remember Mama and cry for her without anyone stopping her. Blinking away moisture, Rebecca changed the subject. "Do you think the green-eyed gentleman truly recognized us or was he just being forward?"

Louise hesitated. "I would like to believe he was sincere, but common sense dictates he is more likely cutting a wheedle."

"Yes, I daresay you're right. Something puzzles me though. He also said he recognizes you. I'm unable to decide if his remark makes it more, or less, probable he was being forward."

Louise rested her embroidery hoop in her lap. "I wonder whether there was a connection between our parents which would account for our names."

Rebecca shook her head. "I asked the duchess about that possibility several years ago. She told me she knew of no connection. She was never able to learn anything about my family and knew nothing of yours beyond your parents' names and your father's occupation."

For a few minutes, the only sound in the room was the ticking of the clock on the mantel as the ladies continued their needlework.

"Something else bothers me." Rebecca paused to thread her needle. "I know we've discussed this many times through the years, but I cannot get our names out of my mind. Is it just coincidence we have the same three names only in a different order, as the duchess believes? Or could there be a person somewhere who shares out names?"

"I often wonder about that too. She would be in Hampshire if she exists. No one ever mentioned any similarity of names."

"Perhaps we should have stayed there." Rebecca spoke from the uncertainty in her heart. "You see, if there is a third one of us, she might be in need. She might not have been as fortunate as we have been."

"I doubt most people would consider themselves fortunate to grow up in an orphanage," Louise told her.

"Perhaps not, but I suppose there are few, if any, orphanages which are as well maintained as where we lived. The Duchess of Dorchester only sponsors one. Besides, we always had each other. Our togetherness counted for quite a lot, do you not agree?"

"Yes, a close friend can make up for so much that might not be what one would prefer." Louise was quiet for a moment, her normally busy hands lying idle. "I don't know how we would go about learning whether such a person does exist. The only information we have is the three names. I should think, though, finding her would be an easier task after we discover who you are. You know I will help in any way I can."

Rebecca nodded. "It would be interesting to know if the green-eyed gentleman would recognize the features of three of us."

They gazed at each other a moment before Louise voiced her thoughts. "He might recognize the features of both of us without ever seeing either of us. Thinking back over his words, I don't have the impression he believes he has seen us in the recent past. Perhaps he has seen our features, or similar features, on different faces."

"He appears too young to have been acquainted with our parents."

"He does appear closer to us in age. Have you given any thought to the other gentleman who we encountered today?"

After a moment of frowning thought, Rebecca answered, "Do you mean the inebriated gentleman who approached me at Hatchard's? I had forgotten about him."

"You brushed him aside earlier, but what do you think about the possibility now? Could he have known your mother? Could she have been presented to King George?"

"I never thought my mother might have been of the quality." In a burst of candor, Rebecca confessed, "I thought my father might have been of a higher class, and perhaps took advantage of my mother, who was of the lower orders."

"The gentleman called you 'Louise'. Could that mean I was named for your mother and you were named for mine?"

"Then how do we account for 'Marie'?"

"I believe this gives substance to our thoughts there might be a Marie Louise Rebecca or a Marie Rebecca Louise somewhere."

"If only there was a way that we could learn the answers to our questions."

Louise tried to alleviate her friend's frustration. "Mr. Wright seems convinced he can find your family. You might see the inebriated man again when he's not in his cups. He might make sense then. Or the green-eyed gentleman might remember by the next time you see him."

"If I ever do." Rebecca took a deep breath. "Yes, I will. I will see the green-eyed gentleman again, even if I must do every one of those nonsensical things which we mentioned the other evening."

"That's the spirit," Louise said. "Determination will carry the day."

Chapter 3

Shelburne Shares His Frustration

"Why can I not remember where I saw her before? The other one too," Shelburne muttered to the liver-colored hound at his feet. Seated in his library, he drummed a tattoo on the arm of the massive leather chair. He seemed to have spent a considerable amount of time there in recent days. Estate paperwork was a poor second to deep blue eyes which haunted him. The earl barely roused himself when voices penetrated from outside the door.

"Never mind, Jenkins, I'll announce myself. In the library, is he?" Major George Stafford entered the room, a limp obvious as he made his way to the wing-backed chair on the other side of the fireplace. Shelburne raised his head to face the cheerful countenance topped by fair hair cut in the Bedford crop preferred by the military.

"George, I'm in a quandary. I saw two lovely young ladies today. Well, I first saw one of them some days ago. The thing is, I know I recognize them, yet for the life of me I cannot place them."

His friend swept him a bow. "A good afternoon to you, too, m'lord. This is a beautiful day, is it not, m'lord? Yes, m'lord, I would like some brandy. Yes, m'lord, I will be pleased to serve myself. How kind of you to offer, m'lord."

Shelburne and George Stafford had been friends since boyhood. His limp grieved Shelburne. Stafford suffered a broken bone during the siege of Ciudad Rodrigo the previous January when his mount was shot out from under him. Napoleon's troops in Spain had a lot to answer for. Only heavenly interference prevented the bone being crushed when the horse fell on him.

Shelburne waved toward the decanter. "You know better than to stand on ceremony in this house."

Drink in hand, George propped an ebony cane against his chair. His long legs stretched toward the fireplace where low flames licked the coal. "Now, what is this about two lovely ladies? I can't imagine you ever forgetting where you met one lovely lady, most assuredly not two."

"Nonetheless, I have. See if these descriptions mean anything to you. Both ladies are taller than average, both are slender but not thin, by any means. The one I saw twice has dark blue eyes with the longest lashes I have ever seen. Her wide-brimmed bonnet revealed raven hair pulled back from her face. The other one has dark reddish-brown hair we call auburn. She has the creamy complexion we often see with that shade of hair. Her eyes are brown but have gold lights."

George let out a low whistle. "You have seen them only a couple of times, yet you can describe them so thoroughly? They impressed you almost beyond belief."

"They did." Shelburne shrugged. Why would he deny the attraction to someone who could read him like a book? "At least the blue-eyed one did."

George frowned in thought for a moment. "I like auburn hair, as you know. It never fails to attract my attention, but I don't know any female who answers your description. She can't have been in Town long, because I would have spotted her without doubt. What age are they?"

"Eighteen or nineteen, I suppose. I'm sure they're out of the schoolroom but not on the shelf by any means."

"Then they should be in Town for the Season."

"If she is, I cannot find her. I've made an absolute cake of myself going to all the *ton* parties, the balls, breakfasts, opera, the theater. Even that stupid Pantheon masquerade. All the things I normally do over protest, if at all, yet I cannot find her. I know I did not dream her. At least, not twice."

George cast a speculative glance at his friend. After a brief hesitation, he inquired, "Are you sure they are, hmmm, *ladies*?"

His meaning was clear and Shelburne answered without hesitation. "Oh, yes, there is no doubt they are ladies although probably not by title. Otherwise without doubt we would know them. Their graceful carriage, the proud tilt to their heads, their very demeanor shouts their gentility." Shelburne paused for breath. "Properly dressed, the dark-haired blue-eyed one would be a diamond of the first water. Even now her gracefulness puts every female I know to shame."

"I must say you're in raptures, which is unusual in a man who claims to be a confirmed bachelor." George shifted in his chair. "You didn't say whether they were accompanied."

A shout of laughter met this remark. "Oh, yes, they were accompanied, all right. A veritable dragon about five feet tall was with them. She has a penchant for horses, if her language is any guideline. She called the girls 'fillies' and, when they walked away, I heard her say I have a queer kick in my gallop."

George joined in his laughter but could be of no help. They sat long over their brandy as their subject changed from the young ladies to the status of Wellington's army.

"The news I hear from Spain is far from hopeful," George said. "The French seem to know our troops' destination, because they're waiting for us when we get there. Their knowledge is uncanny, positively uncanny.

I have wondered if they are intercepting our carrier pigeons, but all of them have reached their destination. As if that isn't enough, we also have this ongoing problem with those upstart colonies that call themselves the United States of America."

Shelburne suppressed a chuckle at George's disgust. He didn't know how Englishmen could object when their former colonists tried to protect their own people from impressment in the Royal Navy. The people who dealt with the war didn't admit their activities—probably never would—but it was an open secret the navy had seized hundreds of American merchant ships. A declaration of war by their President James Madison would not surprise Shelburne in the least.

"Our losses in the peninsula are much too heavy," Shelburne concurred. "Another war might devastate our forces. I miss army life since I sold out. I feel I should be there with my men. I'm sure you can appreciate my feelings on that score. When do you return to Spain?"

"The sawbones refuses to clear me yet. Says he isn't satisfied with the way the bone is healing. I'm eager to get back into the thick of things." George's voice was devoid of expression when he added, "My father is trying to convince me I should sell out."

Shelburne knew George was heir to a barony, but preferred military life. Having estate responsibilities himself, Shelburne could understand why the baron wanted his son at his beck and call, but he could not understand why the baron refused to allow his heir to voice any opinions about the estate. The baroness had only one ambition in life—the immediate acquisition of grandchildren. To that end, she threw every young miss she could find at her son, although she knew he preferred older females. His plight brought sympathy from Shelburne, who then changed the subject by asking what plans he had made for the evening.

"That reminds me of why I came. I have a meeting with our solicitor this evening, then early tomorrow I leave for the country for several weeks, probably all summer. It seems my father needs to consult me about the estate." Stafford's voice held a glimmer of amusement. He reached for his cane preparatory to taking his leave.

Shelburne escorted him to the door, then hurried to his bedchamber to dress before going to dine *en famille* with his sister.

The *ton* generally agreed Lady Becca Cecil, as the daughter of an earl, had married beneath herself when she chose to marry a mere baronet, Sir Julian Haverford. However, the couple's continued affection for each other was obvious.

Shelburne found his quiet brother-in-law most congenial. After Becca and Marie left them at the dinner table, they lingered over glasses of port, their conversation touching on the political happenings of the day. With the Tories in power, the dreadful riots in the Midlands raged on, requiring military intervention. The latest information from Leeds indicated the Luddite fervor had moved from Yorkshire into Lancashire. There seemed to be no end to the labor problems. Was the war with Napoleon not a big enough problem for England to face?

Julian didn't answer the rhetorical question, saying instead, "You seem preoccupied."

Shelburne raised his eyes to those of the older man, but then lowered them to the glass in his hand, swirling the contents around and around. Should he confide in him? Sharing his problem might ease his frustrations. Answering the implied question, he chose his words with care.

"I've seen someone I would like to know better, but I'm unable to find her."

"Is she someone I might know?"

"I have no idea. I'm sure I've seen her before, but I don't know where. I don't know who she is or anything about her except she has the most compelling blue eyes I've ever encountered. They haunt me." The last admission seemed torn from his lips. Glancing at his companion, Shelburne clamped his mouth into a tight line and wished he hadn't opened it. This conversation was not a good idea.

Haverford's raised eyebrows returned to their normal position. "I've never known you to get in a state of turmoil about chance-met females, not even when you first tasted the delights of adulthood."

"Chance met? Well, yes, I suppose yours is a valid statement. But, Haverford, she doesn't seem chance met. Quite the contrary. I'm sure I know her from somewhere, like I've known her forever or at least many years. Yet, I can't fathom when or where that could have been."

"Have you asked Becca or Marie about her? They appear to know everyone in Town."

"I would feel foolish doing so," Shelburne admitted with a rueful smile.

"Nevertheless, the ladies might be able to help. They're having a quiet evening at home, gathering their strength for the final hectic weeks of the Season. Shall we join them?"

The ladies sat in companionable silence with needlework in their hands when the gentlemen joined them in the drawing room.

While waiting for the tea tray, Shelburne caught a glimpse of himself in the mirror over the Adams fireplace. Could that be a sheepish expression on his face? The debonair man about Town, the envy of every schoolboy, the desire of every schoolgirl, the despair of every matchmaking mama—even though he hated to admit any of those things—sheepish? He schooled his features to blandness.

"Ladies, Shelburne has a little mystery you might be able to help him solve."

Marie clapped her hands. "I do adore mysteries. Has someone stolen the crown jewels? Is someone missing? Is there a mysterious stranger in our midst? Oh, do tell us."

Becca shushed her exuberant daughter. "Yes, do tell us, Edward. There has obviously been something on your mind these past few weeks. Or someone, perhaps."

Never one to discuss his personal matters, Shelburne's face grew warm as he forced himself to speak. "Marie is on the right track. I have seen a young lady, rather two young ladies, whom I'm unable to identify, yet I'm sure I know them. I can't find them even though I have searched every place I can conjure for some weeks."

"So, these are the ladies you searched for at our ball. Yet if they are *ladies*, I fail to understand why you have not seen them at the social gatherings you've haunted in recent days."

"Dear, they could be ladies without being a part of the annual matchmaking sweepstakes." Sir Julian's dry words caused a surprised expression to cross his wife's face.

"I suppose so," Becca answered, with obvious skepticism. "In any event, Edward, describe them to us."

He obliged, not realizing how much he revealed. As his voice faded into silence, Marie gazed at him in wonder.

"Uncle Edward, you have seen them how many times?"

"I've seen the raven-haired one twice, the auburn-haired one once."

Marie exchanged a glance with her mother, who commented with obvious restraint. "They made quite an impression on you, Edward. However, off hand, I don't recall anyone who fits those descriptions. Marie, do you?"

"I'm afraid not. The only raven-haired girl I know is Deborah Langford and you're acquainted with her. Catherine Palmer's hair might be considered auburn although it looks plain red to me." Marie patted the curls arranged over her ears. "Fair-haired ladies are in favor this season, have you not noticed?"

They continued to discuss the mysterious young ladies until Shelburne rose to leave.

"You've aroused my curiosity." Becca picked up her embroidery frame. "When you find them, abduct them if necessary and bring them to me. When I see them, I imagine something about them will ring a bell."

A smile settled on Shelburne's face as he bid them good night and turned to leave. He was not any closer to identifying the girl with the haunting blue eyes, but at least he had others helping him search.

The earl was not the only one searching. Rebecca tried to be discreet while she looked for a pair of green eyes in every face she saw, every place she went. He had shown that his initial interest had continued, but what was his real interest? Honorable? Dishonorable? Rebecca wished she knew. As she lay in bed one night, she forced herself to confront her reaction to him.

Why do you care?

He might remember where he has seen me, my features, at least. Rebecca answered the little voice in her head. That little voice had cautioned her to correct behavior since her early childhood. The duchess had called it her conscience and said she could never go wrong if she listened. Too often she hadn't listened and the voice had made a nuisance of itself. *His interest could lead to finding my family.*

Is that the only reason?

Yes.

Truly? Or have you succumbed to his handsome face? You don't even know his name.

Be quiet, do, Rebecca answered, yet had to admit that little voice was right. Why had he not introduced himself anyway? He should have after waylaying them, even following them to the confectionary and sitting at the closest table. He could have a title. He had enough audacity to be a royal duke, at least. They might consider themselves above mere introductions. Punching her pillow into a more comfortable shape, Rebecca again told that little voice to be quiet then settled down to sleep.

On the Sunday following her second encounter with Lord Green Eyes, as Rebecca had begun to think of him, the ladies walked the few blocks to the small Marylebone parish church. Surreptitiously glancing from face to face, Rebecca paid no attention to her surroundings until Louise grabbed her arm, jerking her away from a barrow pushed by a small ragged urchin.

"Missus, why doncher watch whar yer be a-goin'?" The lad struggled to hold upright an overfilled cart much too large for him to handle.

"Rebecca, do watch your step," Amelia scolded. "You were looking everywhere except in front of you."

While trying to control the heat she felt rising in her face, Rebecca scrabbled in her reticule for a penny, which she handed to the grubby boy. "I apologize for upsetting your cart, child. I was woolgathering when I should have been minding my steps."

The urchin scowled, even as he snatched the coin which he pocketed before pushing on without favoring her with further words.

Pull yourself together, Rebecca ordered herself. How could she be so weak-willed as to allow a stranger, even a handsome one, to invade her mind to the extent she could not function? The duchess would not hesitate to express her opinion of such behavior. Matron also.

Mrs. Peters and the young ladies arrived at the church without further mishap then slipped into the back pew of the sanctuary. Maintaining an interested expression as she faced the pulpit, Rebecca allowed her gaze to rove over the congregation dressed in their finest garb, she was sure, much the same as she and her companions dressed.

Rebecca missed the small church in Wickham, where the orphans were in regular attendance. She remembered, with pleasure, the dear old Reverend Layton, who never frowned when the children grew restless during the service, as happened with the smallest girls. He'd always had a special story for the children at the start of each service. He began with "Suffer the little children to come unto me and forbid them not for of such is the kingdom of Heaven." His soothing voice came back to Rebecca as if she were still a grieving six-year-old.

Rebecca's wandering glance stopped on a certain gentleman sitting near the front. Could it be? The set of his shoulders, the proud tilt of his head—yes, surely it was. She forgot her vow not to think of the green-eyed gentleman as she stared at the dark hair. She felt only chagrin when the head turned showing the hawk-like beak. After all, why should Lord Green Eyes attend this small, out-of-the-way church? He would attend St. George's in Hanover Square, if he attended church at all.

Leaving the church a short while later, Amelia again took Rebecca to task. "What is wrong with you today? First, you upset that child's cart. You do have enough presence of mind to remember that, I trust. Then during the service, your mind was miles away. I wager you cannot tell me one thing about the sermon, Rebecca. Can you?"

"The sermon was from the twenty-fifth chapter of Matthew about helping less fortunate people. There are plenty of people in London who need assistance."

A slight smile crossed Rebecca's pensive face. "However, you were right about one thing. Part of the time my mind was miles away in Wickham." She consoled herself with the thought her answer was true, as far as it went. Rebecca turned to Louise. "Do you remember the Reverend Layton? How he was forever giving us sweetmeats when adults were not watching us?"

Louise chuckled. "I certainly do remember those sweetmeats. I've never tasted better ones, perhaps because I wasn't supposed to have them. Do you remember the time he placed his hat on the ground, and you put the toad in it?"

"How could I forget that? We hid behind a tree watching him put the hat on his head. He was so comical when he took off the hat, and the toad hopped off his head!" Rebecca wiped her streaming eyes. "We were terrible children."

They whiled away the walk back to Harley Street regaling Amelia with such recollections. Rebecca was able to push a pair of green eyes to the back of her mind.

However, that didn't last.

Chapter 4

He Finds Her Again

The following morning, Rebecca sat in the tiny room given her by Mr. Wright when he hired her to work in his business office. The door between her room and his opened. "Miss Black, will you prepare tea for us, please?"

This was a normal request intended to bring Rebecca into the vision of the client in his office. As he had explained when he hired her, "One has only to look at you to know your ancestry is quality. I have several upper-class clients. I am confident if I bring you to their attention, someone will recognize your features. We can then find your family."

"Mr. Wright, if they, whoever they are, cared to acknowledge me, they would have done so long before now," she had replied. "I see no reason to believe I am of aristocratic lineage, yet if I am, I must be baseborn." Rebecca cringed with mortification at her language. Properly brought up young ladies should not know that word. "I prefer not to have the embarrassment of my illegitimacy becoming known. After all, there is nothing aristocratic about the name Black, is there?"

Now, as Rebecca carried the tray into Mr. Wright's office, she didn't have a great deal of confidence the visitor would recognize her features. During the few months she had been in London, she'd met many people, but no one recognized her either socially or in the business establishments she patronized. She thought of the older man at Hatchard's bookstore. However, he was in his cups, so she dismissed him and his words from her thoughts. Rebecca had almost given up what little hope she had cherished throughout her childhood that she might have a family somewhere. However, there was still her green-eyed stranger. Something might come of their chance encounters, as Louise had said.

"Here you are at last," an excited voice exclaimed. "This time, I intend to learn your identity before you disappear again."

Rebecca almost dropped the tea tray at the sound of the melodious voice she had dreamed of hearing again. She raised her eyes to meet his—not a dream.

"Lord Shelburne, am I to understand you are acquainted with this young lady?" Mr. Wright took the tray which tilted in Rebecca's trembling hands.

"No, not to say *acquainted*. I'm sure I know her from someplace, but I can't think where it might be." He pushed his fingers through his hair, which had been immaculate only a moment before. "Perhaps if you will introduce us, we can get to the bottom of this mystery."

Mr. Wright studied his client for a long moment. "Your suggestion seems reasonable. My lord, this young lady is Miss Rebecca Black. Miss Black, may I present Edward John Carlisle Cecil, the Earl of Shelburne?"

The earl bowed over her hand, which he held in his firm grasp as he studied her features. "I do not recall any family named Black. Who are your parents? Where do you live?"

An *earl*? His manner was abrupt, yet Rebecca decided not to take umbrage. After all, had she not wished someone would attempt to learn her identity? She hesitated, but raised her chin in a determined manner. "My lord, I know nothing of my father. My mother died of the influenza when I was six years old. I grew up in an orphanage in Hampshire."

"Hampshire? I cannot recall any acquaintances there. Pardon my interruption. Please continue."

"The Duchess of Dorchester owns the orphanage. She observed me on regular occasions, and my appearance never struck any chords in her memory."

The earl released her hand, which Rebecca had been tugging, but continued to stare at her.

Rebecca met his eyes without flinching. She could drown in their green depths.

Mr. Wright moved behind his desk. "My lord, I am quite familiar with the orphanage in question—an enlightened establishment maintained by people who believe in education for the girls, a rarity as you must know. I have known Miss Black since she was a small child and have long been convinced that she is of gentle birth. I believed someone would recognize Miss Black if my clients had the opportunity to see her. This is one reason that I employ her. Although many people have seen her, you are the first to feel any sort of recognition."

Mr. Wright's words embarrassed Rebecca. It sounded as though he wanted the earl, a nobleman, to escort her among society. She smothered a sigh. If this were what it took to find her family, she would agree.

Under Lord Shelburne's scrutiny, Rebecca grew nervous, yet refused to lose countenance. She lowered her eyelids until her gaze fixed on the emerald nestled in his exquisitely tied cravat.

"My lord, you do feel some recognition?" Mr. Wright's voice broke the silence. "You're not simply looking for, uh, diversion?"

Rebecca understood Mr. Wright's quandary. He wished to do his best for her, yet did not want to offend this wealthy client.

Shelburne had not shifted his gaze from her face. "Oh, yes, I know those features. I have never heard her voice, though. The tone is deeper than I expected, yet I don't know why I had any expectations whatsoever."

Shaking his head, he repeated, "I know the features, but they belong to someone else. My problem is that I don't know who."

With a sigh, Shelburne turned his eyes toward his solicitor. "This is frustrating, you must understand. Miss Black's features have haunted me for days. I am no closer to identifying them now than the first time I saw them. Perhaps I would remember if we became acquainted, if I could see her mannerisms as well as her features." A rueful smile on his face, he turned to Rebecca. "Can you forgive me for my rudeness, Miss Black?"

Rebecca lifted her candid gaze to his again. "How can I not, my lord? After all, my sole purpose for being in Mr. Wright's office is to be recognized."

"No, no," Mr. Wright exclaimed. "Your head for figures and the neatness in your penmanship are of invaluable aid in my business."

The earl turned interested eyes upon her. "You obviously were well educated at the orphanage. As Mr. Wright said, education for females is a rarity."

"As Mr. Wright also said, the orphanage is well-known for its advanced educational precepts, my lord." She cast a mischievous glance at Mr. Wright, who returned her smile. "The Duchess of Dorchester can be most persuasive in gaining her own ends."

After a slight hesitation, Shelburne spoke. "Would you be agreeable to becoming better acquainted in the hope that I might remember who shares your features?"

"What do you have in mind, my lord?" Mr. Wright asked before Rebecca could reply. "This young lady is under my care to a certain extent. I feel bound to protect her in any way necessary."

Ignoring him, Shelburne spoke to Rebecca. "That female who was with you when we met on the street, is she your chaperone? Does she live in your home with you?"

"Yes, my lord, that *lady* serves as chaperone to Miss Tracy and me. Mrs. Peters is also our friend."

"Perhaps I could call upon you?" The earl's diffidence following so soon after his arrogance surprised her. She wondered about the change in his attitude.

Rebecca took her courage in her hand. "Yes, my lord, I believe a visit would be acceptable. Is tea tomorrow afternoon convenient for you?"

She managed to hide the fluttering of her heart as they discussed the directions to her home. After returning to her room, Rebecca clasped her hands together. An *earl*, and she would see him again.

With considerable difficulty, Rebecca kept her mind on her duties until she could return to her rooms. There, Rebecca restrained her exuberance until the three ladies were together at the dinner table. When they relaxed over coffee, she could no longer contain her excitement. "You'll never guess who I invited to tea tomorrow."

Amelia and Louise glanced at each other before speaking in unison. "Who?" When she didn't answer immediately, they clamored for information. "Tell us!"

"The Earl of Shelburne."

"Who?"

"Where did you meet an earl?"

Rebecca could contain her laughter no longer. "The Earl of Shelburne is the green-eyed gentleman. He's a client of Mr. Wright and came to the office today and saw me and said . . .

"Whoa, girl! Slow your pace to a canter and tell us a round tale." Amelia's penchant for the turf, which she had picked up from her late husband, was never more obvious. Although she made an effort to curb her use of what she termed "horse cant," excitement brought out the race track jargon in full force. At this moment, Amelia was in alt.

Rebecca told the story of her afternoon experience until her friends' excited comments burst forth.

"At last somebody . . ."

". . . an earl, too . . ."

"What are you going to wear?"

That all-important question brought silence as Louise and Amelia gazed at Rebecca.

Amelia spoke. "You must change to your prettiest afternoon gown, not the somber garb you wear to Mr. Wright's office every day. You're a beautiful gel when you dress the way a lady should."

Louise agreed. "I know what you should wear. The deep rose muslin with the puffed sleeves and the flounce around the hem."

"You can wear my silver amulet, which is the perfect length for that gown. It will show off your beautiful neck to perfection."

"Oh no, Amelia," Rebecca exclaimed. "The amulet is the only thing you have left of your mother's. An heirloom is much too precious to loan to me." The idea she might damage her companion's most valued possession horrified Rebecca. Amelia had told them early in their acquaintanceship of the stratagems she had used to hide this one item from her husband who had sold everything else of value, then wasted the money on horse races. "I might break the amulet."

"Nonsense! There is no reason to think you will break it right here in our own drawing room. Or were you planning to raise a rumpus of some sort?"

Rebecca joined Louise's laughter which met this question. "I feel like it."

"Is it not stupendous that we have Mr. and Mrs. Morton?" Louise asked. "I thank God daily for putting the thought in the duchess' head to supply them. Besides having a cook who bakes the best biscuits I've ever eaten, having a butler to open the door is impressive beyond my wildest dreams."

"Butler!" A sound suspiciously like a snort escaped Amelia's mouth. "He's naught but a footman in fancy duds. Although I must admit he does look quite well in his blue and gold livery."

"I agree he isn't an experienced butler, yet he has managed to announce people creditably so far. Having a cook-housekeeper is, uh, *stupendous* even though we still must do a fair amount of work." Rebecca cast an impish grin at Louise who laughed at the gentle mockery.

When a knock sounded on the door the following afternoon, Rebecca, who looked her best in the agreed-upon rose muslin, glanced at her companions. Amelia was the complete matron in rich purple satin with long fitted sleeves. Louise wore jonquil muslin complimenting her auburn hair. Amelia nodded her approval at the girls as the butler opened the drawing room door.

"Ladies, Edward John Carlisle Cecil, the Earl of Shelburne." The ladies' eyes widened at the deep-throated pronouncement. Without doubt, there was more to their butler than met the eye.

Shelburne glanced around as he entered the drawing room, his eyes lighting up when he saw Rebecca seated on a striped damask sofa near the windows. She rose and stepped forward.

"My lord, may I introduce my friends? This lady is Mrs. Amelia Peters." Turning toward Louise, she said, "This is Miss Louise Tracy, my best friend."

Shelburne managed to tear his gaze away from Rebecca long enough to murmur greetings and bow over the hands of the other ladies.

Talk was general while Amelia filled teacups. Louise passed around the plates of small cakes and macaroons. Rebecca thought of the days in the orphanage when she was learning correct tea table manners. Was she as nervous then as now?

"Ma'am, as I explained to Miss Black yesterday, I am convinced I know her features. I am anxious to remember where I've seen them before. However, the information she gave me yesterday did not bring enlightenment." Shelburne set the cup of tea on the table at his side then turned toward Louise. "Miss Tracy, your features also are familiar to me, although I can't place them either. Can you tell me anything about your parents?"

Louise had been quiet after acknowledging the introduction, now she turned toward him. "My lord, there is no mystery about my ancestry. My parents were John and Marie Tracy. We lived in Wickham until they died of the influenza when I was five years old. The duchess told me that my father was knowledgeable about horses. He spent much of his time obtaining them in Ireland to sell in England."

She paused, waiting for his comment, which didn't come.

"I don't imagine you purchased horses all those years ago," Louise continued. "Therefore, unless you were with someone who did consult my father, it is not likely you ever met my parents. I'm confident they did not move in your circle, my lord."

Shelburne shook his head. "I don't believe I knew Irish horses could be purchased in Hampshire. Yet I do know your features. I know I do. Miss Black's too."

Amelia joined their conversation. "The gels have feminine features, my lord, so they probably resemble their mothers. Could you have known them at some point?"

"That's possible, but I cannot remember when or where," Shelburne replied. After a moment of silence deliberating over his thoughts, he turned to Rebecca. "Yesterday, you said the duchess did not recognize your features. Did anyone else have the opportunity? Were you easily visible to other people in Hampshire or were you kept on the orphanage grounds?"

"We attended church each Sunday in Wickham, which is only a small place," Rebecca replied. "I rarely even visited the village."

Ripples of laughter escaped Louise, causing the others to turn toward her. "The Guy Fawkes bonfires in the village. They were the highlight of the year for us. Do you remember our first one?"

"I prefer not to be reminded," Rebecca replied with feeling.

"Will you tell us what happened, Miss Tracy?" Shelburne asked with a smile toward Rebecca. "Apparently, she prefers not to share what I suppose were her peccadilloes."

"Oh, I shall tell you, my lord," Rebecca responded. "Otherwise, Louise will indulge her penchant for exaggeration."

"I reject your slur on my character, Rebecca Marie Louise Black. I shall remember the affront for future action," Louise told her with mock seriousness.

"Thank you for warning me, you unnatural creature. Now I shall be on my guard."

"Back to the bonfire, girls, if you please," Amelia reminded Rebecca.

"The bonfire was my first, you must understand. I personally believe my action was heroic," Rebecca informed them with an inelegant sniff. "I threw my cup of punch on the fire."

Shelburne stared at her. "Why in the world did you do such a thing?"

"To put out the fire," she answered.

"Put out the . . ." he went off into peals of laughter. When he could control himself, he assured her that her action had indeed been heroic.

"The duchess did try to find her family, my lord," Amelia assured him when their laughter subsided. "No one in Hampshire recognized her. I understand there was a regular parade of people visiting the orphanage to get a glimpse of her during her first weeks there."

"In all the years I have known you, Rebecca, I don't believe I've ever wondered whether you are originally from Hampshire." Louise sounded surprised. "I just assumed you were."

"I never gave it any thought, either."

"Then perhaps you are from a different area. The duchess may have looked in the wrong place," Shelburne exclaimed. "What do you remember about your life before you went to the orphanage?"

Rebecca shook her head. "Almost nothing, sir. I remember riding in a crowded coach for what seemed like many days but probably was not. I remember touching Mama's face while she was lying on a cot. She was so hot. Then I remember a nice lady telling me I would have a new home." Tears stood in her eyes much as they had on that long ago first day at the orphanage. "I couldn't understand why Mama was not there."

Louise crossed the short distance between them in one swift movement. Holding Rebecca close, she whispered, "I told you then we would always be best friends."

Rebecca wiped her eyes on a small handkerchief. "We are."

Much affected, but not wanting to show his emotion, Shelburne asked how, among so many children to choose from, they became such close friends.

The girls exchanged smiles. Louise returned to her chair while Rebecca recalled that day in 1800 when they first saw each other at the orphanage.

"I remember standing in the doorway of a large room crowded with little girls. I barely had the courage to focus on anyone in that sea of faces. Through my tears, though, I saw some flaming red hair standing quite close. The brown spots on her face fascinated me."

"Brown spots?" the earl inquired.

"Freckles. I was covered with them." Louise's laughing eyes met Rebecca's for a moment. "But my hair was not red."

"Was too." Rebecca reverted to the teasing voice she'd used so often in those early days. "I thought your head was on fire."

"Rebecca didn't throw any liquid on me, though," Louise assured the others. "Probably only because she didn't have any."

Amid their laughter, Shelburne was able to say, "Well, Miss Tracy, your hair is auburn now. Not red. Furthermore, your freckles are a thing of the past, for which I congratulate you."

"Thank you, my lord."

Turning to Rebecca, he asked, "So her fiery head drew you to her?"

"Her hair was the first thing I noticed, but I remember best how warm her hand was when she took mine. Her merry heart attracted me too. In the following days, she kept me laughing. We have been friends ever since," Rebecca finished the tale. "Sisters could not be closer than we are. We even share the same names."

"The same names? I don't understand."

"I'm Rebecca Marie Louise. She's Louise Rebecca Marie."

"What an astounding coincidence."

"We thought so," Rebecca nodded. "Our names immediately drew us together."

By the time he had heard the girls' story, Shelburne's visit had far exceeded the normal half hour allotted to afternoon visits. Turning to Mrs. Peters, he asked, "May I come again?"

Mrs. Peters studied his face a moment. "I cannot see what you hope to accomplish, just staring at these young ladies. However, yes, you may come again."

Rebecca breathed a silent prayer of thankfulness.

She would see him again.

Chapter 5

Vanishing in Green Park

On his first visit to Harley Street, Shelburne had blinked in surprise when the doorman asked his identification before directing him up the broad stairs. As the days passed, he grew to appreciate the double protection the ladies had, with Jamison on the ground floor and Morton inside their rooms.

Shelburne made his way to the Harley Street house daily to take Rebecca driving in Hyde Park, either Louise or Mrs. Peters always there to play propriety. Because of Rebecca's employment hours, they were unable to drive on Rotten Row at the fashionable hour; nevertheless, they often arrived in the park before the last stragglers departed to dress for their evening engagements. Their stratagem was to no avail.

After three such late afternoon drives in the park, Shelburne asked if Mr. Wright required her services on Saturday.

"No, my lord, I'm fortunate in that respect. Mr. Wright only requires my presence between ten and four from Monday through Friday."

"Then we will be among the first arrivals and the last to leave the park this Saturday afternoon. I'm confident someone will recognize you." Shelburne paused a moment. He'd wondered about something since the first day they met. Now was the time to appease his curiosity. "Speaking of your employment, I'm curious about your mode of travel. Do you keep a carriage, perhaps?"

Rebecca gazed at him, a surprised expression in her eyes. "No, my lord, we do not maintain a carriage. I sometimes walk, but on most mornings, Mr. Wright sends his closed carriage for me. I return home the same way."

"How does Miss Tracy travel?"

"All of her students are within reasonable walking distance, my lord." Rebecca tightened her lips for a moment. "Lord Shelburne, you must realize we are in service much like many other young females who are not of the aristocracy. Our lives, by necessity, are much less circumscribed than those young females of your acquaintance."

"Yes, I do understand, Miss Black." The earl cast an anxious glance in her direction. "My question arose from curiosity, not judgment, I assure you."

Shelburne had forgotten one important thing, however. In his preoccupation with Rebecca Black, he had stopped attending society functions and, therefore, had failed to realize how few members of the *ton* remained in Town.

On that Saturday afternoon they were, indeed, among the early arrivals and among the last to leave the park. However, the crowd was thin. Although several people greeted them, no one recognized Rebecca.

***

Later, over tea in Harley Street, Rebecca pointed out an obvious fact which they had ignored. "I am not necessarily of the aristocracy, my lord, even though Mr. Wright thinks it possible."

"Yes, I see what you mean. You can be of gentle birth without being aristocratic. Your family might not participate in the Season, perhaps living in a rural area some distance from Town. Indeed, my brother-in-law said much the same thing."

"Your brother-in-law, my lord?" For one heart-stopping moment, Rebecca realized the earl might have a wife. But then she reminded herself that Mr. Wright would never allow Shelburne's attention to her if the earl were married.

"Yes, my sister's husband."

"Do you mean to say your family knows about me?" Rebecca asked in stunned disbelief. She never thought the earl would mention her, a nobody and probably illegitimate, to anyone. Especially not his family. No, a nobleman, would not commit such an impropriety.

"Certainly they do, Miss Black," Shelburne replied. "They helped me search for you until they returned to their country home for the summer. Are you perturbed my family knows of your existence?"

"Oh no," she assured him. He must be serious about finding her relatives if he had told his family about her. Rebecca basked in the pleasant thought until it occurred to her to wonder, yet again, why he was interested in her lineage. After all, Shelburne might be trying to prove she was *not* of his class. He would go about the situation the same way, would he not?

Shelburne broached another subject. "Would you have time for early morning drives before you go to the solicitor's office?"

She glanced at Amelia, who nodded. "Yes, I believe there is sufficient time, my lord."

Shelburne explained. "Since Hyde Park in the afternoon has not helped us, perhaps we might drive in Green Park in the mornings. Many people go there, not just the aristocracy."

"I'm familiar with Green Park, Rebecca," Amelia told her. "I see no problem with you driving there."

Thus, on Monday morning Shelburne's carriage wound its way to the more rural park, well known for cows and dairymaids. There, the earl and Rebecca strolled about within view of the bench where Mrs. Peters chose to sit while she enjoyed the antics of the nursery maids with their lively charges. Rebecca realized Amelia looked forward to these outings as much as she herself did. They probably brought back memories of her life before she made the disastrous marriage.

"Why are those people crowded around that cow?" Rebecca nodded toward a group a few yards away.

"They're purchasing milk from the dairymaid. Would you care for a cup?"

"Does she sell milk to just anyone?"

"Yes, to anyone who has the necessary pennies. Shall we join the group?"

"Yes, let's do, my lord. I have never seen milk coming from its original source. Just wait until Louise hears about this. I admit to being surprised that the matron didn't require us to learn about the extraction of milk from cows. We had to learn how to do so many other chores."

"You did chores at the orphanage? Do you mean household chores?"

"I implore you not to get Louise started on chores. Matron insisted that we could not manage households in a proper manner unless we knew the correct way to do the mundane, routine business of everyday life. How could we learn such things if we did not do them? I must admit she had logic on her side, dislike it though I did. We did everything from polishing the brass, to washing the dishes, to preparing meals, and everything in between. I expect the odor of the blacking we used on the andirons to remain with me to my dying day."

He smiled at her droll tone. "Did all the girls have the same requirements?"

"In this respect, yes, we did. We would all expect to have homes one day, would we not?"

"A telling argument indeed," he agreed with a laugh, which stopped when he heard Rebecca gasp. "Is there a problem, Miss Black? You seem perturbed. What startled you?"

"I just saw ... no, such is not possible." She shook her head.

"What did you see? If there is offensive behavior in the park, I will put a stop to it on the instant."

Rebecca drew her gaze from a point to their left. "Nothing, my lord, nothing offensive."

"Then what bothered you?"

Embarrassed, Rebecca took a deep breath and smiled at the absurdity of what she was about to say. "For a moment, I thought I saw two people vanish into the air. Such a thing cannot be, so let us forget it. A trick of the light, I daresay."

Shelburne agreed, and they turned their steps back toward Mrs. Peters, both forgetting the milk.

Thereafter, mornings often found them in the more rural Green Park where they could talk, uninterrupted by the requirements of society. On their third visit, Rebecca again saw two people vanish. This time the effect on her was different. She stood rooted in her tracks as two figures came toward her. A young woman wearing a deep blue dress had her hand tucked into the elbow of a man in regimentals. Before turning aside, they threw back their heads in a gesture of laughter but made no sound.

"Miss Black, whatever is the matter? You're staring as though you've seen a ghost."

Rebecca met his gaze. "Do you believe in ghosts, my lord?"

Shelburne studied her face for a moment before answering. "I have heard of them, certainly. I do not recall ever seeing one. I admit to skepticism about their existence."

"I have. Seen ghosts, I mean. I just did. At least I believe I did. The female looked like me." Her choppy sentences emerged in an anguished whisper. "Do you think the sighting is an omen, my lord? Is it possible I have seen myself dead at such a young age?"

"Nonsense," Shelburne blustered. "Another trick of the light, nothing more. Shall we return to Harley Street now?"

Rebecca forced herself to maintain a composed conversation, but she didn't believe what she had seen was a trick of the light. The apparitions had been in colors, blue, red, gold, and brown against greenery. To her admittedly limited knowledge, light could not produce such a variety. She avoided Mrs. Peters' questioning glance until Shelburne drove away after seeing Jamison open the door for them. Then Rebecca promised in a near whisper, "I'll explain everything over tea."

They found Louise waiting for them in the drawing room, so Rebecca only had to tell her story once.

"You poor thing," Amelia exclaimed when she had finished.

"What a horrible experience, to be sure," Louise agreed. "Yet I refuse to believe you saw yourself dead. I will not contemplate even the possibility of you dying young." Her voice broke. "You see, life without you is unthinkable."

It was Rebecca's turn to give a comforting hug. She did, but repeated, "The female looked like me—almost like looking in a mirror."

"Did she resemble you in every respect?" inquired Amelia. "Was she dressed like you? Hair and eyes the same color? Was her hair styled the same way as yours?"

Rebecca frowned in thought. "No. Her gown had a full skirt, old-fashioned I suppose one could say. She had blue eyes like mine. Her raven hair was in curls bunched under the brim of her bonnet."

"Well, you don't own a full skirted gown," Louise declared. "Furthermore, you have not had curls since you were a tiny girl."

"Who is to say that dress style won't come back into fashion? Hair styles change too, and I might cut mine someday."

"No, you will not, because I shan't allow such a thing," Louise stated in unequivocal tones. "So, the apparition could not have been you. Now, put her out of your mind."

Rebecca accepted that a part of Louise's concern was for herself—a dread of losing her best friend's friendship after so many years, but at least she believed in the apparition. The earl did not. Rebecca struggled not to resent Shelburne's disbelief. However, he couldn't know she was not an imaginative person.

Shelburne, too, tried to put the entire episode out of his mind. This was the second time Miss Black had seen something unexplainable in Green Park, or imagined she did. Could she have inherited an unbalanced mind? The thought bounced around in his head as he drove himself home. No, if she had an unbalanced mind, he would have seen evidence of it before now. Besides, Obadiah Wright would not champion her in the way he does if she was weak in the head. The solicitor was much too astute. There must be something in the atmosphere at Green Park which did not agree with Miss Black. This was reason enough to avoid the park, Shelburne nodded in satisfaction at his reasoning.

"Several days have passed since we visited Hyde Park," Shelburne announced the following afternoon. "Shall we test our luck there again? Who knows? This might be the day we meet the one person who recognizes you."

Rebecca hesitated, trying to put aside her resentment about his disbelief in the apparitions. Amelia covered the pause by voicing her agreement.

Rebecca had recovered her usual calm demeanor by the time Shelburne flourished his whip, directing his chestnuts through the Hyde Park entrance.

Keeping to what he considered a safe topic, he inquired into Rebecca's schooling. "Mr. Wright considers you well-informed, so you didn't confine your time to learning household chores. Did all the girls receive the kind of education you did?"

"Yes, sir, education was open to all the girls. However, beyond the required reading, writing and simple figuring, the duchess allowed each girl to follow her own aptitude. All females do not have the same capabilities, my lord. We are not all cut from one mold, contrary to masculine belief."

Noticing the tartness of her answer, Shelburne changed the subject. In truth, he was like most men in his attitude toward females. He considered their mental faculties vastly inferior to males and wondered at Obadiah Wright's naiveté in believing otherwise. Shelburne conceded Miss Black might have neat penmanship. She probably could read too. Many females could. Still, he was unable to accept that she was capable of learning more than the simplest figuring. How could such limited knowledge aid Mr. Wright who had several fully capable male clerks? Shelburne would humor her while he guided her into a better understanding of her limited abilities. In doing so, he would become better acquainted with her.

The days flew by. Shelburne took her for a drive in Hyde Park on most afternoons, or if the weather was inclement, they remained in the rooms in Harley Street under Mrs. Peters' watchful eye.

On one of those occasions, he appeased his curiosity about her employment. "Do the people at the orphanage find suitable positions for all their charges or do they depend on the regular domestic agencies for maids?"

"Oh no, they never use a domestic agency. The Triple D always ... "

"The what?"

Rebecca cast an impish grin toward him. "Triple D. Our soubriquet for the duchess."

His mouth twitched as he asked, "Dare I ask what it means?"

"The Darling Duchess of Dorchester."

He controlled his laughter. "Does she know the children gave her a special name?"

"Oh, yes, she loves it. The duchess truly is a very nice person, as you must know."

"No, I don't know because I cannot recall ever meeting her grace. Do go on. What does this paragon among females do?"

"The duchess finds positions for all the girls based on their abilities. She even gives them a small amount of money before she has them taken by carriage to the new positions."

"Is that what she did for you and Miss Tracy?"

"She was even more generous with us because we were not going into a private home. She hired Mrs. Peters to act as our chaperone, for which I bless her every day," Rebecca replied with a smile toward the estimable lady seated close by. "The duchess owns this building, which she converted into four flats some years ago. She supplied funds to furnish our rooms as we chose. She even supplied money to support us until we were earning a sufficient income to maintain ourselves, which we now do."

Shelburne agreed the duchess was generous. "Has she placed others in the same type of situation?"

"No, Louise and I are the first. She called us her experiment."

He briefly joined her laughter, then continued. "She educates the girls above the average, then finds suitable employment for them. Is she as progressive in other ways?"

"Her grace keeps all the girls at the orphanage until they turn eighteen."

"Eighteen? Is that not rather old for females to go into service?"

"I understand so. However, she believes too much is expected of girls at too young an age. The duchess does not educate her girls to be scullery maids. She says they will obtain higher positions and will manage their responsibilities better if they have more time to mature."

"I imagine she's right. Still, her grace's decision is unusual, considering how many females are married by their sixteenth year."

"The duchess is, indeed, an unusual female, my lord. She is quite verbal in defense of her girls." Rebecca smiled as memories of various encounters with the vicar flitted through her mind. "Do you know what I believe is the best thing she does?"

At his raised eyebrows, Rebecca continued.

"Should the girls ever leave their employment for any reason whatever, they return to the orphanage. The duchess considers it our home. The girls stay there until she finds them another place."

"Admirable, indeed. Otherwise, they might end their days on the streets."

One afternoon excursion in Hyde Park, Rebecca remained quiet until Shelburne asked if something bothered her.

"Not precisely bothered, my lord," she began. "We spend a considerable amount of time talking about me, never about you."

"I don't consider myself an interesting person. My life is much the same as that of every other man of my age and station. However, what do you want to know?"

"Anything you care to tell me."

"All right. I am the tenth earl in the direct line. My father is deceased. My mother resides at our country residence in Somerset, although this summer she is a guest of friends in Dorset. I have no brothers, but do have one older sister." He paused in surprise. "I've just realized something. You share the same name, only we call her Becca, so I don't think of her full name. Were you ever called by a nickname?"

"I do not believe so, although I have a vague recollection of my mother calling me Curly Top. She had such a sweet voice. At least I remember she sounded sweet." Rebecca bit her lip to stop the trembling. Even twelve years after her mother's death, the thought of her brought an ache deep within Rebecca's being.

"I am not sure about this," Shelburne cautioned. "It seems to me, though, you ought to remember more about your life before the orphanage."

"Do you remember much about your life before age six?"

Shelburne marshalled his thoughts as he turned his team back toward Harley Street. After several moments, he admitted he had little recollection of his earliest years. He told her of a hobbyhorse with a scarlet saddle. He chuckled and recounted sneaking out to the stable where he found some puppies.

"I hid one of the little fellows under my jacket, even managed to get back to the nursery without being caught. Unfortunately, my misdeeds were discovered when the puppy made a puddle in my bed."

"Your bed?"

"You see, I hid him under the covers. He was so small he hardly made a ripple in the blankets. Nanny found him and the wet sheets when she put me down for a nap. She kept a closer watch on me thereafter."

"Typical boy." Mrs. Peters chortled.

On that merry note, he escorted the ladies to the door and waited until Jamison admitted them before returning to his curricle, unaware he had an interested observer.

Chapter 6

Surprising Encounters

Unknown to either Rebecca or the earl, a silent witness to many of their drives followed them from one park to another. Lord Rushton, who had known Shelburne since their days at Eton, also liked early morning rides.

Rushton had noticed Shelburne with a raven-haired beauty strolling in Green Park. When they stopped going there, he went to Hyde Park with the hope of finding them. Whoever she may be, this beauty hadn't attended any of the *ton* parties with the earl or any other people as far as Rushton knew. Therefore, he reasoned, polite society did not accept her. This could only mean she was Shelburne's *chère-amie*, or if she did not yet occupy that exalted position, Shelburne was moving in her direction.

A bitter expression crossed Rushton's face when he remembered a petite fair-haired Cyprian who had thrown him over a few years before in favor of the earl's deeper pockets. Now was the time to even the score and this raven-haired beauty was just the chit he needed.

Deciding against a possible snub a request for an introduction would almost certainly produce, Rushton followed the pair to Harley Street from a distance. Reining in his mount a few doors away, Rushton watched Shelburne escort the females to the door before driving away.

Returning to Harley Street the following morning in a closed carriage, Rushton settled himself to watch the house. He had not long to wait. The object of his attention hurried out the door and entered a waiting carriage that sped away. Waiting only a moment, Rushton alighted from his carriage, then strolled to the house. He surveyed the large man who opened the door in answer to his knock.

Nonchalantly shaking coins in his hand, Rushton leaned forward. "Ah, good morning, my good man. I believe I observed an old friend leave this house moments ago. Could you tell me if she was Gertrude Billingsley from Somerset?"

"No."

"No? Do you mean 'no' you cannot tell me, or 'no' she is not Miss Billingsley?"

"I mean I cannot tell you anything about the lady." Jamison closed the door in the face of the annoyed inquisitor.

Rushton vowed to learn her identity. He would not be denied. The next morning, he again parked his carriage in Harley Street. When his quarry drove off, he followed at a discreet distance until he observed her enter a building located in a business area. He settled to wait, believing she would not spend much time in such a place. What would she do in there, anyway? No female has reason to visit such an establishment. Particularly one of her apparent lack of gentility.

An hour later, growing impatient, he entered the building and surveyed the interior, a large room where clerks sat at several high desks busily scribbling in books. He approached the first desk.

"I want to see the person in charge." When the clerk answered with a jerk of the head toward his left, Rushton strolled toward an older man.

The senior clerk peered over the steel-rimmed pince-nez perched on his beaky nose. "May I be of assistance, sir?"

"Yes, I trust you can, my good man. I'm inquiring about a young female whom I glimpsed entering these premises an hour ago. I believe she is a childhood friend from Dorset." Responding to the clerk's obvious skepticism, Rushton leaned forward and continued in a confidential manner. "I waited outside rather than have her think me inquisitive about her business affairs. However, I cannot wait any longer. I came to inquire whether she is, indeed, Gertrude Billingsley of Dorset?"

"Sir, I am not at liberty to discuss our clients. I will ask Mr. Wright to speak with you, however. May I give him your name?"

"Rushton," he replied, handing him a card.

The clerk carefully wiped his ink-stained fingers on a cloth before accepting the proffered card. Nodding toward a chair, he left the room.

Mr. Wright glanced up from the papers he was perusing when the clerk handed the small pasteboard to him.

"This gentleman inquired about a female who entered these premises an hour ago. He asked if she is Miss Gertrude Billingsley from Dorset."

"Did he give a reason for his interest?"

"He said he believes she is a childhood friend."

Mr. Wright glanced at the pasteboard in his hand. "Miss Black, are you acquainted with Aubrey James Montclair, Earl of Rushton?"

"No, sir." Rebecca directed her gaze toward the clerk. "Mr. Parker, are you sure he said Dorset?"

"Yes, Miss Black. He said Dorset."

Rebecca turned to Mr. Wright. "Last evening, Mr. Jamison told me a man inquired that morning if I was Gertrude Billingsley, a childhood friend of his from *Somerset*."

"What is your impression of the man?" Mr. Wright inquired of his clerk.

The answer came without hesitation. "He is quality without doubt. However, his manner, almost cunning, raised doubts in my mind about the actual reason for his questions."

Mr. Wright nodded. "Show his lordship in. I will judge for myself. Miss Black, please wait in your room until I call you."

A moment later, he welcomed Rushton into the room. "Good day, sir. I understand you're inquiring about one of our clients." Obadiah Wright prided himself on his ability to measure a man's character on sight. He observed the shifting eyes, the ingratiating voice as his visitor repeated his inquiry.

"You can understand I would like to renew my acquaintance with this old friend."

"Perhaps you should make your inquiries in Dorset. We do not have a client by that name." Mr. Wright escorted his visitor out of the building and watched until his carriage disappeared from view around a corner.

Rebecca waited in his room. "Miss Black, did you get a glimpse of him?"

"Yes, I did. I have never seen him before, to my recollection." She raised perplexed eyes. "Why would he be inquiring for me under that name from two different counties?"

"I fear he saw you some place and now attempts to obtain your identity." Wright paused a moment, frowning. "I dislike forming negative opinions, yet I believe his intentions are less than honourable. I doubt he will stop with these attempts, so be on your guard."

With a preoccupied air, Shelburne glanced up from his periodical when Rushton leaned against a chair facing him.

"Well met, Shelburne. I didn't expect to find you here."

"Oh? I come to Watier's frequently."

"Not since you took up with that raven-haired beauty I saw with you a few days ago. I must say she truly is a beauty, quite out of the ordinary. Where did you find her?"

Shelburne disguised his anger with a casual question. "Do you know the lady?"

"Not yet. Is she your latest bit of muslin?"

"The lady is not anyone's bit of muslin, nor will she be." With those angry words, Shelburne stormed out of the club, muttering deprecations about clods who couldn't recognize a lady when they saw one. The sooner he learned her identity the sooner everyone would recognize her as a lady. Shelburne mulled over his next move as he strode down the street, reaching a quick decision. He would go to Hampshire and talk to the Duchess of Dorchester.

The following day, Shelburne tooled his matched chestnuts along the circular drive leading to Dorchester Park. Arriving at the white columned house, he flung the reins to his tiger with instructions to walk them. His feet crunched on the gravel as he approached the door.

"I would like to speak to Her Grace." The stooped butler accepted his card, then escorted the visitor to a small, sunny morning room.

Shelburne rose to his feet when a white-haired lady entered the room on a waft of lavender scent followed by a footman with a tea tray. After bowing over her hand, Shelburne stood erect, accepting her scrutiny. For his part, he saw a lady of medium stature who stood so erect she appeared taller. Intelligence showed through the fading blue eyes trained on his face.

"Do I pass muster, Your Grace?" he asked, a small smile curving his lips.

"You are the image of your papa, Shelburne. He used his green eyes to some effect, too, as I recall." The duchess waved him to the chair opposite hers. "Your mama and I made our come-out together. How is she?"

"Mama is doing quite well, ma'am. It behooves me to admit that, according to her, I don't hold a patch on Papa," he added.

"Ah well, Olivia was besotted with him from the moment she first set eyes on him at Almack's." The duchess excused her old friend and handed Shelburne a cup of tea. "Now, to what do I owe the pleasure of your visit?"

Shelburne sipped the scalding brew before answering. Driving into Hampshire, he had gone over his questions several times in his mind, convincing himself that his reasons for seeking information about Miss Black were logical. Now, meeting her shrewd eyes, he was not as confident. Placing the teacup on the tray, he began in what he hoped was a confident tone.

"I met a young lady whose features are familiar to me even though I had never met her until quite recently. My curiosity is piqued. I want to know what her ancestry is, so I can place her features."

"She is someone I would know?"

"She is Miss Rebecca Black, who lived for a period of years in your orphanage."

"Where did you meet her?"

The change in her tone from pleasant to sharp surprised, nay shocked, him. Shelburne studied her face which had become remote. Her eyes shot sparks at him. What had he said to warrant this sudden change in her?

"I met her in the office of my solicitor, Mr. Obadiah Wright, Your Grace," he answered. "I have also met Mrs. Peters and Miss Tracy."

"Why do you want to know about Miss Black?"

"I told you ..."

"I heard what you said. Now, I want the truth if you please."

Shelburne shifted in his chair, crossed, then recrossed his legs. Blast the woman. What call had she to demand his intentions? There was no question that she believed she had the right and intended to have his answer. I don't have any intentions beyond learning her identity, he asserted to himself, ignoring the little voice in his head hooting in derision.

"I do not have any dishonorable intentions toward her," Shelburne assured the duchess, meeting her eyes. He ignored that little hooting voice again. Her stillness indicated his answer did not satisfy her. He tried again.

"Miss Black is without doubt a lady, and I find her company enjoyable." Shelburne stumbled through that statement under her sharp gaze. His words didn't satisfy her either, so he continued with a sheepish grin. "The fact is, Miss Black fascinates me. I have been unable to get her out of my mind from the first moment I saw her."

"And?"

"I can visualize her as my countess." Astounded, Shelburne asked himself where that idea had sprung from. He had not admitted the possibility even to himself until this moment. He hadn't even given the idea the remotest thought. However, the sense of relief he felt saying the words lifted a burden from his shoulders. "All things considered, I believe I could accomplish that more easily if I could learn her ancestry."

The duchess studied his face a moment longer then appeared satisfied with his answer. "I wish I could help you, Shelburne. I did attempt to find her family."

"Miss Black told me you had done so, Your Grace. I suppose I hoped you could tell me something, anything you learned, which you would not tell a child."

"Alas, I cannot."

"Then tell me this. How did she come to be at your orphanage? Was she left on the doorstep?"

"No, nothing like that. She was not an abandoned child. The vicar found her with her mother wandering on the street. Her mama, at least that is what Miss Black called her, was ill, so the Reverend Layton took them in. The mother had a fever of some sort and could not speak coherently. The apothecary made every effort to reduce her fever, but she died within hours. That's when the vicar's wife brought the child to us. She knew her own name and age but nothing else. I contacted the vicars in surrounding villages, but no one knew her. I regret that is all I know because someone nearby should have recognized her."

Shelburne mulled over what he had heard. "Miss Black never mentioned any names?"

"None."

They were silent for a moment.

"Rebecca Black was one of my favorite children, bright, eager to learn," the duchess reminisced. "The teachers kept me informed about her regular schooling, but I saw her intelligence for myself in conversation with her."

"I find it surprising Miss Black is employed in the capacity you found for her." Shelburne spoke in an even tone while he studied her face for a reaction. He received a tart answer, her eyes flashing with fire.

"I believe females will one day routinely enjoy employment in the public sector. I do my possible to further that belief through thorough education as Mary Wollstonecraft advocated. Confining females into one role in life is the height of ridiculousness. You don't expect all your cattle to have the same abilities, do you?" the duchess asked in barely suppressed steel, her eyes flashing more fire. Enough to scorch him if he wasn't careful.

"No, ma'am." Shelburne struggled to control his twitching lips. The duchess sounded just like his mother when she got in alt over implied insults to females.

When the duchess fell silent again, the earl encouraged her to continue.

"From the beginning, I have taken upon myself to teach my girls the niceties of life. With some, this type of education is easier than with others. With Miss Black, as with Miss Tracy, learning the niceties of life came naturally. I believe their mothers were from a higher class than was apparent." The duchess shook her head. "I wish I could reassure you about Miss Black's legitimacy, which is what I believe you want to know, but I cannot. I am sorry."

Shelburne accepted her words with a nod. "You are right, Your Grace. Although I'm confident that my family would support my choice of countess, Society being the way it is, I would like to know the circumstances of her birth and ancestry."

"What will you do if her ancestry never becomes clear?"

Shelburne didn't want to consider that possibility. "I know one thing, Your Grace. I will never dishonor her. You have my word on that."

"I believe you, Shelburne. You are too much like your father to take advantage of an innocent female."

"Thank you for recognizing that," he answered. "Perhaps we can go about this from a different perspective."

"How so?"

"Miss Tracy's features are also familiar to me. She told me of her parents, so if I can find other relatives of hers, they might lead me to Miss Black's family."

"I fail to understand how you reached such a conclusion. However, I'm unable to help with Miss Tracy's extended family either. No one in the village had any knowledge of them."

"How did she come to be at the orphanage?"

"Her parents, who lived in a more rural part of the county, died of influenza as did many people that year. Their neighbors brought Louise to me soon afterwards because they had too many mouths of their own to feed."

Shelburne nodded his understanding and changed his line of thought. "I understand you are responsible for Mrs. Peters being their chaperone. She seems quite devoted to them."

"She is the relation of some people I knew long ago. They disowned her when she married a horse fancier when she was little more than a child. As could be expected, he lost whatever funds he had on races. When I found her, she was a recent widow, almost penniless. I have her in permanent employ, so when these young ladies no longer need her, I'll send others to her."

"You chose well, Your Grace."

Rising to take his leave, he smiled down at her. "May I give any message to the ladies from their precious Triple D?"

Her laughter filled the room. "They are precious to me too. By all means, Shelburne, give them my love, as well as my best regards to Mrs. Peters."

Shelburne saluted the scented hand she held out to him in dismissal. He was no closer to knowing Miss Black's ancestry, yet felt he knew her better. He could hardly wait to see her again.

Where is the orphanage? Shelburne berated himself for not asking the duchess. He had given so much thought to his interview with the duchess he had not considered a visit to Miss Black's childhood home.

Pausing at the end of the drive, he gave the matter his attention. He had arrived from his right and hadn't seen anything remotely large enough to qualify. Turning left, a few minutes later he arrived at attractive wrought iron gates built into a curving brick wall. Pulling to a stop, he waited for the gatekeeper to approach.

"I'm Shelburne and have come from visiting the Duchess of Dorchester. Before returning to London, I wonder if I might look around the premises."

He forced himself not to stiffen at the steady gaze of eyes as black as coal directed at him from under bushy brows.

"I will arrange an escort, my lord."

The gatekeeper pulled a whistle from his jacket pocket and gave a blast so loud Shelburne flinched and tightened his grip on the reins.

A breathless young man loped toward them, skidding to a stop not more than one short step from the gatekeeper, who stepped backward.

"Danny, how many times must I tell you to mind your decorum?" The exasperated older man shook his head. "I'm going to show this gentleman around the premises. You stay here but mind you don't open the gate to anyone. Not a single solitary person. Do you understand me? Just tell anyone that I will return without much delay."

"Yes sir, Mr. Dysart. I won't open the gate." Danny stepped toward the lodge.

Shelburne hid a smile as Dysart shot one last glare at the young man then opened the gate. He didn't miss the warning to himself either. He was to have only limited time there. Or so Dysart thought. The Tenth Earl of Shelburne would stay as long as he pleased.

"Come through, my lord." Dysart closed the gate, which he rattled to be sure it latched, then swung himself into the curricle with more agility than his appearance would indicate possible.

Shelburne set the chestnuts into motion with a flick of his wrist then ambled down the smoothly raked gravel driveway while Dysart pointed and talked. Formal gardens lay to their left with a stand of hardwoods beyond. Their size verified they had not been cut within any local person's memory. A stable block was on their right partially visible around a corner of a surprisingly large manor house with extensions on both the right and the left. Shelburne counted windows of four floors plus an attic with its smaller windows. He pulled the chestnuts to a stop in front of steps leading to large double doors.

Before going inside, Shelburne turned toward a corner where children's joyous shrieks reached them. He stood somewhat hidden by a shrub, watching with a smile as a dozen or so girls of various ages ran around an older one in a game of tag. He remained while she allowed a smaller girl with an awkward limp to catch her, and continued to watch to see how the others would react. They were amazingly thoughtful as they kept the disabled girl in the game which surprised him, given his own school experiences as a boy and youth on games day. Perhaps girls were innately more compassionate than boys. He certainly hoped so because he didn't recall compassion toward him.

Shelburne turned back toward the entrance where Dysart said he would wait at the steps. With a nod, the earl banged the lion's head knocker twice then listened for footsteps.

The door opened without a sound revealing a tall, comfortably endowed woman wearing a starched bombazine gown in a cheerful shade of blue. The twinkle in her eyes greeted him.

"Come in, my lord. Her Grace sent word you might stop here. I'm Mrs. Dysart, the matron here." Before Shelburne could speak, she added, "I'm sure you wonder how I received her message this quickly so I'll tell you. She sent a rider across the fields—our most often way of communication."

That explained why Dysart was at the gate waiting for him. Thanking her for the explanation, Shelburne admitted he had speculated about his welcome—an unexpected stranger. "I only decided to come as I left Dorchester Park, so it was astute of Her Grace to realize I might come."

He should have known she wouldn't risk having him turned away by the zealous Dysart for which Shelburne was duly thankful.

"Will you have tea, or perhaps you prefer sherry, my lord?"

For some unexplainable reason, she intimidated him more than the duchess had done at her most austere stare. "Yes, please, Matron, I would enjoy a cup of tea. The roadway is quite dusty. Perhaps you will tell me what you know of Miss Black and Miss Tracy."

Mrs. Dysart ushered him into a small sitting room near the door where she pulled the bell cord. "I doubt I can tell you anything more than Her Grace did. However, I can add that I loved both Miss Tracy and Miss Black dearly. Both were quicker in learning than some of the others, which gave them ample time to get into mischief, which they did on a regular basis." Her laughter rang out. "You must ask Miss Black about gathering hen eggs. Also, Miss Tracy's story about her cat-and-mouse escapade will entertain you, I'm sure."

"I've heard about some of their peccadilloes but not those two." Shelburne laughed. "I look forward to hearing more. They have many happy memories of you and of living here."

They talked another half-hour but, to his regret, Shelburne stepped outside without learning more of the girls' ancestry.

The curricle swayed as Dysart swung onto the padded bench and nodded to Shelburne who set the chestnuts into motion. "I'll see you to the gate, Lord Shelburne."

Shelburne recalled how close to his shoulder Dysart had stood while they watched the girls at play. "I commend you for your carefulness when strangers are here."

"We can't be too careful where our children are concerned." He jumped down when Danny opened the gate. "Good day, my lord."

When the gate clanged shut behind him, Shelburne turned toward the village. At the vicarage door, he asked a woman wearing a smock where he might find the vicar only to learn he had gone to an outlying area for the day.

"May I spend a few minutes in the cemetery?" Receiving her nod, he strolled about a few minutes later searching for the grave markers of Mrs. Black and Mr. and Mrs. Tracy. They were simple stones engraved only with names and dates of their deaths. Mrs. Black had succumbed to her illness less than a year after Mr. and Mrs. Tracy.

Shelburne returned to the curricle where he sat in thought several moments, then set the chestnuts in motion. There appeared to be nothing further he could do in Wickham, so he turned toward London, his thoughts on those haunting blue eyes.

"I talked with a friend of yours yesterday, ladies." Shelburne accepted a cup of tea from Mrs. Peters, but he gazed at Rebecca.

"Who would that be, my lord?" she inquired. "I was not aware we have a mutual acquaintance other than Mr. Wright."

"The Duchess of Dorchester," he stated, smiling at the delight in her face. "Your precious Triple D."

"Oh, is she in London?"

"How is she?"

"Did you tell her you are acquainted with us?"

Shelburne chuckled at their eager questions.

"Oh, do tell us all about your visit, sir," Rebecca pleaded. "We miss her beyond belief."

"I drove into Hampshire to see her because I hoped she could give me some information about you."

"I recall your telling me you had never met her," Rebecca reminded him. "Do you tell me now that you approached her as an absolute stranger and she talked to you about me? I can hardly credit such."

"While it is true that I had never met the duchess, I realized she must be acquainted with my parents. My appearance is much like my father. I felt that would serve as an introduction."

"I see," Rebecca replied. "Did she tell you anything we had not already told you?"

Shelburne recounted his visit, but omitting any reference to his personal feelings for Rebecca. "I also had an interesting conversation with Mrs. Dysart at the orphanage."

"You must tell us everything, my lord. Please," Rebecca pleaded. "Matron was like a mother to all us girls."

He laughed. "Among other things, Mrs. Dysart suggested I ask each of you to tell me something. You're first, Miss Black, something about gathering hen eggs."

Rebecca covered her face with both hands and Louise bent double with laughter.

Shelburne warned, "Your turn comes next, Miss Tracy."

"Oh dear," Rebecca said. "I would rather not remember any of my escapades. However, if you insist, I'll tell the silly story. A few—all right, Louise, *several*—mornings passed without a particular hen laying any eggs. I didn't want her to feel badly, so I gathered one egg from each of the other nests and placed them under her."

"Tell him the rest," Louise insisted.

Rebecca's eyes glittered. "Must I?"

"It's the best part of the story."

"Then I suppose I must. The hen which didn't produce any eggs was a rooster."

After their laughter turned to hiccups, Rebecca defended her action. "I was only seven years old. Besides, why would anyone expect a rooster to occupy a hen's nest?"

"Obviously a peculiar rooster," Shelburne agreed. "Now, Miss Tracy, let us hear about your 'cat-and-mouse escapade', as Mrs. Dysart called it."

Rebecca collapsed into whoops.

Louise shot her a rueful grin when she finally dried her own streaming eyes. "I believe I was nine years old when I decided my life's mission was to emulate St. Francis of Assisi. I smuggled a barn mouse into our bedchamber."

"A mouse?" Mrs. Peters stared at her in patent disbelief."

"Yes, a mouse," Louise agreed with a straight face. "I needed one to feed the cat."

"What cat?" Shelburne didn't know when he'd enjoyed himself more. These ladies had enlivened his life no end.

Louise admitted she'd smuggled a stray Tom into the house. "I couldn't let the poor little mite starve. I knew Cook refused to have a cat in her kitchen. In fact, we weren't allowed to have either cats or dogs anywhere in the house."

"I can hardly wait to hear the rest," Shelburne told her.

"The mouse escaped into the corridor, which scared some girls who created such a stir most of the staff came running to the rescue. The cat came out of the bedchamber to join the fun and spied the mouse under a chest."

By this time, Shelburne was convulsed with laughter. When he sobered enough to speak, he asked her to continue.

"There isn't much more to tell. The cat succeeded in catching the mouse, then ran down the stairs with his dinner. Someone had the presence of mind to open the outside door, so he escaped. I saw the same Tom at different times thereafter, so I suppose he found his own food."

"I'm surprised Matron didn't tell you the whole story, my lord," Rebecca said. "That was her favorite tale for the remainder of our stay."

"I can understand why. Now, I must leave but, Miss Black, I want you to know I left Hampshire knowing the duchess agrees you are of genteel birth even though she couldn't help me. We will continue our efforts to find someone who recognizes your features."

He watched as the uncertainty in her eyes turned to acceptance, accompanied by the smile he hoped for as she agreed to continue their drives.

Shelburne began each ride with eagerness, scanning every face they passed. Yet as the days passed his eagerness faded. He simply enjoyed her company, realizing only as he returned to Grosvenor Square after each drive that he had given no thought to Miss Black's identity noting instead her restfulness and impish sense of humor, which was a constant delight to him.

Yet the day came when she renewed his concern for her emotional stability.

Chapter 7

Friends?

"Miss Black, have you had an opportunity to visit the Kensington Gardens?" Sitting in the quiet drawing room in her Harley Street rooms, Shelburne asked his question as he handed his teacup to Mrs. Peters for a refill.

"No, my lord, that pleasure awaits me."

"Sunday morning is the ideal time to be there because the lower orders are busy elsewhere. Shall we drive there this Sunday?"

Rebecca favored him with a direct gaze. "We attend worship services on Sunday morning, my lord."

"Then, would a visit to Kensington Gardens on Sunday afternoon be convenient?"

At Mrs. Peters nod, Rebecca replied, "Yes, my lord. We would enjoy visiting those gardens."

Shelburne was interested in knowing about life where Miss Black had lived as a child and took this opportunity to ask a question. "Speaking of the duchess reminds me of something I observed at the orphanage. The girls made a point of including a small girl with a noticeable limp in their game, even being slow enough for her to keep up with them."

"Oh yes, her name is Emily. She came to the orphanage soon after her birth. We girls took turns massaging her legs to make them strong until she could walk."

"Was she in an accident?"

Rebecca shook her head. "She was born with one leg somewhat shorter than the other. Her mother died giving birth. The rest of her family rejected her without compunction, but we girls accepted Emily as she is.

Rejection was something we understood because most of us had felt its sting."

Shelburne lightly touched her hand in quick sympathy. "So, all of you formed your own family."

"Yes, both the Triple D and Matron stressed that."

"You once told me the duchess finds employment for the girls. Will the limp hinder Emily in making a choice, or must she learn something which takes into consideration her limitations?"

"The limp would be worse except for the duchess. She has special shoes made for Emily. One of each pair has a thicker bottom than the other. As she grows, Emily becomes more adept at walking in them, so I don't believe her limp will be a hindrance in her employment."

"I don't believe I would have thought of special shoes, but continue."

"Emily's possible employment concerned several of us until we noticed how she enjoyed watching us dress. She often pointed out our choice of shawl didn't look well with our gown, or something similar. She could spend an hour or more brushing our hair too. That gave us the idea two years ago of approaching Matron about training Emily to be a lady's maid. Emily has proven us correct in our suggestion because she is already adept with hair styles which she practices on the girls."

"An excellent solution. She will have considerable experience when she leaves the orphanage."

Rebecca nodded. "Emily is also a good example of how much attention the duchess and Matron give each girl from the beginning for placing them in suitable occupations when the time comes."

Shelburne glanced at his fob watch then rose to take his leave. "I must keep an appointment now, but I do look forward to visiting the Gardens with any or all of you ladies soon."

Thus, on a pleasant Sunday afternoon after a few days of rain, Shelburne arrived at Harley Street in an open carriage. "Ladies would you care to visit Kensington Gardens?"

"All of us, my lord?" inquired Mrs. Peters with a glance toward Louise.

"Yes, Lord Shelburne, you must realize we might chatter until your ears hurt," Louise teased.

"I'll risk the pain. It would give me great pleasure to escort three lovely ladies this afternoon instead of the usual two. The gardens should be especially enjoyable after the rain."

Gathering their parasols, the ladies joined him.

At the entrance to the gardens, Shelburne dismissed his coachman with instructions to return in two hours.

Rebecca took a deep breath of the flower-scented air. "My lord, this is almost like being in the country, more so than being in Green Park even with those cows."

"I thought you would like this place," he replied with satisfaction. Tucking her hand within his arm, he drew her along the crushed stone path. Mrs. Peters and Louise wandered from one flowerbed to another, always remaining in view of the couple, who ignored them.

Nearing a small pond, Shelburne inquired if she would care to watch the ducks for a while. Receiving her agreeable nod, he guided her to a wrought iron bench, which he dusted with his handkerchief before seating her. As usual, the light scent of roses emanating from her hair tickled his nose. Shelburne reveled in the scent as he relaxed beside her. No matter the eventual outcome of his time with Rebecca Black, her scent of roses would remain with him the remainder of his days. They watched the antics of the ducklings in comfortable silence, broken occasionally by a chuckle at the mother duck's efforts to keep her babies in line.

Rebecca's gasp drew his attention.

A gentleman minced forward on shoes with high red heels which threw his torso dangerously forward, necessitating the Malacca cane to support him. His starched shirt points reached his cheekbones, preventing him from turning his head, which rejoiced in a mass of improbable red curls falling across his brow. This wondrous sight wore a yellow coat with heavily padded shoulders above apple green trousers. Numerous watch fobs adorned the red and blue striped waistcoat. Shelburne counted three rings on the one hand he could see.

Turning to Shelburne, Rebecca stated, "There goes my idea of a perfectly attired gentleman."

He turned a thunderstruck countenance toward her. "That is not a gentleman. That's a *dandy*."

Her shoulders shook as she inquired whether there was a difference.

Perceiving the glint in her eyes, he allowed a smile to tug at his lips before he informed her in a haughty voice a *gentleman* would never draw attention to himself by his clothing or accouterments.

"Could you not wear at least two or three fobs? Perhaps a ring or two? And you really need a curl dangling in the middle of your forehead, too, my lord. So romantic," she assured him in a breathless voice.

"Minx!"

Unable to control her mirth longer, she joined his laughter. They were wiping their streaming eyes when Mrs. Peters and Louise joined them. They returned to the carriage explaining the astonishing sight.

That evening, the girls remained in the drawing room after Mrs. Peters had retired to her bedchamber. They sat in silence over their needlework until Rebecca asked a question.

"Louise, do you believe that a gentleman can be friends, just friends, with a female?" She waited with anxious concentration for the reply.

"I fail to see why friendship should be impossible." Louise gave the question her full attention. "It seems to me friendship would depend on the expectations each had, or perceived the other to have."

"Perceived the other to have," Rebecca repeated.

"Was that a hypothetical question?"

The answer was indirect. "I believe I could be just friends with an interesting gentleman if I thought we could have nothing else."

"Are you thinking of Shelburne?"

Rebecca nodded.

"Somehow, I do not believe Shelburne would be content with friendship. Certainly not with you."

"Perhaps you're right. I feel we're friends even if we never become anything more."

Louise agreed friendship is very important. "Just think of ourselves. What would our lives have been, and still are, if we were not friends? Still, I am not sure a gentleman would be satisfied with only friendship with a female."

"I wish simple friendship, no deeper emotions, between a male and a female could be possible." Rebecca changed the subject. "Sometimes I feel like Job."

"You? *Patient*?"

Rebecca smiled but did not allow herself to be diverted. "I've never seen Job as patient. Although he never renounced God, Job did complain a lot. That's the way I am."

"As Matron told us, you recognize your problem, now do something about it."

Rising to her feet, Rebecca reached for her candle. "I know, but I need to be reminded often. This has been a busy day, so I will wish you pleasant dreams now."

"I wish the same for you," Louise replied, picking up her own candle.

Lying awake, Rebecca found it difficult to ignore her growing attraction toward the earl. She was far beneath his touch, a circumstance which might, just might, be resolved if she ever learned her parentage. Why had he never married? Ladies must have been casting out lures ever since he reached his majority. Perhaps even before. How could a female of any age, any station in life resist a wealthy, handsome, virile nobleman? That was a question for the ages, and she doubted there was an answer.

Over teacups the following afternoon, Rebecca gathered her courage to ask Lord Shelburne a question. She had debated with herself whether to mention the matter of a literary society to him because she did not want to give him the erroneous impression that she was a bluestocking, despite her advanced education. Yet when she left Hampshire, it had been with anticipation for the literary people she might meet. She had verified with Mrs. Peters that her attendance would be permissible if the place was reputable. Rebecca decided the only way she could be sure the

Frederick residence was a proper place for them to visit was to ask someone. Mr. Wright might know, but she hesitated to apply to him for anything of a personal nature. The earl was the only other person of her acquaintance who could answer her question, so she would ask him.

"Lord Shelburne, are you acquainted with Lady Augusta Frederick?"

"I'm acquainted with her, yes. However, I don't claim friendship. Why do you ask?"

"I saw a notice in the newspaper that she holds literary discussions on Sunday afternoons. I would like to know if they are open to strangers and whether it is proper for me to attend them."

She waited anxiously for his reply. Her words met silence while Shelburne appeared deep in thought. Not for the first time, Rebecca wished she could read his thoughts.

Shelburne studied her face, seeming to peer inside her head, before answering in a slow voice. "There is a possibility your parents had been London residents, and perhaps literary, which would explain your interest and the education you found easy, according to the matron. So, it is certainly possible that someone among today's literati would recognize your features."

"Recognition had not occurred to me, but I admit the possibility," she agreed.

"Then you want to go for the literary aspect."

"Yes, I would, if the place is reputable, if strangers are permitted to attend."

"As far as I am aware, Lady Frederick's salon is reputable. I have never heard to the contrary. Is there someone special who will be there this week?"

"No one in particular, but the notice indicated Sir Walter Scott attends on occasion. Have you read his *Lady of the Lake*?"

"I must admit I have not."

"Oh." She cast an impish glance from under her eyelashes, then spoke with a die-away air. "I don't suppose you read Lord Byron's poetry, either. Anyone who refuses to wear a curl on his forehead could not possibly appreciate his genius."

Shelburne shouted with laughter. He exhibited no interest, yet he said, "To make up for my lack of reading sensibility, I promise to escort you to Cheney Walk this Sunday afternoon. I will even listen regardless of the subject and no matter how boring."

Rebecca beamed a genuine smile toward him. "Thank you, my lord."

Sunday afternoon proved to be perfect for a drive to Chelsea. However, reaching there, Rebecca soon wondered whether her idea had been a good one. A glance at Shelburne's determined face seemed to confirm her thoughts. Climbing the short flight of steps, Rebecca clasping one of his arms and Louise the other, they endured the high-pitched voice of an overweight female extolling the virtues of wearing trousers rather than the gowns society demanded females to wear. So much more comfortable, she said as she gasped for breath.

Once inside the drawing room Rebecca stood in startled silence when a gaunt, hollow-cheeked gentleman wearing a smeared painter's smock accosted them. He used his hands to frame Rebecca's face, mere inches away, exclaiming he must, he really must paint this enchanting creature on the instant.

Shelburne was not gentle in removing the would-be Gainsborough from their path, his eyes constantly searching for their hostess as they moved deeper into the room.

After a glance at Louise, Rebecca stared, wide-eyed, at all the people. How could they ever be quiet enough to discuss anything? Someone pushed between her and her companions, thus Rebecca found herself struggling to get back to them. Before she could, a pale-faced young gentleman gazed with rapturous intensity at a point to the left of her face. Shoving her onto a spindly chair against the wall, he knelt at her feet, clasping her hands in his and sighing over her shell-like ear.

She stared at him, appalled at his behavior.

"Get up, sir, do," she begged to no avail.

He continued to stare, his face getting closer to her ear until he landed in her lap. Managing to free her hands, she pushed him away, directly into the path of the woman in trousers who fell on top of him with her considerable weight.

Midst the ensuing high-pitched giggles, Rebecca moved away from them, her face hot. She inched her way around the side of the room, searching for Shelburne, until she collided with a solid object that rocked her back on her heels.

"Oh, I do beg your pardon, sir." Rebecca gazed into a pair of dark brown eyes that twinkled at her from beneath bushy eyebrows.

"There's no need to beg pardon, little lady." The rotund gentleman steadied her with hands that clasped her shoulders. "I have never known Freddie's salons to be quite this crowded although she must be in alt. She does like people surrounding her."

"Freddie?" Rebecca asked. "Do you mean Lady Frederick? I have yet to meet her."

"Come, I will lead you to her. I'm Buchanan, by the way. We're informal here." So saying, he clasped an arm around her shoulders using the other to push their way through the crowd to a petite lady ensconced on a high-backed sofa, her feet on a brocade hassock. She interrupted her dissertation on the disgrace of children working in mines to gaze at the newcomers. Raising her pince-nez, she studied Rebecca from the top of her once carefully arranged hair to the blue slippers peeking out from under the darker blue muslin gown. With a welcoming nod, she asked, "Who do we have here, Bucky?"

"I don't know, Freddie, but she was looking for you, so I brought her. She's so pretty I am unable to resist her." He released Rebecca's shoulders.

Rebecca dipped into a curtsy, almost landing in Lady Frederick's lap when someone bumped into her from behind. "Oh, I do beg your pardon, my lady! My name is Rebecca Black. I only recently moved to Town from Hampshire. This is the first time I've been privileged to attend one of your salons. Thank you for permitting a stranger into your home."

Her hostess motioned Rebecca to sit beside her on the sofa. "Child, I enjoy meeting new people. Are you enjoying yourself so far?"

"My lady, thus far I've spent more time apologizing than anything else." Rebecca's confession brought amiable laughter from surrounding people and eased her embarrassment. She joined the conversation on the evils of child labor.

A much-disheveled Lord Shelburne, clutching an equally disheveled Louise by one wrist, found Rebecca an hour later, whereupon he broke into their conversation without apparent compunction. The expression on his face was easy to read. His temper was near the end of its tether. The sight of her being in the center of several people hanging on to her words failed to appease him.

"Ah, Miss Black, here you are. I see you found our hostess."

Rebecca blinked at him, recognized his obvious displeasure, and then met Louise's amused grin. To her chagrin, Rebecca had forgotten the others. She gave herself a mental shake and rose to her feet, an apology on her lips.

"Shelburne, are you acquainted with this delightful child? You rarely show so much discrimination," Lady Frederick informed him.

With a strained smile, Shelburne acknowledged his acquaintance with Miss Black. "I believe I should return her to her residence now. Shall we leave, Miss Black?"

Rebecca had been studying him, not sure what to make of the polite—not censorious—tone of his voice. "By all means, my lord."

Responding to his tug on her hand, she managed a quick curtsy to her hostess. "Lady Frederick, I have had a delightful time. May I come again, please?"

"To be sure you may, Miss Black. It is rare to find a gel as young as you are with so much knowledge. I look forward to seeing you again and delving further on your ideas for curbing child labor." She smiled and returned to her conversation with the others.

Rebecca was quiet as Shelburne guided her out of the crowded room. Once outside, she glanced at the silent earl, who stared straight ahead. Was he angry with her? Risking a snub, she asked, "Did you have a pleasant time, my lord?"

Receiving no answer, she chattered on with a description of the woman in trousers falling on top of the poet. Noticing his twitching lips, she murmured, "He did not wear any fobs or rings, so I suppose he was a gentleman?"

Shelburne raised one eyebrow, but grinned. In perfect accord, they proceeded toward their carriage until they heard his name called by a soldier dressed in regimentals.

"Burton! I was not aware you had returned from Spain. When did you get back?" Shelburne vigorously shook the newcomer's outstretched hand. They talked excitedly for a moment until it occurred to Shelburne to introduce his companions. Turning to them he said, "Ladies, may I present a close friend, Major David Burton? David, this is Miss Rebecca Black and Miss Louise Tracy."

Rebecca acknowledged the introduction before her gaze dropped to the braid on the major's uniform. Her fingers rubbed her left cheek.

Seeing the puzzled expression on Rebecca's face, Shelburne made arrangements with the major to meet at Watier's that evening then handed the ladies into the carriage. Taking the reins from his tiger, he gave the horses the office to start, then he asked. "What is the problem, Miss Black?"

Continuing to massage her cheek, Rebecca raised her eyes to his. "I am not sure, my lord. When I saw the braid on his uniform, my face started hurting. A vague memory flashed into my thoughts of being embraced by a man wearing a red coat like the major's. The braid dug into my cheek."

"Perhaps your father was in the army. You might yet bring forth enough memories to identify yourself. I wish I knew how to speed up the process."

"Perhaps," she agreed and stopped rubbing her cheek although the puzzled frown remained.

Escorting them to the door in Harley Street, he commented on their plans for the following day. "Many people are returning to town for some special functions over the next few days, before returning to the cooler country air again. Shall we drive in Hyde Park tomorrow afternoon? We should see quite a few people who have not yet observed you."

"A drive in Hyde Park would be delightful, my lord," Rebecca agreed and then hurried indoors, eager to hear how Louise had fared in the crowded salon.

After relating her own experiences to Louise and Amelia, Rebecca settled her teacup on a small table beside her. "Now, Louise, it's your turn. Did you meet interesting people?"

Rebecca raised her eyebrows when she received a shout of laughter in answer.

"After we lost sight of you, Shelburne held my arm in such a grip I couldn't do anything except stumble after him around the room as he searched for you. We must have crossed the room, back and forth, at least five times."

Rebecca joined the laughter, but as it faded to chuckles, she sighed. "I don't suppose Shelburne will care to escort me there again."

"You must admit the salon was loud and crowded," Louise told her. "If all literary salons are like this one, I wouldn't care to go to another one."

"I managed to block out the noise as we talked about the horrors of child labor, which, unfortunately, is rampant particularly in the industrial areas. Some children working in those businesses are as young as six." Rebecca remembered being six years old and cringed at the thought she might have ended like those poor children spending long days in the dark holes of coal mines.

Amelia refilled their teacups, a puzzled expression on her face. Her tone was pensive when she said. "I've never understood how anyone could mistreat children, yet abuse happens all around us."

"I would like to be a part of the solution to this particular problem," Rebecca confided on an impulse. She had befriended many small children who came to the orphanage, most often in tears. The conversation at Lady Frederick's salon had confirmed her in her desire to help those unfortunate children who had no one else.

"Perhaps you can someday," Amelia encouraged.

Rebecca nodded. "For now, I'll ask whether Mrs. Morton needs my assistance in the kitchen."

Chapter 8

Tribulations of Separation

Arriving on Rotten Row soon after five o'clock the following afternoon, his matched chestnuts pulled Shelburne's phaeton along the wide carriageway. He had judged the crowd correctly. There were more people than he had seen at Season's end. Gentlemen in curricles vied with ladies in open landaulets, their parasols held high. The younger gentlemen flaunted their expertise in high perch phaetons, gaining the admiration of young ladies but the disapproval of older ones.

Shelburne smiled in satisfaction. Rebecca was already causing quite a sensation. Sure enough, they stopped often as various people, both in carriages and on horseback, sought an introduction to the lovely lady riding with the *Ton*'s most elusive earl. Rebecca acknowledged each person with sparkling eyes and a radiant smile.

"Shelburne, you dog, introduce us to this beauty! How dare you keep her to yourself?"

"Mrs. Peters, Miss Black, I recommend you ignore these fribbles, at least until they learn appropriate manners."

A chorus of indignant replies met this sally. Shelburne grinned as he performed introductions to Major Stovall, Major Honeycutt, and Captain Dixon. "They call themselves members of the Horse Guards when they are naught but Hyde Park saunterers!" He waved away their responses to this impertinence as he moved the carriage forward.

Rebecca chuckled, but before she could comment, they stopped yet again. A matron, accompanied by two giggling girls dressed in identical white muslin gowns, which did nothing to improve their sallow complexions, waved a parasol at them and then stepped in front of their carriage. Shelburne perforce drew the chestnuts to a standstill, his face shuttered, his lips in a thin line. The woman stepped to the side, her gaze focused on Rebecca.

"Shelburne, who's the chit?" The abrupt question came from the overdressed matron whose puce bonnet boasted no less than five plumes.

Shelburne's voice was noticeably cool as he said, "Good day, Mrs. Davenport." Before she could speak further, he put his horses into motion. They moved on, Shelburne muttering about "encroaching Cits."

He spoke to several people as the phaeton made its slow way around the park before leaving by the Stanhope Gate. Rebecca was quiet except for a few comments on the marvelous sight of the *beau monde* on the strut.

"My lord, I noticed several of the gentlemen who stopped us are of the military. I gather from some of the conversation that you are too. Have you served with Wellington?" She corrected herself. "I should call him the Earl of Wellington, should I not?"

He grinned. "I, too, have a hard time remembering Old Hookey is an earl now."

"Old Hookey," Rebecca exclaimed on a gurgle of laughter. "Now it is my turn to ask—does he know you call him that?"

"Oh yes, he knows and revels in the familiarity. Even Spanish peasants called him by his nickname." He explained. "It is his nose, you understand. Have you ever seen him?"

"No. If he was ever in Hampshire, I was not aware of his presence, but I've heard of his exploits. We digress. Did you serve with him?"

"Yes, I was with him in the Portuguese campaign of '08. From there we went into Spain. I had to sell out when my father died last year. I am his only son, you see, so I must manage the estate." There was an obvious tone of bitterness as he added, "I feel I should be with my men, not staying safely in England while they lay dying in Spain."

"I believe I can understand the way you feel," she told him. "Have you taken your seat in Parliament? Or has there not been sufficient time?"

"Not yet although I have given the matter some thought. The estate keeps me busy. I have no interest in political matters anyway, much to my secretary's oft-repeated comments on the subject."

"The war is controlled by politics," she exclaimed. "At least it seems so to me from reading newspapers. Correct me if I'm wrong."

"You're right, but the entire political situation is in an upheaval since the assassination of Perceval in May."

"Does your knowledge indicate Lord Liverpool will become the next prime minister?" Rebecca touched Shelburne's arm. "Oh, please forgive me for asking a question you might not want to answer."

"There's no reason I cannot answer. Liverpool resists the idea because he prefers a younger man. Yet, there does not appear to be another suitable candidate of any age." Shelbourne shook his head in exasperation. "You see, age is the problem. Liverpool is too old to run the party. The Duke of York is too old to command the army."

"I notice you don't include the Mary Anne Clark debacle in his ineligibility."

"Oh, no, no, I assure you that was a mere tempest in a teapot. York would never sell army commissions. The idea is ludicrous, as Prince George recognized when he reinstated York as commander-in-chief last year. Returning York to the post he held for many years was George's first act after Parliament name him Regent. I admire him for doing so. At the present time, age is the deciding factor in leadership. Old age."

"Perhaps the experience needed to run the army, nay the entire nation, comes only with many years of service in various capacities."

They had drawn to a stop in front of her residence. Shelburne studied her serious face a moment. "I had not thought about experience in that light, so I must give it more thought. There may well be some way I can be useful, after all."

She chuckled. "While you gain the experience you need to assume either position at some point in the future?"

"The mere thought of either possibility is enough to send me to Bedlam." Throwing the reins to his tiger, he escorted the ladies to the door where Jamison waited to admit them.

Rebecca showed her dimples. "Does the House of Lords require members to wear much jewelry?"

He laughed as he bowed over her hand and took his leave.

Late that evening Rebecca stood by the open window of her bedchamber, unable to sleep because of the heat. If the weather was this hot in June, what should they expect in August? She wafted a fan near her face, recalling the pleasant ride.

The memory of the friendly soldiers made her smile. Still, try as she might, she could not stop thoughts of the earl's rudeness to Mrs. Davenport from intruding. He treated other people of the lower orders with politeness. What was different about Mrs. Davenport? Then she realized. A woman of the lower orders had brought forth his rudeness. Encroaching Cit, he had called her.

Rebecca's fan came to an abrupt stop, even as her heart seemed to stand still.

A tap on the door interrupted her thoughts. Louise peeped inside. "I saw your candle light. Can you not sleep either?"

When Rebecca shook her head, Louise pointed her toward the bed. "Do you remember when I used to sit on your bed while we whispered secrets after everyone else was asleep?"

"I do. Those were some of our happiest times." Rebecca plumped the pillows against the headboard. She then pulled her knees to her chest and laid her forehead against them. Louise pulled a chair to the side of the bed. After a moment, without raising her head, Rebecca gathered the courage to tell her about the afternoon ride.

"What if I'm a Cit? Will he reject me out of hand if we learn one or both of my parents were residents of the City? Employed in the City?"

Louise shook her head. "You're upsetting yourself for no cause."

"You're saying I should not be concerned about how Shelburne would react about my parents being Cits until we learn whether they were."

"Yes."

"You ignore one thing. I'm employed in the City, so that makes me a Cit, does it not?"

Louise was cautious. "His lordship knows of your employment but he hasn't rejected you, so that must mean you're not truly one."

Pretending to be convinced, Rebecca issued a huge yawn then declared she could sleep now. Louise assured her with a laugh she could take a hint and returned to her own bedchamber.

Rebecca snuffed her candle but did not lie down. Rather, she went back to the window, again twisting the fan in her agitation. She pondered Louise's words even as she wondered why the earl had not already rejected her. Perhaps he did not believe she belonged in the City. He did not believe her features belonged to any merchant or banker he had met. Perhaps the possibility of her being a Cit had not yet occurred to him. What would happen when he thought of it?

Rebecca Marie Louise Black might be uncertain about many things, yet in her heart, she knew one thing beyond doubt—Shelburne would bid her a civil, but definite, good-bye. The fan snapped in her hands, bringing her thoughts to reality.

The knowledge his emotions could be so shallow saddened her. Still, in honesty, she had to admit that she might well feel the same way under the same circumstances. They differed in so many ways, could they ever reach a compromise?

This business of lower orders, for instance. Seeing them as different, lesser in many ways, was natural for him because of his station in life. Rebecca, on the other hand, had always lived with all sorts of people paying no attention to class distinction. Even the Duchess of Dorchester with her wealth and high rank had treated everyone without prejudice.

Rebecca straightened her shoulders turning away from the window where the first signs of a lightening sky greeted her. She must get some sleep before she went to her employment in the City. She dozed off with the thought it would be well if, in the future, she guarded her foolish heart with more care.

A couple of days later, Rebecca and Louise sat with their teacups in hand, each lost in her own thoughts. The drawing room door opened, gaining their attention. Rebecca's heart quickened when the earl strolled across the expanse of carpet, his hand outstretched. She schooled her face not to show her pleasure at the sight of him, but allowed him to take her hand.

"Good afternoon, ladies. I trust you are both well?"

Rebecca ordered her leaping heart to behave as she reluctantly withdrew her hand from his. Despite her resolve, she had been staring into space, thinking of him, and his sudden appearance flustered her.

"A good afternoon to you too, my lord. Yes, we are quite well, thank you. I'm sorry Mrs. Peters is not here to greet you. She will be sorry to have missed you. Errands demanded her attention this afternoon."

"Will you have tea, my lord? Morton has just this instant brought a fresh pot." Louise busied herself with the teacups.

"Thank you, Miss Tracy." He glanced at Rebecca over the cup rim. "I came by unannounced because I have just received word that I need to go to Shelburne Park for a few days. I have not been there as much this summer as I normally am. I wanted to take proper leave of you before I go."

"I trust there is no problem, my lord."

"Nothing serious. Merely decisions which only I can make. I have an excellent steward, but he can do only so much without my directions, which I can't give from a distance."

After chatting for a few minutes, the earl rose to leave. He captured Rebecca's gaze. "I shall miss you."

"We look forward to your return, my lord," Rebecca answered him as calmly as she could manage. She could not find the words to admit how much she would miss him, how the time would surely fall heavily on her hands until his return. She couldn't have said them anyway. Most improper, the duchess would say, too brazen for a lady.

When the door closed behind Shelburne, Rebecca turned to Louise, who stared at her with a troubled expression. "Is something wrong?"

"No, nothing is wrong," Louise replied, refraining from sharing her thoughts.

Rebecca realized Louise would miss him too even though she didn't see him as often as did Rebecca.

Amelia's return brought a discussion of their respective days, so both Rebecca and Louise allowed thoughts of the earl's absence and its effect on their lives to slip from their minds.

By the third day of Shelburne's absence, Amelia was ready to pull out her hair. She was fortunate the gel went to Mr. Wright's office for part of each day, otherwise they might have come to cuffs. Rebecca moped. Rebecca sighed like a love-struck chit not yet out of the schoolroom. Rebecca stared into space failing to hear half of what anyone said to her. Amelia decided she'd had enough of such behavior.

"Rebecca?" Receiving no reply, she waved her hand in front of Rebecca's face. "Rebecca, will you pay attention to me, please?"

With a blink, Rebecca returned to the present. "Whatever is the matter, Amelia? Must you raise your voice to me?"

"I believe so since you ignore me otherwise." Amelia glared at her. "Now listen to me, my girl. This nonsense must stop. You have languished around this house ever since Shelburne left. I'm surprised you still have employment with Mr. Wright if you mope around his office the way you do here."

Rebecca bit her lip, misery evident on her pale face.

Amelia's voice softened somewhat. "My dear girl, I believe you have lost your heart to Lord Shelburne. Is that wise?" Receiving no answer, after a moment, Amelia persisted. "What will you do if he ever leaves never to return?"

Biting her lip, Rebecca hurried from the room.

Amelia listened to Rebecca's footsteps pacing behind the bedchamber door. She knew the younger woman was upset with her, but Rebecca was also intelligent. When she thought through her behavior, she would get past her anger. Amelia sat in thought about a solution to Rebecca's problem when Louise returned home.

"Sit here beside me, my dear. I want to talk to you about something important."

Louise joined her on the sofa, her eyes wide, her face solemn. She clasped Amelia's hands in her own. "What is the problem? Have you received bad news from someone?"

"No, this isn't about me." Mrs. Peters took a deep breath. "I want to talk with you about Rebecca. You've noticed how she is reacting to Shelburne's absence, have you not?"

"I could hardly avoid seeing her staring into the distance. I've given up trying to communicate with Rebecca. I can only hope Shelburne will return before she goes into decline."

"We need to distract her, so what do you think about having a party?"

Louise's eyes shone and she released Amelia's hands into a clasp of her own. "A party sounds just the thing. I'm sure hosting a party will be a lot of fun even though we've never had one."

"Whom shall we invite? Do we even know enough people?" Amelia asked. "Do we have enough space for a big crowd?"

"I shouldn't think so. Small parties are much the best anyway, I feel sure. I must admit, though, I have never been to any party except our birthdays at the orphanage. They were fun but not like an adult party." Louise added with a small laugh, "Any size would be stupendous."

They had their heads together thinking of names when Rebecca joined them, her face again serene. "Are you talking secrets?"

"We're going to have a party, Rebecca! Is that not stupendous?" Louise fairly bubbled in her enthusiasm.

"Sounds like fun, but who can we ask to a party? We hardly know anyone."

"We are just now discussing that. I thought of Toby Williams …"

"You said you had never met him." Rebecca interrupted without compunction. "You cannot invite a stranger to a party."

"His sister introduced us since then," Louise explained. "He's nice. So is his sister Josephine. We will invite her too."

Amelia frowned. "I don't recall you mentioning her before. Is she one of your pupils?"

"No, she doesn't care to learn to play the piano. She has reached her twentieth birthday and is betrothed to a clerk in her father's business. His name is John, I believe. We can invite him too."

"I realize extensive knowledge about all your students isn't necessary," Amelia assured Louise.

"However, before we invite them into our home, should we not have some personal information?"

Louise agreed. "Yes, of course, I agree with you. I must have neglected to tell you that, in my interview with Josephine's parents about teaching the younger girls, they questioned me about my morals. They quizzed me on various points."

"Then inviting them is not a problem."

"Now, who else shall we invite?"

Rebecca hesitated. "I could ask Mr. James Lowell, I suppose."

"Who is he?" Amelia asked.

"A gentleman I met in Mr. Wright's office when he came in to receive information about an inheritance. He's employed as librarian to Lord Worthington and seems quite nice. On several occasions, he invited me to share luncheon with him in a coffee shop. I always refused."

"Has Mr. Wright heard of these invitations?"

The anxiety in Amelia's voice brought quick nod. "Although he has no reservations about Mr. Lowell, he told me going to a coffee shop without a chaperone is not proper for a young lady."

"Then we can add him to the list." Amelia nodded to Louise, who wrote the name.

"Amelia, who would you like to invite?"

"Mr. Jamison introduced the gentleman who lives in the rooms above us. Mr. Samuel Rogers has been congenial each time we've spoken."

They continued to add to the list until they had twelve, including themselves, and decided that was enough.

The dinner party proved successful, resulting in some return invitations. They hesitated over accepting a surprise invitation from Josephine Williams for an evening of whist. Gambling was abhorrent to them, even if they could have afforded chicken stakes, but with the assurance playing whist was only for fun, they spent an enjoyable evening.

Mr. Rogers, who did not feel competent to prepare a meal for guests, was their host for dinner in a coffee house. They could hardly control their mirth as he regaled them with stories of the trials and tribulations of being a tailor's assistant. Mr. Lowell and Mr. Williams became familiar visitors to Harley Street, as did Mr. Rogers who gazed upon Mrs. Peters with admiration. Amelia blushed rosily when her charges teased her about her conquest. Still she walked with a lighter step in the following days.

In Somerset, Shelburne busied himself with his estate agent who had been surprised to see him. Although he had been less than honest with the ladies in Harley Street, honesty now compelled Shelburne to admit to himself there had been no need for him to return to the country although his first question to the agent pertained to the foal due any day.

Reassured that the little guy had arrived in good health the day before, he strolled out to the stable to admire the tiny creature standing on wobbly legs next to his mother. Shelburne stroked the mare's mane and murmured his congratulations on a job well done before turning to the groom who couldn't hide a grin,

With an answering smile, Shelburne said he expected great things on the racetrack from the newcomer in a year or so. He turned the subject to the rest of the stable. Do the stable boys exercise each horse every day? Do they have the necessary light touch?

The steward hid his surprise at questions which the earl knew were unnecessary because all the hands had been with the estate for many years.

As the days passed, he discussed with his agent the possibility of putting more fields under cultivation. Together, they inspected each barn roof with an eye toward repairing them before harvest, in the event restoration was necessary. Shelburne rode out every morning and talked with the tenant farmers. In the afternoon, he spent time going over the record books. He made a point of conferring with the housekeeper then shocked her beyond measure when he inquired about the number of sheets needed to maintain the household. Shelburne even invaded the kitchen premises to consult his chef about a newer model of enclosed stove.

All this to forget a pair of blue eyes that haunted his days as well as his nights. Nothing worked for the simple reason she was there in the house. At least, Shelburne corrected himself, he felt her presence there, which was impossible, yet he couldn't convince himself otherwise.

Shelburne paced the terrace one evening while he tried to puzzle through his thoughts.

He sensed Miss Black in the drawing room, but not the library; in the dining room, but not the estate office. When he traversed the broad stairs, the feeling she was there was almost tangible. It was enough to drive a man insane and Shelburne was beginning to think he had reached that point.

A sudden idea sent Shelburne in long strides from the terrace around the corner of the house to his mother's rose garden. There, he stood between trellises where red, yellow, and pink roses climbed in a riot of color, their scent floating on a slight breeze. Inhaling deeply, he thought of the scent surrounding

Miss Black and the bowls of potpourri in her drawing room.

Nothing. He had no feeling of her presence.

Shelburne returned to the house none the wiser.

Chapter 9

Unwelcome Attention

Rebecca saw the apparitions again.

Mr. Lowell had suggested they visit Green Park. Afterwards, Rebecca could not decide if she was pleased or sorry. She only knew the apparitions were there, regardless of what others might think. And she wanted to see them, perhaps be close enough to look her other self in the face.

Strolling across the grass, Mrs. Peters and Mr. Rogers walking behind them, Rebecca exchanged idle pleasantries with Mr. Lowell. Fluffy pillows of clouds drifted across a wide expanse of deep blue sky while in the shrubs, chaffinches added their song to the lowing of the ever-present cows, but the odors created by those cows soon became insignificant to Rebecca.

Glancing around, she gasped, and came to a complete stop, unaware that her companions stopped also. Rebecca was aware only of the two people who stood in front of her. Perhaps stood was not the correct word. Rather, they floated a few inches above ground, swaying in the slight breeze, aware only of each other. Rebecca gulped for air, and then forced herself to concentrate.

This time the woman wore a gown of deep rose with a lace fichu tucked in the décolletage, but her raven hair was still in curls bunched around the brim of her chip straw bonnet.

Rebecca shifted her gaze to the man who still wore regimentals. He had fair hair and dark blue eyes she could only describe as laughing.

If the female apparition was herself, who could the gentleman be? Rebecca felt a hand shaking her shoulder and turned to gaze into Mrs. Peters' worried eyes.

"My dear, are you unwell? Perhaps we need to return home."

"Yes, I believe returning home is an excellent idea. I suddenly feel somewhat faint."

When they reached her Harley Street residence, Rebecca apologized to Mr. Lowell for cutting short their walk, then hurried indoors barely acknowledging Mr. Jamison's greeting.

Once inside their drawing room, Mrs. Peters was the first to speak. "Are you ill? Or did you go off into a daydream again?"

Rebecca denied such had happened with a vehement shake of her head. "I saw those apparitions again."

"I'm beginning to think you're all about in your head," Mrs. Peters declared. "If you continue this way, you will end up in Bedlam.

After a long pause, Rebecca shook her head. "The woman is too much like me not to be me, but I don't know who the soldier could be. I have never been acquainted with anyone in the military."

Mrs. Peters stared at her in consternation. "My dear, Rebecca, you must put that notion right out of your head. You cannot see into the future. Holy Scripture makes clear the impossibility. There's no such thing as ghosts anyway. They're the product of disordered minds. However, considering the way you have acted in recent days, your mind may well be disturbed."

Rebecca shrugged but agreed when Mrs. Peters suggested that she avoid Green Park. Rebecca didn't confess that she would return there if the opportunity presented itself. Those two apparitions fascinated her. How often did one see one's self as a ghost?

Through sheer determination, Rebecca managed to stay out of her daydream world while she was with others, yet when she blew out her candle at night, her thoughts turned to the earl. What was he doing at Shelburne Park? When would he come back? After yet another restless night, she woke early and stood by the window watching dawn break through the early mist. Not for the first time, she wondered whether this day would bring the return of the earl. Could she be happy if he never came back?

Rebecca's mind transported her into the past, to the orphanage and her last conversation with the duchess. That, too, was early one morning. The duchess had come to the orphanage to bid her and Louise good-bye. Rebecca had never asked Louise what the duchess said to her, nor did Louise volunteer the information. However, Rebecca remembered her own last advice from her preceptor and now relived their conversation, which had pressed itself on her mind.

"Good morning, my dear." The duchess motioned Rebecca to a chair. "Today you begin your journey of adulthood. I am extremely proud of what you have learned during your years here, as well as how you have matured. I am as proud of you as I would be if you were my own daughter."

Rebecca wondered whether the duchess gave this same speech to every girl who left her care. "You are most kind, Your Grace."

The duchess ignored the interruption. "I realize Mr. Wright believes you are of genteel birth. I do not disagree. Still, I would be failing in my duty to you if I did not warn you that you may never find your family. Furthermore, even if you do, they may reject you out of hand."

Rebecca clamped her teeth into her lower lip before relaxing her facial muscles to nod her comprehension.

"If you do enter what is termed 'Polite Society,' you will find glamour is an illusion. Titles do not guarantee happiness. While it is true surroundings can influence happiness, this is only a fleeting happiness. You will find that contentment is the result of your own attitude toward life. Next to God, your mind and your friends are the most important elements in your life, so be sure to cultivate both."

The duchess smiled at the young woman sitting in front of her. "There, now. That is the last homily I will give you."

Rebecca rose to her feet. Was the duchess dismissing her? Would she ever see her again? Would she ever see any of these people again? The thought of confronting her future without the presence of this person who had nurtured her for twelve years overwhelmed her.

The duchess rose from her chair and took the younger woman in her arms. "You go with my blessing, Rebecca. I want you to remember you are always welcome here. Under any circumstances, do you understand me? This is your home. You may always come back to us."

Bright sunlight shining in Rebecca's eyes brought her thoughts back to the present. She shrugged away the memories vowing yet again to forget the earl though she knew she'd set herself a difficult task.

However, the duchess was right. Rebecca must make her own happiness. She ignored the fact this was not the precise meaning of the Triple D's final homily. Rebecca would begin this very day by cultivating other friendships. Mr. Lowell, for instance. He had shown he enjoyed her company. Rebecca determined that she would avoid all titled people. With that determination made, Rebecca dressed for a day of pleasure. No work today.

"Good morning, Amelia, Louise. Is it not a glorious day?"

They smiled their delight that she was in such a happy mood, replying in unison. "Good morning!"

Pouring herself some coffee, Rebecca inquired their plans for that day.

"I need to return some books to the library," Amelia said. "Otherwise, I have no plans."

Louise twinkled over her coffee cup. "We can always stroll through Mayfair and dream of the future in one of the mansions."

"Yes, by all means, let us take a walk," Rebecca agreed. "I thought we might have a whist party tonight. We should get responses by early afternoon if we hand deliver the invitations."

"What a stupendous idea, Rebecca! Whom shall we invite?"

An hour later, with invitations in hand, the ladies departed on their day's activities. Late morning found them leaving Hatchard's with a couple of books each. As they descended the steps, Rebecca stopped when a hand grasped her arm. All three ladies stared in amazement at the gentleman who accosted them.

"Good morning, Miss ..." he raised his eyebrows. Receiving only a frosty glare, he continued. "I'm Rushton, a close friend of Shelburne. I thought we should get acquainted while he's rusticating in Somerset." His voice trailed off as he glanced from one haughty face to another.

How dare he—a complete stranger—approach her in this way? Mr. Wright had been correct in his assessment of this gentleman. Rather this man who masqueraded as a gentleman. This man had not ceased his efforts to learn her identity. This time Rebecca must deal with the situation. She ordered him to remove his hand from her arm. "At once!"

Rushton stiffened his shoulders, the cynosure of several pairs of eyes. He stared at her, a glitter of determination in his eyes but released her arm.

Mrs. Peters, her voice dripping disdain, stated, "Sir, we do not know you, nor do we choose to know you." The three ladies descended the steps and hurried down the street.

Rebecca quivered with temper. If this is what she could expect from Shelburne's friends, she preferred not to be around any of them. The duchess was right. A person could not trust titled people. That this was not what the duchess had said did not cross Rebecca's mind. Deliberately calming her nerves with a deep breath, she smiled at her friends, who gazed at her with anxious eyes.

"That was an experience I prefer not to repeat. Now let us forget the unpleasantness."

Louise could not contain her curiosity. "Who was he, Rebecca? Has Lord Shelburne ever mentioned him?"

"No, his lordship has never mentioned him to me although I recognized him. He's the gentleman who approached Mr. Wright at the office inquiring whether I was Gertrude Billingsley. Presumably he is the same gentleman who had approached Mr. Jamison with the same inquiry."

"Determined creature," Amelia commented.

"Are you going to mention his audacity to Lord Shelburne?" Louise asked.

Rebecca sniffed. "I have no reason to think I will ever see the earl again."

Amelia gasped. "Child, what kind of maggot do you have in your brainbox now?" When Rebecca shrugged, Amelia continued. "I see what it is. You've worked yourself into a dither because he hasn't writ you a billy-do. Let me tell you something you need to know, Missy.

A female can't keep stallions on a short rein nor break them to bridle neither, so you might as well put that notion right out of your noddle now."

At first miffed with her friend, Rebecca could not prevent a smile at her friend's pronunciation of *billet-doux* and she joined Louise's laughter when the horse cant continued.

Amelia stared at them in amazement. Then, red in the face and speaking in her most genteel voice, she said, "I have done it again, have I not? Will I ever lose my tendency to use language suitable only to the stables?"

Rebecca gave her friend a quick hug. "We like your, uh, colorful language, truly we do." She grew serious. "Amelia, I wouldn't want a husband I could keep on a short rein. I want one who is strong enough to know who he is, know his self-worth, but not one who would consider me a possession with no brains. I realize you're right about Lord Shelburne. There truly is no reason for him to be in touch with me. He surely has much to do on his estate. I have decided to put Shelburne out of my mind." She would too. On that, Rebecca was determined.

"Have you indeed?" Louise's teasing voice held a modicum of skepticism.

"Yes. Now let us forget all about men while we enjoy ourselves perusing shop windows."

They spent a pleasurable two hours without spending a penny. Back in their rooms, they found five acceptances, so they had enough for two tables, the perfect number for their whist party. After luncheon, they began preparations for the evening.

"Louise," Rebecca grinned at the wary expression on her face. "I will help Mrs. Morton in the kitchen if you will help Amelia prepare the drawing room for our card party."

Louise heaved a mock sigh of relief declaring her undying gratitude. "I do dislike the idea of serving burnt food to guests."

With a laugh, Rebecca left the room, and joined Mrs. Morton in the kitchen where she soon started rummaging through the pantry.

Rebecca made a determined effort to concentrate on her cards throughout the evening, partnering both James Lowell and Toby Williams. She believed she had not disgraced herself beyond all hope. It was just as well she didn't aspire to being a gambler, Rebecca acknowledged at one point when she forgot which suit was trumps causing Mr. Lowell to lose his bid. He graciously accepted the loss, much to her chagrin. Nevertheless, at the end of the evening Rebecca felt she had acquitted herself reasonably well, better than she had thought she would do.

Clearing away the remnants of small cakes, Rebecca teased Louise about Mr. Williams' attention. "He did not so much as frown when you bumped his elbow, causing him to drop his cards. That is affability, indeed."

Louise made a wry face. "I doubt Toby will ever accept another invitation from us."

Amelia chortled. "I'll own my surprise if Mr. Lowell agrees to partner Rebecca ever again. Buffle-headed. Beyond a doubt, that's what you are, my girl, buffle-headed!"

Rebecca joined their laughter. "I daresay you're right, Amelia." With a wide yawn, she wished them a good night.

The day after their card party found the three ladies making their way home from church. "What shall we do this afternoon?"

Louise answered Rebecca's question. "The day is much too nice to stay indoors. Shall we take a walk and enjoy the sunshine while it lasts? We're still looking for someone who recognizes your face. Perhaps today is the day."

With surprise, Rebecca realized she had not given any thought to that in several days.

After a quick luncheon and with parasols shading their eyes, the ladies enjoyed a stroll through the streets of Mayfair. Rebecca eyed the houses with their shining doorknockers, their gleaming windows. She felt as though she belonged there—should know the insides of the houses as well as the people who lived there. Preposterous thought. Rebecca admitted that the City was more likely her home area. The females in these houses wouldn't dream of living the way she found necessary. Riotous laughter brought her back to the present.

A small crowd gathered around a Punch and Judy man. He manipulated the puppets with considerable dexterity as they quarreled their way through a domestic crisis caused by Judy's extravagance.

Laughing as Judy threw an armload of gowns at Punch, Rebecca heard a familiar chuckle near her ear. Lord Shelburne! She froze in embarrassment at being caught enjoying such childish antics. Turning to meet his gaze, Rebecca realized his amusement duplicated her own. They watched the remainder of the show in harmony.

After tossing some coins onto the puppet stage, Shelburne strolled along the street with the ladies. "I have just this minute returned to Town. May I escort you ladies to Gunter's Confectionary for some ices?"

Both Rebecca and Louise turned eager faces toward Amelia, who agreed after a hesitant glance toward Rebecca.

Over their ices, the earl inquired whether Rebecca cared for riding.

"I rode almost daily in Hampshire but have gotten out of the way of riding since coming to London, my lord."

"I took a chance and sent a couple of ladies' mounts to town from Shelburne Park. Would you care to ride with me one morning soon?"

Rebecca again glanced at Amelia. "Mrs. Peters does not care to ride, my lord, and Louise's schedule might preclude her from accompanying me."

Turning to the older lady, Shelburne inquired, "Ma'am, would you permit Miss Black to ride with me if my groom is in attendance?"

Amelia studied his face a moment before replying. "Yes, my lord, I believe that will be acceptable."

Rebecca schooled her features not to betray too much enthusiasm. "Then, yes, my lord, I would enjoy riding with you."

Shelburne thought for a moment. "I must take care of business the next two mornings, so will Wednesday morning be convenient?" When she agreed, he took his leave of them.

Louise clasped her hands together. "He sent *two* ladies mounts to Town! That means I can ride, too, do you not agree? Amelia? Rebecca?

They agree with her and retraced their steps to Harley Street.

Rebecca was overly talkative the rest of the day yet avoided any mention of the earl. Nevertheless, when she stood beside the open window of her bedchamber—where she spent too much time staring out on the noisy street—she could no longer deny the obvious. Rebecca Marie Louise Black was an idiot. Definitely lacking in sense. A little voice inside her head made sure she knew it.

So, you were finished with him, were you? You were not going to think of him ever again.

I intended to put him out of my life, yet how can I when he turns up without warning and catches me off guard?

You could have refused to go to Gunter's for ices.

Refuse ices? Impossible!

You could have refused to ride with him. Instead, you almost went into alt over the idea.

"Oh, do be quiet!" Rebecca spoke aloud hoping no one had heard her. She must stop arguing with that little voice, she admonished herself. It was always right.

Shelburne lounged in his study staring into the empty grate, his thoughts roving over the dilemma that was Miss Black. A delightful dilemma without a doubt, nevertheless a dilemma. On the one hand, she was a pleasant companion, lighthearted and gay. On the other, Miss Black was seriousness personified. She could change from one person to the other in the blink of an eye. Her divergent personalities kept him on his toes trying to determine when the change might occur.

Light flickered from the candelabrum at his elbow, casting the rest of the room into shadows, which fitted Shelburne's mood. Miss Black was an enigma, a challenge he could not resist.

True, the earl had needed to make decisions at Shelburne Park, but he admitted to himself he had not needed to stay so long. He had forced himself to stay almost two weeks in his effort to clarify his thoughts about Rebecca Black. He could not think about her with any degree of clarity when he saw her almost every day. Yet, he could not restrain himself from seeking her company as often as he could.

Shelburne also had to admit he had not reached any conclusions. Quite the contrary. The days he spent at Shelburne Park had served to deepen his consciousness of her, of her haunting blue eyes. How could he feel her presence there when he knew for a certainty that she had never been to Shelburne Park? Yet he had felt her presence in various places.

Chapter 10

Military Intrusion

Shelburne sat in an austere room at Whitehall the following morning waiting to confer with Colonel Hayes. Driving back from Shelburne Park, he had decided the time had come to put into action his belief he might be of some help to the army. Now he was anxious to start. Waiting had never been easy for him, and he struggled to control his impatience.

"Welcome, Lord Shelburne." The colonel eyed his newest recruit. "I understand Sir Julian Haverford is a relation of yours."

"Yes, sir, Haverford is married to my sister. I don't recall he has mentioned being acquainted with you, however."

"Oh, yes, he is a member of this committee also, although he could not meet with us this morning." Colonel Hayes indicated the other gentleman present who had stood when Shelburne entered the room. "Are you acquainted with Viscount Beaufort, my lord?"

Shelburne shook the other man's hand while standing up to the keen scrutiny. "I'm familiar with Lord Beaufort's name although we have not met. I believe you hail from Yorkshire?"

Beaufort nodded his acknowledgment then asked if Shelburne was familiar with the military problems in Spain.

Shelburne detailed his war activities. "My first action was in Portugal in '08. From there, we went to Spain. Oporto. Talavera. I believe I saw enough before my last battle in Barossa to have a clear idea. The foot soldiers' uniforms by then were in tatters, their boot soles reinforced with whatever they could find. At times, we were perilously close to starvation as of course were the horses. Too often, we slogged through mud on foot because our mounts were too weak to carry us. Unfortunately, I have no reason to think there's been any improvement in the army's condition since I left the military."

"There hasn't. If anything, the problems are worse simply from passage of time, if nothing else. The soldiers must scavenge more than they should," Beaufort told him, and pounded the table. "We cannot allow that situation to continue."

Of no more than average height, Beaufort gave the impression of great physical strength. His face grew harsh as they discussed the problems in Spain. His thorough knowledge of the problems facing Wellington as the army moved toward the French border was distressing to hear.

Beaufort continued, "Finances are another serious concern. Troops not only can't travel on an empty stomach—they also can't move on threadbare boots as you described them. Their mounts face the same problems."

"That is certainly true, but not the primary problem we face at the moment." The colonel rose to his feet. "Shelburne, I am due at a meeting with Liverpool and York, so we will not go into details now. I called this meeting for the purpose of meeting you, my lord. I look forward to discussing the problem in depth at our next meeting."

Shaking hands all around, Colonel Hayes hurried from the room with Shelburne and Beaufort at his heels.

Shelburne had felt an immediate affinity with the compactly built colonel who had studied him through eyes so dark they rivaled coal. Sharp, eagle eyes which would miss little, Shelburne surmised. Hayes exhibited a controlled vitality which impressed the earl, who parted from him with an eagerness to meet again.

While Shelburne discussed the military situation, Rebecca dealt with her own uncertainty.

On Monday, Rebecca greeted dawn with a sense of urgency. She came fully awake with one thought uppermost in her mind. She must see her apparitions again. They had floated throughout her dreams during the night, the female alternately wearing gowns of blue and rose, but the male always wore regimentals. Rebecca struggled to contain her impatience, while she waited for Louise to finish her breakfast before approaching her in a cajoling voice.

"Louise, best of my friends, in actual fact, my only real friend, will you do something for me?"

A distinct twinkle accompanied the reply. "I'll do anything you desire—there's no need to empty the butter boat on my head."

Rebecca's chuckle belied the seriousness of her request. "I want you to accompany me to Green Park. I don't wish anyone else to know."

"Yes, certainly, I will go with you, but may I know why? Do you have an assignation with an undesirable *parti*?" Louise asked in jest. "I wasn't aware you know any."

"In one sense I suppose you are correct in your assumption." Rebecca became somber. "I want to find the apparitions again."

"Oh." Louise's voice bore evidence of her disquiet. "Any particular reason?"

"I want to make a little experiment. You will see if we find the apparitions."

"Then let us go now while Amelia is at the market."

They spoke little as they walked in a purposeful manner toward Green Park. When they arrived, Rebecca's glance darted around until, with a gasp, she fixed her gaze at a point to her right.

"Do you see an apparition?" Louise asked in an urgent whisper.

"Yes, she's standing near that large oak tree, by herself today. Please tell me you can see her too," Rebecca pleaded.

"I wish I could, I assure you. Perhaps you are the only living person who can see her, for some reason. What's your experiment?"

"I'm going to walk through her, or perhaps allow her to walk through me, if she begins walking while I'm near her. Come with me."

Rebecca set a steady pace until she reached the apparition. There she took a deep breath, then stood face to face with her look-alike. There was love in its dark blue eyes but also controlled impatience, something Rebecca had seldom been able to achieve. She released Louise's hand, stepped forward, merged with the ephemeral form, then came out the other side. Turning, Rebecca stood inside the apparition a moment savoring the warm sensation. Reluctantly stepping away, Rebecca addressed Louise through stiff lips. "That proves the theory. There is no doubt that the apparition is me."

Unmindful of dairy maids in their vicinity, Louise shook Rebecca's arm. "You are not to say that, do you understand me Rebecca Marie Louise Black? You are not."

"I must. It's true."

In despair, Louise briefly closed her eyes. Through clenched teeth, she asked for an explanation of Rebecca's absurd conviction.

"In every book we've ever read about ghosts, there are comments about cold, the person is chilled, a cold wind blows, a room suddenly becomes chilled. Am I not correct?"

Accepting Louise's nod, Rebecca continued. "The people experiencing the cold air manifested by these apparitions were strangers to them. Is that not also correct?"

Unable to speak, Louise again nodded her head.

"This apparition is not cold. On the contrary, I felt distinct warmth as our bodies merged, both stepping through it and then returning through it. The heat proves she is me. We must accept I will die young."

"I refuse to believe your early death. That's final," Louise informed her. "If this were your ghost, I'd be able to see the apparition. Our minds are too closely attuned for the situation to be otherwise."

"Maybe God is using this way to let me know I'll die young, that I shouldn't count on a future." With the earl, she added in her thoughts.

"I still don't believe the apparition is you," Louise declared. "Rebecca, just listen to yourself. You're putting words into God's mouth instead of waiting for Him to work things out for you. How many times did Matron correct you for your impatience? Too many to remember, I daresay. Yet, now, even as an adult, you persist."

"Perhaps you're right. I hope so." Rebecca looked once more on the apparition that now moved forward, a smile lighting her face as she reached for the arm of the soldier in regimentals.

Rebecca watched them float away. A tug deep within her urged her to follow, joining in their obvious happiness. Instead, she hooked her arm through Louise's and they left the park.

As agreed upon during their visit to Gunter's, Wednesday morning found the earl in Harley Street to take Rebecca for the promised ride. She had spent those two days berating herself for her impatience to see him. His face persisted in coming between her eyes and the letters she was transcribing for Mr. Wright. To her chagrin, she had wasted a few sheets of his engraved paper. Rebecca took herself severely to task over the expenditure then forced herself to concentrate.

Nevertheless, it was with a rapidly beating heart that she glimpsed Shelburne's arrival while she stood at a window drinking a cup of chocolate. He'd sent a note round earlier inquiring whether Miss Tracy could join them.

"He's here, Louise! Shelburne has arrived with two beautiful mounts. Hurry, let's don't keep him waiting. We don't want the horses to stand long."

Without taking time to return the cup to the kitchen, Rebecca hurried down the stairs, Louise at her heels. They paused only to remind themselves of proper decorum before motioning for Jamison to open the door for them.

Shelburne sat relaxed yet controlled his big black gelding that sidled around, shaking his bit. Despite her effort to hide behind the drapes, he had spied Rebecca at the window watching for him. His heart lifted with the hope his life would always be thus—Rebecca waiting for his return home. "Good morning, ladies. I'm pleased you can join us, Miss Tracy."

"As am I, my lord."

A groom handed Rebecca onto a roan mare that didn't seem the least bit perturbed by her restless companion.

Rebecca, in a dark blue riding habit with the white ruffles of her muslin shirt showing at the neck, settled herself easily in the saddle. "She's beautiful, my lord. What do you call her?"

"Her name is Lady, which I find most apt. Although she's lively, there isn't a grain of vice in her. Miss Tracy, your mount answers to Ginger because of her color, not her disposition. She's lively at the moment because she's impatient for activity."

"Thank you, sir. You're most thoughtful," Louise said as the groom lifted her into the saddle. "I'm confident I can handle her."

When they reached the park, they released the restraint they had exercised over their mounts and raced side by side for the length of the avenue before pulling the panting horses to a stand.

"My lord, I enjoyed that," Rebecca assured him. "I did not realize how much I've missed riding."

"Nor I," Louise chimed in.

"You need not miss riding any longer. I stabled the cattle in the mews behind your rooms, so feel free to call upon their services at any time."

Louise thanked him, but Rebecca refused, albeit in an unhappy voice. "We could not take advantage of your offer, my lord. Such behavior would be improper beyond anything."

"Nonsense. They must have exercise on a regular basis. The stable owner knows only you ladies may ride them. In truth, you would be doing me a favor to ride every day."

Shelburne met Rebecca's uncertain gaze for a long moment before she capitulated.

"If you're sure, we will be happy—nay overjoyed—to exercise them for you."

After a brief hesitation, the earl spoke quietly, but firmly. "There is just one thing I need to mention. It is not acceptable to gallop in the park even in the very early morning."

Rebecca glanced at Louise then lifted her firm chin. "We will make it a point to remember your admonition, Lord Shelburne."

He leaned toward her. "Now please do not poker up on me, Miss Black. I was not being critical—after all I started the gallop. I just did not know whether the duchess had seen fit to advise you of that fact among her conversations with the girls."

Rebecca relaxed enough to smile while they retraced their route. After a few moments of silence, Shelburne spoke.

"I did it, Miss Black." Meeting her interested gaze, he continued. "As you suggested several days ago, I thought about what I might do to help the war effort. Yesterday I talked with some people at Whitehall who said I can be of service to them based on my battle experiences."

"That is wonderful news," Rebecca congratulated him with a warm smile. "Can you tell us about your work?"

"I am not yet sure of my exact duties, though I understand that at least some of my work will be confidential." Shelburne recounted his meeting with Colonel Hayes. "The problems are much the same in Spain as when I was there."

"Can you tell us anything of your experiences?"

Shelburne grimaced. "If you ladies expect glorious accounts of battles, I am afraid I cannot oblige you."

"I assure you that we do not believe battles are glorious, Lord Shelburne. We are not totty headed."

Louise concurred with a brief nod.

"Now please do not fly up into the boughs, ladies," Shelburne begged. "I offer my apologies. Most people who inquire about my war experiences expect to hear about battles fought in full dress uniform under cloudless blue skies, the enemy fleeing for their lives with us at their heels. Or they believe we spend our evenings at balls, and the enemy approach us while waving a white flag."

The dismal emotion expressed in his voice caused Rebecca to answer gently. "That cannot be the way of battles. People should have better sense—common sense if not actual knowledge."

Time receded. Shelburne heard again the clash of swords, the screams of men and horses when cannon balls found their targets. he stiffened his spine against the memories, then gave a succinct answer.

"The Peninsula was either incredibly dry and dusty or incredibly rainy and muddy. There was no happy medium. The flies were unbelievable, the food was often hard to find for ourselves as well as for our cattle. Horses must eat too. Their need of stamina is urgent because they carry a large load. Napoleon's army had ransacked the land, plundering the gardens, leaving the peasants fighting starvation. There were times when we were close to starvation ourselves. This puts the entire matter of what the army faces as mildly as possible."

In his mind's eye, Shelburne again saw the hollow eyes of starving peasants who watched without hope as Wellington's troops passed through their villages when searching for food.

Rebecca apologized. "I am sorry I upset you with my thoughtless question, my lord."

Shelburne pulled himself together then clasped her hand for a moment. "Now ladies, shall we make a visit to Gunter's?"

Louise, who had remained quiet throughout his comments on the war, agreed. "Yes, my lord, I accept for both of us."

"I rather thought you would," Rebecca teased her. "When did you ever resist ices?"

A few minutes later, seated in the confectionary, Shelburne commented they were receiving steady stares from across the room.

They glanced in that direction, then declared they had never seen the ladies before.

Two women several years older than Shelburne approached the table to apologize for staring. "We thought we recognized these ladies, my lord. Upon seeing them more closely, however, we realize we don't. They're too young, yet, there's something about them ..." The ladies shook their heads in puzzlement as they moved away. Suddenly, one of them turned back. "There ought to be three of them. There are always three."

Rebecca and Louise glanced at each other at the mention of three. Before they could speak, Shelburne nodded in satisfaction. "You see, I'm not the only one who recognizes your features. We will solve this mystery yet. I *know* we will. Perhaps the two of you together triggered their memories. So, Miss Tracy, you must accompany us more often."

With a mischievous grin, Louise asked, "When we drive, do I get to take the reins?"

"My tiger would never forgive me if I allowed a female to do the driving. Would you want me to risk his disfavor?"

"Oh, no," Louise quipped. "I would not dream of coming between a gentleman and his tiger."

On a note of laughter, they retrieved their mounts, the girls forgetting the reference to three people.

Shelburne sat alone in his study staring at the burgundy drapes that encased the tall windows shutting out the overcast skies. He had meant to do some paper work this morning before his secretary took him to task again, but he could not concentrate. His thoughts kept turning to Rebecca—how the sun had brought out blue highlights in her raven hair on their ride the day before, how her absurdly long lashes lay against her cheeks when she thought he'd reprimanded her. Shelburne inhaled and seemed to capture again the scent of her rose water which had floated on the light breeze.

He admitted to himself knowledge of her ancestry was no longer important—even her legitimacy or lack thereof. Shelburne had found the one woman in the world for him. Nothing was going to stand in the way. The thought of never hearing Rebecca's gurgling laughter again, never seeing those haunting blue eyes again, never to see those eyes without shadows was more than he cared to contemplate.

Shelburne frowned at an unwelcome thought. How did Miss Black feel about him? She always seemed to enjoy his company. Her face did light up at his appearance. His anxiety eased. He would ask for her hand in marriage. But from whom? Mr. Wright? Mrs. Peters? The duchess? He'd have to think about that later. First, he would approach her and would not take no for an answer, Shelburne told himself. He'd never proposed marriage, hadn't expected to for several years. Forgotten was his earlier stated vow to remain unencumbered with a wife until he reached five and thirty. Now was the time, not seven years into the future. He turned to his paper work with renewed energy.

Determined not to waste any time, Shelburne visited Harley Street that same evening, finding only two of the ladies present. Directing his intense gaze toward Mrs. Peters, he asked, "Ma'am, will you permit me to talk privately with Miss Black?"

Mrs. Peters gazed at him a moment, searching his solemn face as though for a clue to his thoughts. After a glance at Rebecca's face, which turned a delicate pink before becoming pale, Amelia nodded and left the room, leaving the door ajar.

Shelburne cleared his throat before speaking. Who would ever have thought a simple offer of marriage could be so difficult? He'd never given thought to a proposal before. He'd never met a female who inspired him to consider marriage. He took a deep, steadying breath, gathering his scattered wits. "Miss Black, I love you. Will you do me the honor of becoming my wife?"

A startled gasp escaped Rebecca's gaping mouth.

Whatever she had expected, Shelburne realized an offer of marriage had not occurred to her. He waited with barely concealed impatience for her reply, a foregone conclusion in his mind. Apparently, their minds were not in tune.

Rebecca took a deep breath before answering, then shook her head and looked straight into his eyes. "My lord, you cannot wish to marry me. I am a nobody, with no known lineage, not worthy of a peer of the realm. Polite Society contains any number of ladies endowed with the perquisites to be your countess. The Earl of Shelburne can choose any one of them with the full knowledge of acceptance without giving the matter any thought."

He pulled her to her feet, slipping his arms around her. "Yes, the Earl of Shelburne can choose whom he wants. My choice is to marry you. I not only want to marry you, I intend to do just that, so you might as well say 'yes' immediately."

Rebecca almost smiled at the teasing threat in his voice, but then she turned her face away before answering with heart-wrenching sadness. "Even if we learn who I am, who my family is, or was, the fact remains I am probably baseborn. A nobleman cannot marry so far beneath him. You know that better than I do. That truth has probably been instilled in your brain since your boyhood."

The Tenth Earl of Shelburne was not accustomed to rejection. Dashed if he would accept it now. He turned her face toward his. "You must marry me, Rebecca Black. I have waited all these years to find someone like you. I will not, absolutely will not, take no for an answer."

Struggling to free herself from his grip, Rebecca surprised him with a display of temper. "I will not marry you. I can survive being ignored by Polite Society, but I refuse to be ostracized for something over which I have no control, something which is not my fault."

"Nonsense," Shelburne countered. The arrogance of several generations of earls behind him stiffened his voice. "No one from King George to the lowliest street sweeper would dare ostracize *my* countess."

"If they did not actually ostracize me, they would laugh behind their fans, which would be worse."

Shelburne struggled to get a grip on his emotions. Recognizing her distress, he forced himself to use the quietest tone he could muster under these difficult circumstances. "Understand this, Rebecca Black. Your ancestry is of supreme indifference to me. I care not whether your parents were married or chance met strangers. I shall not press you now, but I also shall not change my mind. I am going to marry *you*, not your family no matter who or what they are or were. So, will you give some serious consideration to my marriage proposal? I promise not to press you," he assured her, "difficult though it will be.

Shaking her head, Rebecca regained control.

With an inward sigh, Shelburne realized he would have to redouble his efforts to learn her identity. "With most of the *ton* in the country again, there is a limited number of places I can take you where people might recognize you. However, when people return to Town in the autumn, will you attend society functions with me?"

A shocked expression settled on her face. "No, I will not, my lord. The idea is absurd. To attend Society functions would be highly improper until I know if I am acceptable to Society."

Nothing he could say would change her mind, so he tried another tack. "My mother rarely comes to Town, but would you visit my sister with me when she returns from the country?"

"She surely cannot want to meet me."

"Yes, she does. Becca even suggested I abduct you, if necessary, and bring you to her."

The idea caused Rebecca to smile. "Then, yes, I suppose paying her a visit would be permissible, but only if you're sure she truly desires to meet me and only at her convenience."

Shelburne had to be content. Caressing her face, he kissed her parted lips, then drew away with only that feathery touch.

"No, you must not."

"Only a chaste salute, my dear. Your precious Triple D could not possibly condemn it." He cradled her cheek in one palm then strode from the room.

When the door closed behind the earl, Mrs. Peters returned to the drawing room, her eyes bright with curiosity. She found Rebecca staring into space, her arms held rigidly at her sides, fists clenching and unclenching.

"I heard raised voices and debated whether to come to your rescue." Receiving no reply, Amelia continued. "Rebecca?" When she still didn't receive a reply, she tried again. "Why did he want to talk to you alone? Can you tell me?"

"Shelburne asked me to marry him." The sadness in her voice brought a gasp from her companion.

"That is wonderful, Rebecca. Why do you sound unhappy? Surely you did not say no." The idea was so preposterous that Rebecca's answer stunned her.

"Of course, I said no. An earl cannot marry a nobody, or worse still, less than a nobody. A nobody might be respectable. A baseborn nobody is beyond the pale." The words released her stiffness, and she began pacing the floor.

Before Mrs. Peters could reply to Rebecca's blunt statement, Louise's return from a piano lesson brought forth more exclamations. Still Rebecca refused to yield. The Earl of Shelburne could not marry an illegitimate nobody, thereby cutting himself off from Society. She ended the conversation by entering her bedchamber, closing the door after her.

Rebecca's words were adamant, yet her heart didn't listen. She enjoyed being with Shelburne, felt a oneness with him that made her ache to throw caution to the wind, accept his offer, let the future take care of itself.

During the earl's many visits since his return from Shelburne Park, Rebecca had often caught him looking at her with puzzled eyes. He would produce the lopsided grin she had come to love, shrug, and assure her he did know her features from somewhere. She should send him away but didn't have the strength.

So, Amelia was right, announced a little voice in her ear. *You have lost your heart to the earl.*

Arguing with a disembodied voice which was always right was difficult to the point of impossibility. Honesty compelled Rebecca to acknowledge she had lost her heart to Shelburne. How could she have been so stupid when she knew deep in her heart that pain was inevitable?

Chapter 11

Uncertain Tempers

"What do people do in Town during the summer?" Shelburne muttered to himself but received a reply from Hodges, who was picking up discarded cravats as soon as the earl dropped them, unhappy with the way they appeared around his neck.

"I'm sure I cannot say, my lord, since we have never been in Town during the summer."

Shelburne ignored the valet's disgruntled remark and continued muttering his thoughts. "A ride on the Thames, perhaps? No, the stench is terrible. Besides who would see Miss Black on a boat in the middle of the river? I suppose we will just continue our rides in the park. Or we could attend Lady Frederick's salons." Remembering his only other visit there, Shelburne cringed at the idea of returning. However, should a visit prove necessary ...

Since proposing to Rebecca two days before, he had given considerable thought to displaying her in public places. Display! Shelburne almost exclaimed the word aloud. How could he even think of such a term, as though she were a possession instead of a human being—a precious human being too.

Nonetheless, he must escort her to places where people might recognize her. He had cast the die, risking his all on a positive outcome. The Tenth Earl of Shelburne had never contemplated any other than a positive outcome in his endeavors, whether simple or complicated, and would not now. He recalled his talk with the duchess. At that time, he could bring himself to say only that he would not dishonor Miss Black. Now Shelburne admitted he would marry her regardless of her objections while still acknowledging the outcome would be easier if they could prove her legitimacy. That was his only real concern, because her ancestry appeared to be her only objection to marrying him.

"Am I to understand that your lordship intends to remain in Town the entire summer?" Disapproval showed in every line of Hodges's body although he kept his voice submissive.

"My work at Whitehall demands my presence in Town a considerable amount of time," Shelburne replied and left his bedchamber.

Unable to concentrate on his agent's reports, he shuffled papers on his desk. When they were in a neat stack, Shelburne sat back, staring into space. He felt a deep yearning for something. He knew not what, but something which gave him the serenity Miss Black demonstrated. Except when she was in a temper, that is. Shaking off the feeling, he rang for his secretary.

After clearing the paperwork, Shelburne nodded his dismissal and, calling for his horse, Shelburne left Grosvenor Square on his way to Harley Street, stopping on the way to get Lady for Rebecca.

Entering the park in hot sun, they rode along Rotten Row, gradually moving into the shade, the groom stopping at a respectful distance. The slight breeze rippling the leaves overhead helped some. How he longed to be in the cool country air.

"Several people have told me so much sun is a rarity in London," Rebecca commented. "I can hardly credit it."

"They told you correctly. We're more accustomed to overcast skies and muggy air."

"I met one of your friends while you were at Shelburne Park," Rebecca told him. "Rather, I should say I encountered one of your friends."

"I notice the distinction. Who was this person?"

She frowned in thought. "I've heard his name, but I cannot bring it to mind." She told him of the incident at Hatchard's, as well as the gentleman's visits both to Harley Street and to Mr. Wright's office.

Shelburne turned his thunderous face toward her. "I cannot imagine who would have the effrontery to do such a despicable thing. Can you describe him more fully?"

"I fear not," she said before an impish grin crossed her face. "I must admit I cannot say definitely that he was a gentleman. I was so surprised at his audacity I failed to count his watch fobs and rings. I did notice he wore an exquisitely tied cravat, however," she assured him while gazing at his own simply tied neckwear.

Shelburne chuckled, and their banter continued as they turned toward the gate.

They rode in comfortable silence until she said in a low voice, "There he is, my lord! The gentleman I mentioned is standing near the gate. See, he tipped his hat to us."

"The Earl of Rushton is an acquaintance only," Shelburne stated and nodded curtly to him as they passed. Rebecca kept her gaze forward as they left the park.

On a more pleasant subject, Shelburne asked about Louise. "Is Miss Tracy always so happy? I've never seen her but what we ended in laughter."

"Oh, yes, she has a merry heart. Even on the first day we met, she had me laughing through my tears. She has never failed to lift my spirits."

"That's important in a friend."

"The only time I've known her to be completely out of countenance was when we were small children, maybe seven or eight. On one of our rare visits to the village, we saw a bigger boy kick a dog. Before Matron could intervene, Louise attacked the boy with both fists.

He held her off with one hand all the while laughing at her. Her temper erupted with a vengeance."

"With good reason," Shelburne told her.

Arriving back at Harley Street, Shelburne escorted Rebecca to the door where he took the hand she extended. Their eyes met for a long moment. He then turned her hand palm upwards and planted a light kiss in the middle before closing her fingers over it. Without speaking, he tipped his hat and returned to his mount.

That evening, Shelburne paced the length of his study. He had felt at loose ends ever since dinner, unable to settle to anything, so having rejected the various clubs, he ordered his phaeton for a drive to Harley Street. In the usual way of things, he only visited Rebecca upon a specific invitation or after sending round a note and obtaining an answer. Shelburne could only remember one occasion when he went there without prior notice—the day he went to Shelburne Park. A trip to get away from Rebecca's haunting eyes, which had been a dismal failure, he reminded himself. He was sure of his welcome at Harley Street.

Arriving there, he hurried up the stairs ignoring Jamison's startled expression. When Morton opened the door in answer to his knock, Shelburne heard lively sounds emanating from the drawing room. He handed his hat and gloves to the butler, noting his surprised expression before Morton opened the drawing room door.

Shelburne surveyed the room, which grew quiet. He spotted Rebecca standing next to the fireplace, talking to a young man wearing a turquoise coat with heavily padded shoulders and a wasp waist over biscuit-colored trousers. His starched shirt points impeded movement of his head, requiring him to turn his entire body to gaze at the newcomer. Shelburne's lip curled, the word fribble entering his mind.

His gaze was dwelling on Rebecca when she realized his presence. He saw joy leap into her eyes and answered it with his own.

She moved to his side, hiding her thoughts as she greeted him with polite enthusiasm. "My lord, how nice to see you."

"I hope you will excuse me for barging in on your party like this." Shelburne raised her hand to his lips, noting her surprised reaction. He wanted to demand why she had not invited him but refrained.

"Nonsense, Lord Shelburne. You are welcome in our home." With a bright smile she added, "Now, allow me to introduce some of our other friends."

They moved around the room until they reached Mrs. Peters where Shelburne lingered, a glass of iced punch in hand, and surveyed the room. It was odd he had never given any thought to Rebecca having other friends, other acquaintances even. She existed only for him. Shelburne gritted his teeth with rage at the fawning imbeciles practically drooling all over *his* Rebecca. How dare they?

Mrs. Peters' prosaic voice brought him back to his senses. "Don't look so murderous, Shelburne. They're harmless colts, haven't found their feet yet. Not one of them is even at the starting gate for all their fancy rags."

Somewhat relieved by her directness, Shelburne grinned, then stood chatting a few minutes more before excusing himself. He paused at the door, his eyes seeking Rebecca, mentally commanding her to look his way. When she did, Shelburne sent her a slow, sweet smile and lifted his hand to her. She was his, no matter what others think to the contrary.

However, Shelburne was soon to learn there was a real threat to his happiness.

Strolling along Piccadilly the following afternoon, Shelburne glanced to his left when he heard a familiar gurgling laugh. With a smile, he turned his steps but came to an abrupt standstill, stunned at the sight before him.

A man of slight build, well above average in height, tucked Miss Black's hand under his elbow, close to his body, leaning down to gaze into her face as they conversed.

Shelburne gritted his teeth as he watched their progress down the street. He remembered seeing that man at Miss Black's party. Who was this upstart who appeared to be on intimate terms with the ladies at Harley Street? Not a member of the *beau monde*, else Shelburne would know him. He was too pale to be a sporting gentleman, so he was probably a Cit, a clerk in somebody's office. This was what came of allowing a female to associate with businessmen. The duchess should know better regardless of her forward thinking.

Shelburne's plan to meet Colonel Hayes for a short review of the army problems deserted him. Visions of Miss Black with that nobody filled his thoughts to the exclusion of everything else. He would get to the bottom of this. He would demand to know just what that mushroom meant to Rebecca. *His* Rebecca. His? For the first time, doubt grew in his mind.

There were also doubts in Rebecca's mind, although of a different nature.

Shelburne's presence at the party the evening before had surprised her. The idea to invite him to any gathering of her other friends had never entered her mind. His suave demeanor, his garb, muted but elegant, had underlined the lack of sophistication of the others. Rebecca had watched him from the corner of her eye while he stood with Amelia, not liking his expression as he looked at her guests. Her temper rose at the memory. What right had Shelburne to condemn her friends? She tried to avoid the knowledge she had often compared every man she met with the earl and had found them lacking in every aspect imaginable, not just one or two traits. Rebecca determined not to make such comparisons again. With that decision, she turned toward Mr. Lowell when he hailed her.

Rebecca had been walking home from an errand when he approached her. They talked with ease as they strolled toward Harley Street. She was aware Mr. Lowell was clasping her hand between his elbow and his body, but she couldn't think of a way to alter the situation without being missish. After bidding him goodbye at the door, Rebecca hurried up the stairs, her thoughts in turmoil. She moved around the drawing room while arranging some roses she had purchased from an old woman on the street. Rebecca had excused her extravagance by assuring herself the emaciated woman needed the pennies more than did she.

"Amelia?"

Mrs. Peters put down her embroidery frame to give the girl her undivided attention. "What troubles you, my dear?"

Rebecca tucked a rose in the vase, then stood back to study the effect. Twitching it again, she said, "I met James Lowell this afternoon. He escorted me home."

Amelia gave an encouraging murmur.

Rebecca's quiet voice filled the room. "I believe he is becoming particular in his attention."

"Are you encouraging him?"

Rebecca stared at the wall, twisting a rose in her fingers. "I dare not encourage him even if he appealed to my senses. He doesn't. Can you not see? I'm not free to encourage him for the same reason I cannot encourage Lord Shelburne. My probable illegitimacy places me beyond the pale, therefore I am unable to encourage any man. I might as well enter a convent."

With those words, the flower broke into pieces. Rebecca ran from the room, her tears as numerous as the rose petals she scattered.

Therefore, two people in uncertain tempers met later that evening. From within the drawing room, Rebecca told her leaping heart to be still when she heard Shelburne's voice.

"Good evening, Morton. Are the ladies in?" Shelburne had only nodded when Jamison allowed him to enter the building, now he didn't wait for a reply from Morton. He opened the drawing room door and surveyed the occupants.

"Miss Tracy, may I speak to Miss Black alone?"

His starchy tones caused Rebecca to stiffen her spine. No matter what the earl said, she refused to be intimidated. Without taking her gaze from Shelburne's face, she spoke. "Yes, Louise, do leave us. I gather his lordship has something of import to say to me."

Louise opened her mouth to reply, but one glance at Rebecca's face changed her mind. She left the room, closing the door.

From her seat on a sofa, Rebecca nodded toward a chair. He ignored her. "Have you something you wish to say to me, Lord Shelburne? Your note failed to give a reason for this visit."

Rebecca kept her voice level and her face blank. Neither apparently penetrated Shelburne's brain, so focused was he on his words.

"Who was that man I saw with you this afternoon?" he demanded with a glare. He rushed on before she could reply. "If he can be called a *man*. His paleness shows he does not pursue manly activities."

The earl's sneer rankled almost leaving Rebecca speechless. Almost, but not quite. "Mr. James Lowell is, indeed, a man. He works for a living, not like the dilettantes who live on the funds their ancestors earned by working."

"Miss Black, I'll have you know my ancestors did not work for their funds," he stated as he raked her face with a haughty stare. "They received the earldom together with a sizeable fortune through service to King Charles the Second."

"I hardly see having ancestors who cozened up to a king of questionable morals is sufficient reason for your arrogance," Rebecca snapped.

"How dare you malign my ancestors? Your *Mister* James Lowell probably cannot account for his lineage for more than one generation."

Fury replaced the hurt in her thudding heart. "Then *Mister* James Lowell and I are well matched because neither can I!"

Her words brought Shelburne to his senses. "You are not going to marry him. Do you understand me? You're *mine*."

Rebecca fueled her anger to stop the hurt. How dare he assume her compliance? Typical arrogance of the upper classes, expecting others to bend to their demands. Rebecca rose to her feet and bit off her words. "I. Am. Not. Yours. I. Am. My. Own. Person. I. Will. Not. Submit. To. Your. Demands. Now, do you understand *me*, Lord Shelburne?"

Rebecca watched the dawning realization in his eyes that he had gone too far, that she was furious. Good.

"I apologize, Miss Black. My temper got the best of me, and I spoke without thinking. However, there's no need to look daggers at me."

Shelburne watched anger begin to fade from her face, which softened the slightest bit. He must not overwhelm her. He began caressing her cheeks with his thumbs, his lips became feather-light moving across hers until she stopped resisting him.

Pulling back, Rebecca reminded him of his earlier promise. "You said you would not."

"I know I did. I did not intend this to happen. Still, you must see you're mine, that we belong together."

"Nothing has changed."

"That's where you're mistaken, Rebecca Black. There's no going back now. You are mine." With that emphatic statement, Shelburne left the room, closing the door after him.

What had possessed her to allow Shelburne's forwardness? Rebecca Marie Louise Black was a proper lady. Matron had taught her well, so why was she so flushed from a simple kiss? Maybe she wasn't so proper after all. The thought should concern her. It didn't.

I let him do it again, Rebecca admitted to herself. The earl had disarmed her with his rueful admission that his behavior was wrong. She must squelch this tendency to succumb to his caresses. No true lady would be so weak-willed, especially one who had reached maturity under the auspices of the Duchess of Dorchester. But, then, could Rebecca Marie Louise Black lay claim to being a lady despite the duchess and the matron?

Louise peeped around the open door. She had heard the earl leave. then had waited a few minutes before returning to the drawing room. Their shouting match had stunned her. Rebecca simply did not lose her temper. Louise couldn't even remember the last time her friend had raised her voice in anger. She found Rebecca pacing the floor.

"What happened, Rebecca?"

Rebecca didn't slow her stride as she admitted, "He kissed me."

Louise asked, "Did he renew his offer? Does he want to marry you right away?"

"I'm not going to marry him."

"What?" The incredulous question burst out before Louise could think of diplomacy. "You *must* marry him. What would the duchess say if you don't? And Matron? Kissing a man whom you won't marry. They would be horrified. Hurt, even, because you ignored their teaching, rejected their moral standards. How can you possibly justify such behavior?"

"Nothing has changed, Louise. I still don't know who my parents were." Rebecca swallowed a lump. "Shelburne certainly made clear his opinion of people who are unable to trace their lineage back several generations."

Louise managed to modify her words. "Rebecca, the earl gives every evidence of caring very deeply for you."

"His arrogance truly passes all bounds," Rebecca continued as though Louise had not spoken. "Lord Shelburne believes he can order me to marry him, that I will bend to his will."

Louise persisted in her argument and enlisted the aid of Mrs. Peters when that lady entered the room.

Amelia listened with close attention to the details of the encounter, then spoke to Rebecca. Both her mien and her words were serious. "My dear, you have accused Lord Shelburne of being arrogant. Have you considered your own guilt of the same trait?"

Rebecca gazed at her in surprise. "What can you possibly mean?"

"It appears to me you're as self-important as you accuse him of being. You have convinced yourself you're right. You refuse to listen to anyone who has a different view of the matter. Is a refusal to listen to others not a form of arrogance?"

Rebecca frowned, not speaking for a moment. "I suppose that is a fair assessment. However, I still cannot marry him."

Remembering Rebecca's response to his kiss, Shelburne drove away from Harley Street with a light heart, his pulse racing. His simple kiss had settled her temper. *She is mine*, he exulted. *She cannot deny the fact. Rebecca Black can't refuse to marry me.* A frown settled on Shelburne's face because she had done just that, refused an offer of marriage from the biggest catch on the Marriage Mart. That arrogant thought bothered him. Not one person had ever accused him of arrogance. Until Rebecca Black. Shelburne drove in silence for a few moments before addressing his tiger.

"Am I arrogant, Henry?"

"Arrogant, m'lord?" Henry had held the exalted position of the earl's tiger ever since his lordship returned from Spain. Now, he spoke his mind with the ease of familiarity. "Just who is this chit who has her claws in you? She must be beetle-headed. Not up to your standards. An addle pate for sure, making you think you're arrogant."

Shelburne ignored most of his words. "Yes, Henry, arrogant. Set up in my own conceit. Convinced that I'm always right."

"No, m'lord. At least no more than any other who is all the crack."

Shelburne remained silent, not quite comfortable with Henry's answer. A few minutes of thought convinced him his behavior was proper, therefore logic followed that he was not arrogant. Yet if he was arrogant, it was only as befitted the Tenth Earl of Shelburne. He nodded in satisfaction at his tortuous reasoning. He had no reason to think ill of himself. If others did, Miss Black included, their opinion showed how wrongheaded they were. Shelburne knew he could change her attitude, her response to his kiss convinced him. What anyone else thought mattered not in the least.

Shelburne's mind was clear when he entered the colonel's office at nine o'clock the following morning. Colonel Hayes fidgeted while Shelburne greeted first Lord Beaufort and then Sir Julian. The latter brought him up to date on family news. Hearing the colonel's grunt, Shelburne turned to him with an apology.

The colonel waved away Shelburne's apology. "I have just received news of another battle in which the French were waiting for us."

"Did we lose many men, sir?" Beaufort spoke immediately while Sir Julian sat in grim-faced silence.

Shelburne stared from one to the other, waiting to hear details.

"No, thanks to the Almighty," replied the colonel. "The front scouts sounded the alarm early enough to prepare Wellington. Gentlemen, we must double our efforts. This leakage must stop." He pounded his fist on the table, sending papers flying.

While Beaufort gathered up the papers, Shelburne asked, "May I know the problem?" His voice held an edge of impatience. How could he be of assistance if they kept him in the dark?

The colonel nodded at him. "Yes, now is the time to explain."

Their problem was simple yet unimaginable. Plans for British troop movements reached Napoleon's army before they reached Wellington's troops. The problem was not only that the French knew the British were planting false information to them about Wellington's movements. They also knew the correct information. There had to be a leak in the colonel's office because the couriers carrying the messages were above reproach.

Wellington's loss at Ciudad Rodrigo in January indicated beyond doubt there was a traitor at work. The decimation of his troops, even though he had captured a French eagle, left Wellington in helpless rage, which he made clear when he had notified headquarters of the battle.

The loss at Badajoz in April enraged him further. Only his last-minute change in plans at Salamanca permitted him to crush Marshal Marmont's forces decisively capturing two more eagles in the process. Now on his march to Madrid, Wellington demanded action on the home front. Who could blame him? At the rate of troop losses this year, they would soon be slinking home in defeat.

"That's the problem in a nutshell, my lord. At first, we thought it was coincidence or the excellence of the French front scouts, but we have changed our minds. Someone on this end is a traitor. So tell me. Who has access to the written plans?" demanded the Colonel. Normally even tempered, his raised voice showed his frustration with the situation. He glared at each man in turn. "Well?"

"Only those present at this meeting, sir," Beaufort answered quietly in his effort to calm Colonel Hayes. After a pause, Beaufort added, "The head clerk who prepares them naturally reads them."

The colonel shook his head. "Somebody else must be seeing them. Shelburne is the only new person involved. We started experiencing these problems several months before he joined us."

Shelburne recalled George Stafford's comments on this same point. Now he inquired whether the clerk was reliable.

"Beyond question." Sir Julian's reply was definite.

The colonel stared around the table. "Does he require assistance in writing the plans in code?"

"Never, insofar as I have been able to ascertain," Beaufort answered.

"Perhaps we should alter the code?" Shelburne was diffident in his inquiry, feeling somewhat less than competent to help.

"How often we change our code has no bearing on the matter. Napoleon's troops still know Wellington's movements before he does."

"Then the information must be leaving here by spoken word rather than written." Shelburne stated the obvious. "Yet how is that possible?"

They discussed the matter, voicing, then rejecting, several solutions. They had lost another of their pigeon posts in France forcing them to depend on human carriers. Arranging another safe post was in order but difficult to do under present circumstances. At length, they agreed to end the conference to meet again when their minds were fresher.

While waiting for his tiger to return with the curricle, Shelburne stood in the outer room where the clerks perched on high stools involved with their work. Glancing idly around, he met the eyes of a pale-faced youth who turned away. Shelburne wondered about the expression on the young man's face, deciding it was simple curiosity.

Shrugging, the earl hurried out the door. Tooling along the crowded street, he decided not to think of the army problems any further that day. Instead, he allowed his mind to veer to Miss Black and how best to proceed with her. He respected her feelings regarding her legitimacy—she had only his welfare at heart—but he must find a way around them.

Chapter 12

An Unexpected Visitor

On a beautiful sunny morning, Rebecca decided to walk the short distance to Mr. Wright's office. She started out briskly, but soon her steps slowed, her thoughts on the earl. What would she do if he didn't solve the mystery of her ancestry? Could she contemplate working in Mr. Wright's office the rest of her life? Should she return to Hampshire and help at the orphanage? That was an idea worth considering, Rebecca thought. The duchess had assured her that the girls could always return.

Her footsteps came to a standstill when a bundle of rags, falling out of a speeding wagon, landed at her feet. Rebecca stared in amazement at the whimpering bundle which rose in front of her. Bending over, she gazed through a tangle of black curls into a child's terrified blue eyes.

"You poor dear! Do not run away. I shan't hurt you. I promise."

The tiny girl stood still, clutching her tattered garments close to her thin frame while she eyed Rebecca.

"What is your name? Where is your home?"

The child's lips quivered, her eyes filling with tears at the mention of home. She would have run away had Rebecca not been holding her arm.

Rebecca glanced at the gathering crowd. "Do any of you know this child?" Receiving no reply, Rebecca studied the urchin in her grasp then reached a decision. "I cannot leave you here, so I will take you to Mr. Wright. He will know how to advise me. Come with me."

A stylishly dressed young woman walking hand-in-hand with a filthy urchin, wearing what can charitably be described as rags, is bound to attract attention. Rebecca did just that. She arrived at Mr. Wright's business establishment with a crowd at her heels and nonchalantly entered the building. She wanted to believe she was nonchalant. However, if truth be told, she was quaking in her half-boots as she pulled the crying child who resisted with all her might.

"Miss Black!" The senior clerk stared in horror at the spectacle invading the hallowed premises of a respectable businessman. "Who are these people?"

"Good morning, Mr. Parker," Rebecca replied with commendable calm. "I have no idea who they are or why they followed me here. Feel free to send them away."

Passing from the outer office into the private passageway, Rebecca heard a babble of voices as Mr. Parker attempted to move the crowd. After tapping on the door, Rebecca stepped into her employer's private room where she braved his incredulous stare.

The child's sobs turned to gulps. The sight of a man caused her to clutch Rebecca with both hands.

"Good morning, Miss Black." Mr. Wright's voice was cordial under the circumstances. "Do you care to tell me why you brought this child here?"

Unable to speak for a moment, Rebecca looked downward into terrified blue eyes. Her mind swung back to her first day at the orphanage. She, too, had been a terrified raven-haired, blue-eyed child. Except for the grace of God and the charity of the Duchess of Dorchester, she might have ended up like this child, alone. She shivered at the thought. This child was friendless no longer.

Facing Mr. Wright, Rebecca raised her stubborn chin. "She landed at my feet after someone pushed her from a moving wagon. She has not spoken, so I have no way of knowing who she is."

Suddenly tears stood in her eyes. "I could not just leave her there, sir. Truly! Do you not see? This could have been me."

"It's all right, Miss Black, I assure you. Sit down while we discuss the matter." He pulled the bell rope summoning Mr. Parker.

Refraining from staring at the child, the clerk said, "Yes, sir?"

"Mr. Parker, we need to determine this child's identity. In the meantime, please obtain food for her."

"Milk, too, please, Mr. Parker." Rebecca smiled at the child whose eyes lit up at the mention of food.

During the few minutes before Mr. Parker returned, Rebecca wiped the child's dirty hands hiding a grimace at the resultant stain on her dainty handkerchief. With an apologetic smile, she accepted Mr. Wright's proffered larger square of linen and continued wiping.

"Child, can you speak?" Mr. Wright watched the little face for any sign of understanding. Although he received only a nod in answer, he was satisfied for the moment.

The odor of a meat pasty preceded Mr. Parker through the door. The child swallowed convulsively and gazed with pleading eyes at Rebecca who blinked back a rush of tears as she settled the starving child at a side table.

"First, you need to drink some milk while I unwrap the pasty. Drink it slowly, so you won't strangle," Rebecca cautioned. She watched the little girl eat, surprised at the restraint the child showed. Instead of gobbling the food down, she took small, dainty bites chewing each mouthful. When the food was gone, she curled up on Rebecca's lap easing into sleep.

Rebecca turned her attention to the gentlemen.

After discussing the matter at length, Mr. Wright realized he could not obtain more information from Rebecca. The child could offer none. Mr. Parker assured them he had been unable to get any answers from the crowd which had followed Rebecca.

"I hardly know where to begin. There are so many children abandoned on the streets, I doubt we will identify this one. However, we will try." Mr. Wright turned to Rebecca. "In the meantime, Miss Black, I will take the child home to Mrs. Wright, who is forever taking in strays."

"No, sir." Rebecca ignored his astonished reaction. "This child will come home with me until you find her family."

"My dear Miss Black, what are you thinking? You cannot take a ragged urchin into your home. There is no telling what kind of vermin she carries on her person or how destructive she is."

"I found her. She is my responsibility at least for now. God might be giving me an opportunity to return some of the help I received from the duchess."

"Perhaps He is, but have you considered what Mrs. Peters and Miss Tracy will say?"

"No, sir, I don't need to consider their reaction because I know they will welcome her. I believe you forget that, until a few months ago, the only home Louise and I could remember was the orphanage. You will recall, too, that Mrs. Peters lived in a small attic room. They will understand why I want to give the child a home for a while."

Rebecca glanced down into the upturned face of the little girl who now stared at her with unblinking eyes. She set the child on her feet. "You're coming home with me. I'll take care of you. I promise."

"If you are sure." Mr. Wright asked Mr. Parker to find a hackney to take Rebecca and the child to Harley

Street. As he handed them into the cab, Mr. Wright assured Rebecca he would commence his efforts to identify the child that day. "Miss Black, I suggest you take a few days off work to care for her."

"Thank you, sir. You are most kind to me."

When they arrived at her Harley Street home, Rebecca ignored Jamison's raised eyebrows at the sight of a dirty child being ushered into his clean lobby. She wished him a pleasant day then continued up the stairs, clasping the child's hand. Her white gloves would never be the same.

Rebecca withstood Morton's stares as she entered the drawing room. She had told Mr. Wright the others would welcome this unknown urchin into their home, still she quaked in her half boots when Amelia stared from her to the child, raising eyebrows to Rebecca.

"Amelia," Rebecca said in a rush, "we have a house guest for a few days." Pulling the resisting child forward, she waited for Amelia's reaction.

"Welcome to our home, my dear." Amelia smiled at the cringing child but spoke to Rebecca. "Perhaps you will introduce us."

"You see, an introduction is a problem. I do not know her name because she has not yet spoken." Rebecca explained the circumstances, assuring Amelia that Mr. Wright was putting forth his best efforts to learn the child's identity.

"Then the first thing we must do is see to a bath. You take care of that while I send Mrs. Morton to obtain some clothing for her."

When Louise arrived home from work, the first face she saw was unsmiling and framed by a mop of unruly dark curls. Big blue eyes stared at her without blinking. Louise smiled as she stooped down to the child's level.

"Who are you?" Receiving no reply, Louise tried again. "Can you take your finger out of your mouth?

Can you tell me your name, dear?" Louise glanced at Rebecca who stood near the windows. "Who is she? Something about her tugs at my memory." Louise studied the child's face while she listened to Rebecca's recital of the day's happenings.

The little girl ran as close to Rebecca as she could manage, one forefinger tucked securely in her mouth. Her eyes darted from one speaker to another.

Suddenly Louise demanded Rebecca put her finger in her mouth.

"Do *what*?"

An expression of amused determination crossed Louise's face. "You heard me. Put your finger in your mouth like she has," nodding toward the child.

Rebecca shrugged but complied. Louise chortled. "I knew it. That is exactly how you looked the first time I saw you—dark curls, blue eyes, unsmiling, your finger in your mouth. Truly, this child could be *you*, Rebecca."

"I know. That's one reason I brought her home with me."

"Who have we here?" Shelburne smiled at the bright-eyed little girl who gazed at him in wonder. Several days had passed since he last called upon Miss Black. His work with the colonel required more of his time, so he spent long hours there every day. Shelburne had learned he must deal with a variety of problems at a time. Some were minor but still needed attention. Arriving in Harley Street unannounced, he hoped for a tête-à-tête with Rebecca during the few minutes before he had to return to his desk. Instead, a small girl with a finger in her mouth greeted him inside the drawing room door.

"Do you have a name?" Receiving no answer, he sat on a small sofa while he studied the elfin face presented to him. With a twinkle, he started calling out names. "Thalia? Calliope? Diana?"

She stared at him with solemn concentration.

"Terpsichore? Clio? Narcissus?"

"Tell Lord Shelburne your name, dear." Rebecca watched the child with a beaming smile.

The child removed her finger from her mouth. "Miranda." She scurried across the room to Rebecca's side.

Shelburne raised inquiring eyebrows toward Rebecca. "Am I to know anything more about her?"

"Yes, of course, my lord," Rebecca assured him. Turning to Miranda, she suggested Mrs. Morton might have some gingerbread if Miranda cared to go to the kitchen. "Will you ask her to bring tea, please?"

The child started to run from the room but then skidded to a stop. Turning toward the others, she dipped a quick, if unsteady, curtsy then hurried from the room.

Rebecca seated herself in a wing-backed chair facing the sofa and recounted her acquaintance with the child, who had landed at her feet the day before.

"How long do you intend to keep her here?"

"As long as necessary," Rebecca replied. "Mr. Wright is looking into the matter of her identity. He will come by this afternoon with a report on his progress. Or lack thereof as the case may be."

"He has his job cut out for him, finding the family of one street urchin among so many. She's a pretty child, apparently with some degree of intelligence since she learned to curtsy so quickly."

"We didn't teach her to curtsy. In fact, this is the first time she attempted the move in my presence. Oh, I can hardly wait for Mr. Wright to get here."

Shelburne quirked an eyebrow toward her but refrained from speaking until Morton set the tea tray on a small table in front of Rebecca. Thoughtfully sipping his tea, Shelburne asked the reason for her impatience.

"Can you not see Miranda is not an ordinary street child? I noticed yesterday how daintily she ate her food even though she was very hungry, ravenous even. Also, last night she sat up in bed, folded her hands in an attitude of prayer and mouthed several words."

"Mouthed? She did not speak aloud?"

"No. Miranda spoke for the first time this morning. Shelburne, she has a refined voice and the nicest manners. Someone has taught her well. She cannot be a street child."

Mr. Wright's arrival interrupted her. Rebecca hurriedly crossed the room, her hand outstretched. "Mr. Wright, what have you learned?"

Her impatience brought a gentle rebuke from Mrs. Peters whose teacup clattered in a dish. "Perhaps you will wait until Morton brings more tea?"

Rebecca accepted the rebuke with a penitent smile. After pouring tea for Mr. Wright, she spoke again. "Can you tell us anything about Miranda, sir?"

"Miranda? Do you mean the child has spoken at last?"

"Just this morning," Rebecca told him. "The only thing of value she has said is her name and her age, which is six, although she has chattered some. Not just some, almost endlessly is more accurate."

"I believe you've forgotten something important," Mrs. Peters said. Seeing the puzzled expression on Rebecca's face, she continued. "The kitten."

"Oh, yes!" She turned to Mr. Wright. "Miranda picked up Mrs. Morton's kitten then announced 'not Fluffy' and put the cat down. She must have had a kitten at home, do you not agree? A pet seems improbable for a street urchin."

Before Mr. Wright could answer, Shelburne spoke. "Have you learned anything about the child?"

"Nothing," he replied. "I must admit I never had a great deal of confidence I would."

"Mr. Wright, do you not see? You inquired about a street urchin. I'm convinced Miranda is not one. She speaks well, all her consonants are in place. She does not use any of the coarse words one would expect from a street child."

The solicitor was skeptical, but before he could reply, Shelburne rose. "I must attend a meeting, so I will take my leave of you." He bowed over Rebecca's hand. "I shall call tomorrow if I may?"

"We will look forward to your visit, my lord," she assured him with a smile. "Perhaps you can help us with Miranda's problem."

"That was not what I had in mind," he commented, then with a nod toward the others, quitted the room.

Rebecca ignored Mrs. Peters' sharp look. Turning to Mr. Wright, she told him he must see Miranda, hear her for himself. Seeing the cleaned-up child would convince him, she was sure. Rebecca hurried from the room, returning with Miranda holding to her hand.

"Do you remember this gentleman, Miranda?"

The child trained her blue-eyed stare on Mr. Wright, then a smile settled on her face. Miranda crossed the room until she stood beside his chair. "I members you, sir. You sended the other gentleman to get me something to eat. I hasn't drinked milk in a long time," she confided. "Not since I lived in the other house."

"Can you tell us who lived in the other house with you, Miranda?" Mr. Wright studied the child standing beside his knee.

"Mama and Papa and Nanny and Betsy." Miranda swallowed and continued. "Other people lived there, too, but I forgetted their names."

Rebecca exchanged pleased smiles with Amelia. Despite some incorrect grammar, the child's gentility became more obvious by the moment. Miranda was not awkward amid strangers nor did her surroundings intimidate her. To Rebecca's mind, this proved she came from a prosperous family.

Mr. Wright continued his questions. "Do you know where that house was situated?"

"What's sit– what you said?"

"Situated means where was the house? Was it near where Miss Black found you?"

Miranda stood in frowning concentration for a moment. "We drived a long, long way from that house to the new house. The horse wasn't pretty like my pony. I rided in the bottom of the wagon. The man gave me a drink and puted sacks over me," she complained in an indignant voice.

"She was abducted, drugged!" Rebecca breathed in horror.

Mr. Wright ignored her. "Did you know the people who took you away from your home, Miranda?"

She shook her head. "He said he was taking me to a new mama." Miranda's lips trembled and tears drenched her blue eyes. "I not want a new mama, sir, I want my old mama." The tears overflowed.

Rebecca swallowed her own tears and cradled the child in her arms until she stopped sobbing. "Darling, can you tell us anything about the new mama?"

"She was sick. She called me Susie. I telled her my name was Miranda, but she still called me Susie."

"Who pushed you out of the wagon, child?" Mrs. Peters' quiet voice broke the silence following Miranda's disgusted statement.

Miranda's face paled, and she clung to Rebecca. "I not want to go back there. Please not make me go back. He hurted me." She broke into hysterical sobs that took several moments to abate.

Rebecca wiped her tears. "Miranda, I promise. You are not going back to him."

Mrs. Peters patted the child's arm. "I did not mean to upset you, dear. We will not send you back to him."

Mr. Wright cleared his throat. "Miranda, the reason we need to know the man's name is because we need to ask him where to find your old mama."

Miranda turned her tear-drenched blue eyes toward him. "His name is Jack. He lived with the new mama until they tooked her away."

"Who took her away?" Mr. Wright's quiet voice soothed the child's fears.

"Some men. They wrapted her in a sheet, then tooked her away." Exhausted after her hysterical pleading, Miranda yawned and snuggled closer in Rebecca's arms, her eyes closing.

"This has been a trying afternoon for the poor dear. The best place for her is her cot." Preparing to leave the room with her small burden, Rebecca asked the solicitor to stay, so they could discuss the matter further.

Returning a few moments later, Rebecca stared the solicitor in the face. Her voice indicated she would brook no nonsense. "The child was abducted. How do we go about finding her family?"

"I would like to find her family, too, Miss Black. The proper procedure would be to contact Bow Street, which I will do as soon as I leave here. If they have no helpful information, an item placed in the newspapers will be our next step." Mr. Wright rose to his feet. "In any case, newspapers will take a few days at least, so you will have her for that long."

"Should he fail to find her family, Rebecca, what then?" Mrs. Peters' question broke the silence after Morton escorted Mr. Wright out the door.

"Could we not keep her with us?" Rebecca bit her lip then answered her own question. "No, we can't. She needs to be with other children."

Mrs. Peters remained silent, allowing Rebecca to work out the situation for herself.

With a sigh, Rebecca acknowledged the obvious. "We will take her to the duchess, although I would love to help her the way the duchess helped me."

"You are helping her, my dear, help no one else would have offered. Even if she's only here for a short time, you're following God's will in what you're doing."

"God's will," Rebecca repeated. "Yes, that's a comforting thought. We can make her life here on earth much better than if I had left her on the street where she might never hear about God's love."

Yet it was also God's will that she die young, Rebecca reminded herself, turning away to hide her tears. This could be her only opportunity to repay a small amount of what she owed Him for placing her with the duchess.

So be it. She'd go to her grave knowing she'd done her best.

Chapter 13

Shelburne Intervenes

Shelburne drove away from Harley Street, his mind in a whirl. Who was the child? How would she affect his time with Miss Black? The child could not be the center of her life. He would not, nay could not, allow anything to take Rebecca's attention away from him for any length of time. If that was arrogance, then he was arrogant. He handed the reins to Henry instructing him to return in three hours. Hurrying to Whitehall, Shelburne's mind was already on the work facing him.

He had promised the colonel he would address the House of Lords on the military's immediate need of funds. The earl didn't look forward to his maiden speech in the House, but he at least had a subject close to his heart—the war. He thought back to the deplorable, often calamitous, problems the army faced every day. When he had filled several pages with his ideas, Shelburne carried them to the colonel's office for his comments.

"Very good points, my lord," the colonel assured him. "They will be the better received because you have experienced these same problems. Now, are you going to write this speech, or will you leave the preparation to your secretary?"

"Patterson will do a much better job of it than I could," Shelburne admitted. "He's in alt because I'm finally taking my seat. He's had more than a few choice words on the subject several times. Probably sees me as the next Prime Minister, or some such nonsense."

Colonel Hayes chuckled. "Patterson will keep you up to the mark, I make no doubt. You may well find yourself in an exalted position one day." He rose to his feet in dismissal. "Let me see the speech draft, if you will."

"Certainly, sir." Shelburne shook the outstretched hand and quitted the room.

Placing his hat at a jaunty angle as he left Whitehall, Shelburne accepted the reins from his tiger, then urged the horses into motion.

Shelburne thought of returning to Harley Street as soon as he gave the pages of notes to his secretary but decided against it. Instead, he would apply his mind to finding a different way to learn Rebecca's ancestry and Miranda's family. He muttered, "I must identify, not one but two beautiful raven-haired, blue-eyed females."

"Did you speak to me, m'lord?"

"No, Henry, I was only muttering to myself. Getting to be a habit of mine, I fear." Shelburne pulled the horses to a stop at his front door, tossing the reins to the tiger. "I'm staying in this evening, Henry, so you're free until morning."

As expected, his secretary went into raptures when Shelburne handed him the notes with a brief injunction to write a speech. Insisting he needed to know more of the circumstances giving rise to the speech, Patterson questioned Shelburne about his battle experiences until the hour grew late. The astuteness of the queries from a non-military person surprised Shelburne.

With his secretary's curiosity finally satisfied, the earl's thoughts reverted to Rebecca and this new responsibility she had undertaken.

Rebecca did not consider Miranda a responsibility as much as a gift for whatever period the child stayed with her. After dinner, she joined Amelia and Louise as they discussed the day's events over needlework. Yet her thoughts were on Miranda, who was sound asleep in the cot Rebecca had placed in her own bedchamber. She smiled as she thought of the child's chatter. After once beginning to talk, Miranda had hardly stopped although she didn't say anything that would help identify her. Rebecca wondered if she herself had talked so much at age six.

Without attempting to hide her yawns, Rebecca excused herself. Opening the bedchamber door, she crossed the room to watch the sleeping child. She moved the tousled black curls away from the tiny face. Her heart ached at the sight of the innocence living on the streets would destroy. This precious little being could even end up living in a workhouse. Or worse. That was not going to happen, Rebecca assured herself. Mr. Wright would locate Miranda's family, or the duchess would take care of her.

Either way, Rebecca knew the outcome was out of her hands. How she would like to keep the child with her, give her a loving home again! Miranda could be the beginning of her long-held dream of helping little girls just as the duchess had helped her so many years ago.

A few hours later, whimpers woke Rebecca.

"What's wrong, Miranda? Did you have a bad dream?" Rebecca pushed the tangled curls aside then gasped as her hand touched the hot forehead. Hot? Why would she be so hot? Rebecca gave no thought to donning her dressing gown or slippers when she hurried to Mrs. Peters' bedchamber.

Shaking the older woman on the shoulder, she almost shouted. "Amelia, wake up. You must wake up right now, I tell you, right this second. Miranda is sick, I'm sure she is. She might even be dying. Oh, do wake up, Amelia."

"Can't a body get any shut eye around here? Stop shaking me, I'm awake." Struggling to sit up, Amelia pushed her nightcap out of her eyes. "Missy, I trust you have a good explanation for waking me in the middle of the night."

"Miranda is sick—horribly, horribly sick. Come help her." Rebecca tugged at the bedcovers.

"All right, all right, don't work yourself into a pelter. I'm coming." Amelia grumbled. Pushing her feet into house slippers, she followed Rebecca into the other bedchamber, where a yawning Louise joined them with a demand for an explanation.

"This merry-begotten brat is cutting up stiff."

"She is not merry-begotten," Rebecca snapped. "She lived with her parents. She said so. She is not cutting up stiff either. She's feverish. Go ahead, touch her forehead," Rebecca ordered. Hardly had she stopped talking when Miranda cast up her accounts. Before they got that mess cleaned up, the child heaved again, then collapsed against Rebecca who held her while Louise changed the bedding again.

While Louise attempted to calm Rebecca, Amelia cradled the child's face in her hand and agreed she was feverish. "I apologize, Rebecca."

Rebecca gave her a tremulous smile. "You must tell me what to do. I've never dealt with a sick child before."

"I have," Amelia stated. "I should think she just has an upset stomach. You stay with her while I prepare a brew to bring down her fever. Louise, you stay too in case Miranda casts up her accounts again."

The next few hours were harrowing in the extreme for Mrs. Peters. But not because of Miranda's upset stomach, Rebecca overheard Amelia tell Mrs. Morton. No, Rebecca was fast driving her into an early grave. She had sent for the doctor at Rebecca's insistence, giving up in her arguments that the child didn't need a doctor. Rebecca understood but could not curb her anxiety.

Mrs. Morton commiserated with Amelia, even tried to calm Rebecca's fears with assurances the child's problem came from eating the rich food she did not consume as a rule.

The cook didn't convince Rebecca either.

In midafternoon, Shelburne arrived in the drawing room in time to hear Amelia admonish Rebecca to sit down before her pacing wore a permanent groove in the carpet. He clasped Rebecca's shaking hands in his own. "What is wrong, my love? What has you so upset? Tell me so I can help."

Rebecca twisted her hands until she could grasp his. "Miranda. Oh, Shelburne, she is so ill. She isn't able to keep anything down, not even barley water or lemonade." Her shoulders shook with sobs as he gathered her into his arms.

"Have you sent for the doctor?" His words were muffled as he buried his face in her rose-scented hair.

"Aye, we sent for him all right." Mrs. Peters' clipped words showed her disgust with the medical profession. "Quack, that's what he be. Naught but a quack," she repeated. "He wanted to bleed her! Can you imagine bugs being stuck on that precious baby? He's addled for sure."

"Not bugs, Mrs. Peters. Doctors use leeches." The earl kept his face buried in Rebecca's hair in his effort not to laugh. "I understand leeches are the normal way to bring down a fever."

"Bugs," Mrs. Peters repeated. "No matter what kind of fancy moniker you give 'em, they're still bugs. I won't have 'em put on a baby." She directed a frown of ferocious proportions at him. "Besides, her fever ain't so high. She has a belly ache. Do you think that quack would take my word for it? Oh, no! Brandy-faced, that's what he was. All he could do was blather break-teeth words. Trying to hide his ignorance, he was, the numskull, but no quack can pull the wool over my peepers! I'm more than seven, and so I told him!"

"Ah, yes, just so," Shelburne agreed, struggling with laughter.

Rebecca raised her face from the earl's chest, smiling through her tears. He mopped her face with a large square of white linen, urging her toward a sofa where he sat beside her, his arm resting along the back.

Shelburne glanced toward Amelia who chewed her lower lip, looking sheepish.

"I fear I got carried away, your lordship," she said in her most refined tones. Indeed, since being in close attendance upon Rebecca and Louise, her speech had reverted to the quality of her youth. Mrs. Peters rarely lapsed into the cant she had picked up from her unlamented husband. "Please excuse my lack of—um—finesse."

Morton entered with a tea tray before Shelburne could answer. Urging Rebecca to drink the hot brew, he inquired for Miss Tracy.

"Louise is sitting with Miranda," Rebecca told him. "Amelia insisted I take a break, but now I need to go back to her."

"Not until you finish your tea and eat a slice of this cake," Shelburne insisted then talked while she did as he said, albeit with poor grace.

"I imagine she ate something that disagreed with her," he soothed Rebecca. "If she is not much improved by morning, I will call in my own doctor to see her. No leeches, I promise." He smiled at Mrs. Peters whose face turned rosy red.

Turning to Rebecca, Shelburne clasped her hands. "You should not take the child's illness so hard, my dear. I remember when my niece was that age. Marie was forever eating too many sweetmeats, then casting up her accounts. Your own health is in more danger than Miranda's." He hesitated a moment. "Is there any hope you will come out for a drive?"

His only answer was a belligerent stare.

"I thought not!" Shelburne pressed a warm kiss on each of her hands and left the room before she could speak her mind.

Taking the reins from his tiger's hands, Shelburne set the chestnuts in motion turning toward Grosvenor Square. Rebecca Black filled his thoughts. She really should not worry about a child she had met only a few days before.

"Hold it, m'lord!" Henry clapped Shelburne on the shoulder, recalling him to his surroundings. They had come upon a wrangle among three cart drivers who blocked their way.

"See what you can do, Henry."

"Yes, m'lord." He jumped down from his perch, then waded into the midst of brawling men and rearing horses. Shelburne surveyed the crowd, his eyes lighting on a vaguely familiar face on the edge of the street. The young man was paying no attention to the crowd. He bumped against a gentleman and then dusted him off talking all the while before striding away. The gentleman hurried off in the opposite direction. Recognizing Rushton, Shelburne thought he must be in a brown study about something, otherwise he would have torn a strip off the young man's hide. Rushton's temperamental outbursts had been part of their daily lives at Eton to the point the authorities regularly sent him down for extended periods of time. Why they accepted him back every time was still a mystery to Shelburne. Arriving back in Grosvenor Square, he flipped the reins to Henry and thought no more about the chance encounter. He settled down at his desk to deal with the everlasting paperwork.

Rebecca stirred and blinked her eyes open, only to draw back into her pillows. A pair of solemn blue eyes stared at her from a distance of perhaps six inches. "Miranda, darling, how are you this morning?" Rebecca smoothed the tumbled black curls from the child's face. Cool to her touch, she was thankful to note.

"I all better now," Miranda assured her. "I feeled bad yesterday, did I not?"

"Yes, you did. Now, hop down so I can get dressed. Do you think you could eat some breakfast?"

Miranda bounced off the bed. "May I have an egg and some toast and some marmalade and some milk and …"

Rebecca interrupted with a smile. "We must talk with Mrs. Peters about your diet. We don't want you sick again, do we?"

Amelia and Louise greeted them warmly at the breakfast table. When they heard Miranda's chatter, both Mr. and Mrs. Morton stuck their heads around the kitchen door directing beaming smiles toward their little darling. After some judicious discussion, Miranda delved into the breakfast of her choice while Rebecca limited her own intake to her usual tea and toast with Mrs. Morton's orange marmalade.

The earl stopped in long enough to inquire about Miranda.

"Oh, she is in rare form this morning, my lord. The child has not had a quiet moment since she got up. Nor have we," Rebecca admitted.

"Then she does not need a visit from my doctor, so I will be on my way to Whitehall."

"Will you be busy all day, sir?" Rebecca explained her question. "We might take Miranda to the park this afternoon if she continues to feel well. She needs fresh air, according to Mrs. Peters. Perhaps you can take a breather from your work to join us?"

"Nothing would give me more pleasure. However, I expect my work will require all my time today."

Rebecca nodded her understanding. "Perhaps another day while she is with us."

After a morning filled with the child's energy, Mrs. Peters agreed a trip to Green Park was just what they needed. A hackney deposited them at the entrance. Soon Rebecca and Amelia sat on a bench in the shade watching Miranda playing with other children. The slight breeze was welcome after the heat of their rooms. Rebecca glanced around, breathing a sigh of relief when she didn't see herself floating in the vicinity.

"Good afternoon, ladies. Is it not a beautiful day?" A suave voice interrupted her thoughts.

A quick glance at their interrogator identified him. Rushton. Rebecca turned her face away and lay her hand on Amelia's in a gesture to keep her quiet.

"Your child is quite charming—the image of you." When he didn't receive an answer, he persevered. "I haven't seen the child with you when you have been with Shelburne. Does he know his inamorata has a child? Or perhaps she is his child?"

Rebecca had had enough, but he was standing so close she could not stand without pushing him backward, which she was inclined to do, the Matron's admonitions about violence notwithstanding.

Amelia not only could stand, she did, drawing his attention around to her. Drawing on her early genteel upbringing, she spoke in her haughtiest voice. "Sir, your manners leave a great deal to be desired. Now, please leave us."

When Rushton turned to stare at Mrs. Peters, his movement allowed Rebecca to rise to her feet and step away. Keeping her face blank, she never uttered a word. Taking Amelia by the arm, she walked to Miranda, and the three prepared to leave the park over Miranda's protests.

The proud Earl of Rushton would not allow her snub. He grabbed Rebecca by the arm, causing a pain that made her shriek. "Oh, no, my proud beauty. You cannot evade me so easily."

"Unhand the lady this instant, you scoundrel!" Shelburne spoke from behind Rushton in a loud, furious voice. The earl grabbed Rushton's shoulder and whirled him around, his fist raised, his intentions clear to passersby.

"No, Shelburne, please don't hit him. 'Vengeance is mine, saith the Lord. I will repay.'" In an effort to calm the situation, Rebecca repeated the words the orphanage matron had required her to memorize when she wanted to hit a girl who had pulled her hair. She didn't recall what punishment the girl received, but Rebecca was sure there had been discipline at least by Matron if not directly by God. This was more serious.

What if they fought a duel over her? Rushton might be the better shot. Rebecca could not have Shelburne's death on her conscience. She glanced around at the gathering crowd of shrieking nursery maids. "We are attracting too much attention, my lord. Let us just leave, please."

Shelburne lowered his fist but shoved Rushton away. "Should you ever approach this lady again, I will beat some sense into your head. I do not make idle threats. Now get out of my sight before I change my mind and finish what I started!"

Straightening his coat with as much dignity as he could muster, Rushton turned away and retrieved his horse. Once mounted, he stared at Rebecca a long moment, turned smoldering eyes toward Shelburne, then rode away at breakneck speed, sending the crowd scampering to safety.

Noticing Rebecca was rubbing her upper arm, the earl took her hand in both of his. "Did he hurt you?"

"Not enough to matter." She managed a tremulous smile. "How did you happen to come along at just the right moment, my lord?"

"I faced my desk as long as I could," he answered with a grin, "An afternoon with my favorite ladies was more attractive, so I went by Harley Street. Jamison told me where to find you. Come, I will drive you ladies home." He smiled at Miranda. "I brought my carriage because I planned to take this young lady for a ride."

Rebecca clasped her hands together to stop their shaking on their ride back to Harley Street. What was it about her that made a gentleman like Rushton approach her in such a manner? Certainly, the duchess, reinforced by Matron, had given her lady-like training, so something inherent in her being, a flaw, must betray her teaching. She couldn't imagine what the defect was, so how could she control it? In their rooms, Rebecca sent the chattering Miranda to the kitchen for her own tea while the adults had theirs in the drawing room.

"I don't believe I will ever go to Green Park again." Rebecca struggled for calmness. "That was Lord Rushton, was it not, sir?"

Shelburne set his cup down and managed to speak in a reasonably calm voice. "Yes, that was Rushton."

"I have tried to make clear to him my lack of interest, yet he persists. He thinks I, you, that ..." Her face a fiery red, Rebecca clamped her lips shut.

"What did he say to you?" The steel in Shelburne's voice demanded an answer.

Rebecca bit her lips before forcing them to open but found she couldn't utter another word. Amelia spoke instead.

"Rushton believes Rebecca is your *chère-ami*, that Miranda is her child and speculates that she is your child too." Amelia's blunt words caused the earl to shake his head in wonder.

"When Rushton gets an idea in his poor excuse for a brain, he refuses to let go of it. I have told him that Miss Black is a lady above reproach. Since he has not mentioned you in recent days, I thought he believed me, but I was wrong." He frowned in thought. "I don't know what either of us can do except stay away from him."

"I can, but can you?"

Amelia agreed. "Have you considered you, too, are in danger from him, Shelburne? Can you ignore the murderous look in his eyes just before he rode away?"

The earl didn't have an answer, so he changed the subject from the encounter to the child. "Miranda seems to have enjoyed her visit to the park. When I approached, I noticed she was playing with several children, which indicates she is comfortable with others her age, not only adults."

"Oh, yes, she truly enjoyed our outing," Rebecca told him. "I suppose she had never seen cows before because she hung back for a moment, but then acquired the courage to pat one on its head."

"Intrepid little soul, is she not?" the earl said in his lightest voice. "Since she is no longer ill, will you ride with me tomorrow?"

"Oh, no, Shelburne," Rebecca stated. "I intend to spend my time with Miranda."

"All your time? I want to have time with you, too, Miss Black. Miranda is a precious child to be sure. I can understand your attachment to her. I imagine you had much the same appearance when you were her age. However, need you spend all your time with her? Can you not trust her to the care of Mrs. Peters or Mrs. Morton?"

"It is not a matter of not trusting them, my lord. I will have Miranda with me such a short time and I might never see her again. I don't want to miss a moment. Can you not understand?"

His lips tightened, but he said no more. Rising to take his leave, he sketched a bow before closing the door behind him.

In the silence following Shelburne's leaving, Amelia asked, "Are you being wise, Rebecca? Since you found Miranda, you have had no time for him at all. This after spending an inordinate amount of time with him, almost daily."

Shaking her head, Rebecca repeated, "She will be with us such a short time, Amelia. And she's such a joy to have here. You must admit she livens our lives no end."

"You're showing an independence of mind that surely exceeds what the duchess instilled in you. The extreme isn't a becoming trait."

Rebecca ignored Amelia's blunt words. "I must be with her while I can."

"Do you think Shelburne will come when you beckon after she is gone?"

Rebecca clamped her mouth shut as she gathered the tea things together before leaving the room. After leaving the tray in the kitchen, she hurried to her bedchamber where she stared out the window not truly seeing anything, just thinking about Shelburne, her situation, and their future possibilities, happy or otherwise.

Her eyes focused outward to the busy street, but her thoughts turned inward. Would Shelburne return when she was ready to spend more time with him? Or would he decide she was not worth the effort? Considering she was most likely illegitimate, besides being employed as a Cit, the current situation might convince the earl not to return. Rebecca heaved a sigh as she contemplated her future without him. Unbearable, yet she must spend this precious time with the chance-found child. Their time together would end all too soon.

After dinner that evening, with Miranda asleep in her cot, Rebecca told Louise of the park encounter. When Louise's gasps of horror faded, Amelia drew their attention.

"Girls, I have given the matter of your public safety considerable thought since this afternoon and have reached the conclusion that you must learn how to defend yourselves."

"How can we, Amelia? Lord Rushton, like most gentlemen, is larger than we are," protested Rebecca, rubbing her arm which he had grasped. "What chance do we have against him when he is determined to gain our attention?"

"She's right, Amelia, however, you are right also. Rushton appears determined in his pursuit of Rebecca."

Amelia agreed. "I am much smaller than either of you, still my husband believed I could protect myself with the necessary training. He was right. I only had to defend myself once, but the maneuver worked for me. I am confident it will for you too."

"What will?" Rebecca inquired.

"First, you must forget you are a lady. Return to those wild women of yesteryear, which your ancient ancestors surely were. Stomp his feet or kick him in the knee. Stick your fingers in his eyes. A man will be so busy blinking you can get away. Don't be afraid to scream or kick up a rumpus. In this instance, forget that the duchess and the matron told you ladies don't draw attention to themselves. On the contrary, attract as many people as you can. Rushton will leave rather than face the humiliation of jeers from the crowd. His sort cannot accept that."

Rebecca and Louise giggled. Seeing Amelia's raised eyebrows, Louise said, "Rebecca can defend herself for sure. She has experience kicking shins."

"Poor Eddie! Rebecca wiped her eyes. "I truly was a terrible child."

Nothing would do but the girls had to tell the whole story of the little village boy who believed he could take Rebecca's sweetmeat. He learned differently in a painful encounter. In the aftermath, Rebecca learned a lady's manners.

In her bed that night, Rebecca twisted and turned. Could she bear living if Shelburne did not return? Why would he not understand her need to spend her time with Miranda? Surely, he could understand she saw herself in Miranda. Could he not see that Rebecca didn't want the child to have the same lost feelings she herself had at the same age?

Rebecca drifted off to a sleep filled with dreams of Shelburne and Rushton facing each other in a hazy morning light with pistols steady in their hands. Miranda floated into their range just as they fired. She lay motionless on the ground and no matter how she strived, Rebecca couldn't reach her.

Near dawn, Rebecca woke with her throat sore from her efforts not to scream. She threw back the covers then stood beside the sleeping child. Nothing and nobody would keep her from this child as long as it was possible for them to be together. Rebecca nodded her head in determination then crawled back between the sheets.

Chapter 14

Happy Yet Unhappy

Regardless of Rebecca's absorption with the child, Shelburne intended to spend time with her, which meant he would have to spend time with Miranda also. This business of winning his love was more involved than he had thought possible. The possibility he must compete with a child for any female's attention never occurred to him. The following afternoon he appeared at the Harley Street flat determined to amuse the child in whatever way possible. The *ton* would not believe the ever-correct, suave man-about-town, the Tenth Earl of Shelburne was soon down on all fours with Miranda on his back, while Rebecca and Amelia watched their game with amusement.

Patting his shoulder, Miranda informed him he was a good pony, then ordered him into a trot. "Faster, sir, faster!"

Upon seeing the others' amusement, Shelburne increased his speed for the length of the room but then called a halt to the proceedings. "Down, child. If we keep this up, my valet will take me to task over the ruination of my trousers."

With a giggle, Miranda clapped her hands. "That was fun. Can we do it again?"

Rebecca intervened. "Perhaps you can tell Lord Shelburne about Fluffy instead."

"Fluffy is my kitten," Miranda informed him as she made herself comfortable on his lap. "Mama gave him to me for my very own. He's supposed to sleep in his basket, but mostly he sleeps on my bed," she confided. Miranda turned her sad face upward and asked, "Will I ever see Fluffy again, sir?"

Shelburne smoothed her curls. "Mr. Wright is doing his best to find your family, my dear. In the meantime, you can play with Mrs. Morton's kitten."

Miranda nodded and cuddled next to his shoulder, her eyes closing. He watched her sleep for a few minutes then carried her to her cot.

The following afternoon, Shelburne arrived at Harley Street carrying a small package which he handed to Miranda.

Tearing the paper apart, she stared at the bunch of slender sticks. "What are they?"

"This is a game called spillikins. Here, I will show you how to play." Sinking to the floor, Shelburne introduced Miranda to the game he had most enjoyed when he was her age.

Soon Rebecca was also on the floor playing the game. Amelia declined to join them, saying her bones would creak, bringing a spate of giggles from Miranda.

The next afternoon Shelburne made a suggestion. "If you believe Miranda won't be scared of the large animals, we could take her to see them at the Tower of London."

"Oh yes, let us go there. Louise and I have not yet been to the Tower. Louise loves animals."

Louise clasped her hands. "Lions? Tigers? I never hoped to see them, my lord. Thank you."

Mrs. Peters declined the pleasure saying she visited the Tower in her youth. The steps would be too much for her now.

Shelburne agreed to be free the following afternoon, regardless of his workload. He was to rue the moment the idea of a visit to the Tower occurred to him.

Keeping two ladies and a dancing child together in the large crowd proved a daunting experience. Yet, with the exception of being jostled, no real problem arose until they reached the caged animals. There, Louise created a disturbance of major proportions involving the crowd.

The moment she saw the small, cramped cages that housed the animals, her temper erupted. Some people backed away while others voiced their opinions as loudly as did Louise. Animals should be allowed to roam free as God intended. But, then, no one would be able to see them. God allows them to be in cages, so it must be acceptable. The cages are too small.

As more people added their opinions, Shelburne picked up Miranda and put his other arm around Louise's shoulder pushing their way through the crowd, leaving Rebecca to fend for herself. They arrived outside disheveled but unbruised.

In embarrassment, Louise apologized. "I believe animals should have enough space to move more than three or four steps in each direction."

Miranda patted her on the arm. "You're right, Miss Louise. I wouldn't want my Fluffy to live in a cage."

Rebecca met Louise's rueful eyes with a glint in her own. "Oh, the memories this provoked."

Returning to Harley Street, they regaled Shelburne with some of Louise's daring rescues of various animals, some of which didn't want to be rescued.

"You were obviously a challenge for the matron, Miss Tracy." At the door, Shelburne told them he would be busy all the next day, but his evening would be free. "Miranda might enjoy a trip to Astley's Circus. Would you and Miss Tracy care for that?"

Louise shook her head. "As much as I would enjoy the circus, I must decline, my lord. However, perhaps Mrs. Peters would enjoy going to the Circus. She has not mentioned a prior engagement."

Rebecca answered with caution yet with a twinkle in her eyes. "Yes, my lord, I believe Miranda would find pleasure in that. However, are you sure your credit in the *ton* will stand your attendance at such an entertainment?"

Miss Black's casualness did not fool him. He had seen her eyes light up. She would appreciate the outing at least as much as the child. Nevertheless, he gave due thought to her question.

With an answering twinkle, Shelburne reassured her. "Just barely, I should think, but only because most of the *ton* is out of town. However, never let it be said that I should place my standing in the *Beau Monde* above the pleasure of an enchanting six-year-old," he declared with twitching lips. "Mrs. Peters, would you care to join us?"

Shelburne wondered which of the females in his party was the most excited as they alighted from his carriage at Astley's Royal Amphitheater the following evening. They gazed in awe at the theater itself, its stage illuminated by a huge chandelier. They gasped in astonishment at the trapeze artists. "How did he do that?" was repeated over and over as the conjurers performed. The equestrian feats held them enthralled. Miranda spoke for the first time when John Astley rode around the arena while standing on his magnificent white horse.

"Someday, I will ride my pony that way." A shadow crossed her face. Turning to Rebecca, she asked with trembling lips, "Will I ever see Brownie again?"

Rebecca hugged her. "Yes, darling, we will find Brownie for you." She stared at Shelburne, daring him to contradict her.

He nodded in sympathetic understanding. Taking Miranda onto his lap, he explained. "Little girls do outgrow their ponies, my dear, so in the event we fail to find Brownie, we will get you a horse all for your own. How would you like that?"

A brilliant smile greeted his words. "Yes," she breathed. Then with a penetrating look, she asked, "A real horse?"

"A real horse." With his assurance, she patted him on the cheek and cuddled against his chest. Glancing at Rebecca, Shelburne said perhaps it was time to return to Harley Street.

Later, with Miranda asleep in her cot, Louise came in from a party insisting upon hearing all about the circus. While they were discussing their evening, Morton came in carrying a salver on which rested a folded sheet of paper. With apologies, he admitted he should have given the message to Rebecca upon her arrival home. He had forgotten.

Rebecca accepted the paper. "There is no need to worry, Mr. Morton. We have been back only a short time." She scanned the message, her face turning pale as she read the words again.

"You're upset, Miss Black. What is the message?" Shelburne moved to her side on the sofa and scanned the note she handed to him. "This is what you wanted, is it not? This is what you asked Mr. Wright to do."

Rebecca blinked away her tears. Turning to the others, she said, "Mr. Wright believes he has found Miranda's parents."

"Oh, 'tis wonderful news to be sure." Amelia beamed while Louise added her own enthusiasm.

"Rebecca, this is what you want, to return the child to her parents." Shelburne reminded her.

Rebecca nodded her agreement. "I will miss her."

"We will all miss her, dear. Does the message say anything else?" Amelia asked.

"Mr. Wright received several inquiries after the newspaper message was published, but none of those missing children were a match to Miranda. He seems convinced these people are her parents."

"Shall I be here when he brings them tomorrow morning?" Shelburne held Rebecca's hands in his, giving what comfort he could.

"Oh, would you? I should be so grateful." Rebecca turned her hands until she could clasp his. "I trust Mr. Wright, truly I do. He is ever faithful to his word, but I would like your opinion too. I must be convinced beyond any doubt before I let Miranda go to anyone. You can appreciate that, can you not?"

Louise assured her. "Rebecca, we do understand your need to be certain about Miranda's future. We feel the same concern."

Shelburne rose to leave. With a smile and a small squeeze of her hands, he assured Rebecca he would be there before ten o'clock the following morning.

Rebecca dressed for bed but didn't lie down. Instead, she sat beside Miranda, watching her sleep, praying for the strength to do what she knew she must. Near dawn, Rebecca dozed off waking a couple of hours later with a stiff neck. Slipping out the door, she went to the kitchen where she stoked the fire and put on a kettle of water for tea. Taking a cup of the reviving brew back to her bedchamber, she again sat beside Miranda's cot watching her sleep until Louise tapped on the door.

The strain on Rebecca's face told its own story. "Have you had any sleep?"

"Not much," Rebecca admitted. "I want to look at her for as long as I can."

"Come now, Rebecca, you must accept the fact Miranda is leaving, whether to her family or to the orphanage."

"Yes, I do know, still it's hard to let her go. Now, I must get her dressed. I want her to be as pretty as possible, so they will know we took good care of her." Rebecca touched the child on the shoulder.

When Shelburne arrived a few minutes before ten o'clock, Rebecca greeted him with a smile, even managed to carry on her end of the conversation while they waited for the visitors. When Morton announced them, she stiffened her shoulders, raised her chin, and walked forward to greet them. She saw a couple who appeared to be in their late twenties, dressed quietly yet fashionably. The solicitor introduced them as Michael and Amanda Abernathy of Oxfordshire. The strain in their faces was obvious as they darted quick glances around the room.

"Where is she? Where is our Miranda?" Anguish colored Mrs. Abernathy's soft voice.

From the moment Amanda Abernathy walked into the room, Rebecca knew this was Miranda's mother. The resemblance was quite clear, the same big blue eyes, the same black hair although Amanda wore hers in a neat chignon at her nape instead of the riot of curls Miranda sported. Rebecca smiled at the distraught woman.

"She is in another room, Mrs. Abernathy. I will bring her to you now." She hurried to the kitchen where the Mortons were caring for the child. They questioned Rebecca with their eyes. She nodded before turning to Miranda.

"Miranda, dear, Mr. Wright brought some visitors to see you."

The child hung back a moment, her thoughts easy to read as they flitted across her face. Miranda still was not quite sure she wouldn't have to go back to that man who pushed her out of the wagon. She had tried to be a very good girl and not cause any trouble so this nice lady wouldn't send her away. Now Miranda sensed she had to leave.

"Is it the man who tooked me away from my old mama?" she whispered in anguish.

Rebecca gathered the child in her arms to soothe her fears. "No, darling, I promise you this is not that man. I would never let you go back to him. I truly believe you will want to see these people." Taking her by the hand, she led the child into the drawing room.

Miranda clutched her hand, hanging back while she glanced around the room. When her eyes met those so much like her own, she flung Rebecca's hand aside and ran. "Mama! It's my old mama!" she shouted throwing herself into the outstretched arms.

Pandemonium reigned a few moments before Michael Abernathy wiped his streaming eyes. "Why did she call Amanda her old mama?"

"As well as we understand the situation, someone abducted Miranda and gave her to a woman whose own little girl had died." Rebecca told the story of her involvement with Miranda, much of which Mr. Wright had already told them.

Mrs. Abernathy said, "We believe Miranda slipped outside to find Fluffy. We didn't realize she was gone until we found the kitten outside the door."

Mr. Wright declined to stay for lunch, but the others sat long over the meal talking over the Abernathys' efforts to locate their child.

"My brother, Simon, has walked the streets of London searching for her," Michael said. "We called in the Bow Street runners to no avail."

"I imagine the abductors kept her indoors," Rebecca said. "She doesn't appear to have picked up any street talk. I must wonder why the Runners didn't mention her language when Mr. Wright approached them."

"There are several Runners and I'm not sure how much communication there is between them," the earl said. "I imagine Mr. Abernathy and Mr. Wright spoke to different ones."

When the time came for the Abernathy family, now complete again, to leave, Amanda glanced at Michael who turned to Rebecca. "Miss Black, you have given our precious daughter back to us. We have been in despair for the past three months, thinking we would never see her again. How can we ever repay you?"

Rebecca protested. No payment was necessary. "You must realize we quickly came to love Miranda. She is a precious child. We will miss her."

"Would you care to visit us in Oxfordshire?" Mrs. Abernathy asked. "I know Miranda will enjoy seeing you again. We would like to get better acquainted."

Before Rebecca could answer, Mr. Abernathy. spoke. "Dear, as much as we would like to know them better, I imagine they are too busy with their London friends to leave Town."

"Nonsense," Rebecca said. "I would like nothing better than to have you as friends. I am sure Mrs. Peters and Louise feel the same way." She glanced around for confirmation.

Shelburne agreed. "Even after knowing Miranda for this short while, we would not want to lose touch with her."

"My lord, you do us too much honor. We would be pleased to have all of you pay us a visit as soon as you can arrange to be out of Town."

"For as long as possible," Mrs. Abernathy added.

Miranda had been sitting in her father's lap, her eyes going from speaker to speaker. Now she added her vote. "Oh, yes, all of you must come and meet Fluffy. Brownie too." She turned an enchanting smile on her father and pointed to Shelburne. "He said if I have growed too big for Brownie, he will get me a horse. A *real* horse."

Her earnest words brought laughter all around. "Well, Poppet, you have not yet outgrown Brownie but when you do, you shall certainly have a real horse."

Mrs. Morton stepped into the room carrying a valise holding Miranda's clothing and toys. Handing it to Mr. Abernathy, she said, "My husband and I will miss Miranda. She has been a delightful guest."

"Thank you for your care of her, Mrs. Morton. We appreciate the care all of you have given our daughter more than you can ever know."

With hugs all around, they agreed the house party would convene as soon as they could make arrangements. When the Abernathy family started toward the door, Miranda ran to Rebecca and bestowed a wet kiss on her rescuer's cheek, standing still long enough for a hug. Then with a bright smile, Miranda grasped her parents' hands as they followed Morton from the room.

There was a moment of silence after the door closed. Everyone watched Rebecca. She took a deep breath. "We haven't lost her altogether. I hope we can visit them in Oxfordshire before too long. We don't want her to have sufficient time to forget about us."

Louise agreed. "It will be stupen-uh, marvelous to get out into the country. Beyond doubt, cooler than London." She waved her fan back and forth seeking relief from the heat.

Shelburne left Rebecca's flat with a light step. Miranda had returned to her parents, so Miss Black's time was his again. He signaled Henry to bring the curricle forward. Taking the reins, Shelburne urged the mare to a trot. He needed to go to Whitehall for a conference with the colonel. During the past hours, the earl had suppressed all thoughts except those directly concerned with Miranda's circumstances. Now he could no longer hold off his speculations about the encounter he had witnessed that morning.

While driving to Harley Street, Shelburne saw Rushton and the same young man who had collided with him several days before. This time they were standing in the shadows of an alley, Rushton listening then speaking to the young man who nodded. While Shelburne puzzled over this, the conversation ended. The men went their separate ways.

"Henry," he addressed his tiger, "did you notice that young man talking to Rushton?"

"Yes, m'lord."

"I know I have seen him someplace, but I can't think where it might have been."

"Probably at Whitehall, sir. I've seen him leaving the building when I've had occasion to wait for you."

"You're right, Henry, he is one of the junior clerks there. Now, just what would he be doing in close consultation with Rushton?"

Henry had no answer, so he remained silent.

With Miranda's problems behind him, Shelburne applied his mind toward Rushton's behavior with the clerk. Could Rushton be at the root of the army's current difficulties? However, he must not allow his personal antipathy to the man to cloud his judgment. Shelburne resented Rushton's treatment of Rebecca, but the fact Rushton confined his ardor to members of the lower classes, who had little protection from him, did not mean he was a traitor to his country. Arriving at Whitehall, Shelburne tossed the reins to Henry with instructions to return in an hour.

Striding into the colonel's office, Shelburne's eyes lit on his brother-in-law. "Good. I'm pleased to see you here, too, Julian."

With a grin, Haverford cocked an eyebrow at Shelburne. "Good afternoon, Edward. You seem to have news of some sort. Have you found the solution to the question of life?"

"Life in general? No, but perhaps the lives of Wellington's troops."

The earl's serious statement wiped the humor off their faces. They listened to him detail his sightings of Rushton and the clerk. This clerk couldn't be the only person involved since the problem arose before his time there. Nevertheless, they would start with him. The colonel yelled for the head clerk to present himself. The junior clerk in question, one Mr. Cooper, was not working that afternoon. The colonel nodded dismissal to the clerk.

"One moment, Colonel." Haverford spoke. "Could a clerk be dispatched to bring Beaufort here? I believe he should hear this immediately."

After giving a terse "do it" to the clerk, Colonel Hayes settled down to question them about Rushton.

Sir Julian left them reeling with a question of his own. "Are either of you aware that Rushton's maternal grandmother was French?"

The subject of their discussion had no inkling he was of interest to Colonel Hayes. Rushton sat in his study pondering the news he'd learned when he met with Cooper earlier in the day. Why would Shelburne concern himself with army business? He had sold his commission a year ago, that much Rushton knew beyond doubt, so what possible reason could he have for involving himself with the war? That new chit of his surely kept Shelburne occupied.

The object of Rushton's thoughts lay in bed thinking over the long conference in Colonel Hayes' office making plans to trap Rushton and Cooper. The clerk was the weak link. No question of that. He could lead them straight to the real culprit, almost surely the dishonorable English nobleman. Shelburne gritted his teeth as he remembered so many of his comrades-in-arms lying dead on several battlefields as the result of Rushton's treasonous activities. While Shelburne waited for sleep, without realizing what he was doing, he lifted his thoughts toward heaven and asked the Almighty's guidance.

Cooper was also waiting for oblivion. He had a full stomach. Hopes for the future too. What more could a man ask? This tiny attic room in the shabbiest part of the City would not always be his home. He had decided on that several weeks ago. It was Cooper's lucky day when he first met Major Rushton. He couldn't call their meeting an accident because Major Rushton had approached him, a lowly clerk. He had been real civil, too, he had. All the major wanted was a little information. And he paid good money. What harm could it do to tell a former soldier what his comrades were doing? Him what had been right hand man to Wellington himself. Heartbreaking it was to hear him grieving because he couldn't be in Spain with "Old Hookey" as he called the great man. The very least Cooper could do was tell the former soldier what routes the troops would travel, so he could trace them on a map. After all, it wasn't Major Rushton's fault the men at Whitehall were jealous of his friendship with Wellington.

On that note, Cooper turned on his side recalling his evening with cronies at the King's Arms. He couldn't treat himself to good beef and ale often, but in the future his life would be different. Cooper drifted into dreams of a life of leisure, unaware of what the future held for him.

Someone else lay in bed thinking of the future. Rebecca hugged herself in glee as she thought of her coming visit to the Abernathys. Who knows? This might even extend into other visits through the years. She would so enjoy watching Miranda grow into a young lady. As Rebecca drifted into sleep, Miranda's features dissolved into her mother's, and Rebecca realized Miranda didn't resemble herself at all. They only shared superficial coloring. Miranda's future was safe. Rebecca slept with a peaceful heart.

She woke as peacefully as she had slept. Stretching like a cat, Rebecca performed her ablutions then joined the others for breakfast. "Good morning. I trust both of you slept as well as I did."

"A good morning to you too," Louise greeted her. "Do you go to Mr. Wright's office today?"

Rebecca made a small grimace of displeasure. "I fear I have become indolent because a day in the park appeals more than one in his office. Yesterday when

Mr. Wright left, he told me to expect his carriage this morning, so that means work."

Throughout the following morning, Rebecca forced herself to concentrate on her work. Mr. Wright's handwriting was truly a challenge. She pondered an unlikely combination of letters before reaching the decision to consult him. He entered her room before she could rise.

"I have almost finished the last of the letters, Mr. Wright."

"You've accomplished a great deal this morning, Miss Black." He placed a sheaf of papers on her desk. "I want you to copy this. Afterward, you are free to leave."

"Yes, Sir."

"I'm leaving now and don't expect to return until late. Just leave everything on my table, if you will, Miss Black. Oh, yes, Mr. Parker will see you home." With a smile, he closed the door after him.

Rebecca had forgotten to ask him about the strange word. Perhaps Mr. Parker could help. She answered a knock on the door. "Oh, Mr. Parker, I was just thinking of you."

"Yes, Miss Black," he answered, leaving the door standing wide. "Mr. Lowell is asking for you." His tone alerted Rebecca he was not pleased.

"Asking for me, Mr. Parker? I fail to understand why he would want to speak to me."

"I'm sure I cannot say."

Rebecca's surprise turned to perplexity. This was outside her experience. She appealed for Mr. Parker's advice. "This has never happened before, sir. I don't know what I should do. What do you suggest?"

His attitude softened. "I expect you should see him, Miss Black."

"I suppose so. Will you stay in the room, please?"

With a benign smile, Mr. Parker bowed himself out of the room, returning with Mr. Lowell close behind.

Rebecca inclined her head in answer to Lowell's bow.

"I wonder whether I may speak with you, Miss Black." He glanced at the head clerk who made no move to leave.

Rebecca allowed her surprise to show. "This is a business office, Mr. Lowell. Mr. Parker is in charge in Mr. Wright's absence. You should properly speak to him, not to me."

Mr. Lowell flushed at her tone. "I'm not here on a business matter, Miss Black."

"Not a business matter, Mr. Lowell? Then why have you approached me here? Would it not be proper for you to send a message to Harley Street?"

"I hoped you might agree to have lunch with me," he stammered.

Rebecca had no hesitancy in refusing. "I must decline your invitation, Mr. Lowell. I dine at my desk, as I have told you on several previous occasions."

She turned to the clerk. "Mr. Parker, after you have seen Mr. Lowell out, will you return here? I need your assistance with some work."

When the clerk returned, Rebecca studied his face. Did he hold Mr. Lowell's visit against her? "I hope you don't think I encouraged him to come here."

"Young men don't need encouragement, Miss Black. They follow their own inclinations. You are not to blame in any way."

"Thank you, Mr. Parker." Rebecca changed the subject to her work. Yet if she thought her words to Mr. Lowell was the end of his attention, she mistook his intentions. He approached her again that same evening. The dinner hour had passed. The ladies were in the drawing room discussing their day over their embroidery frames when the door opened, admitting Morton.

"Ladies, Mr. James Lowell."

Rebecca nodded but allowed Mrs. Peters to greet their visitor.

"Mrs. Peters, ma'am, may I speak to Miss Black, please? Alone."

Mrs. Peters turned to Rebecca, who stared at him in surprise. "I believe you should talk with him, my dear," Amelia said then left the room taking Louise with her.

Silence reigned for several moments until, growing more puzzled by the moment, Rebecca broke the silence. "You wished to speak to me, Mr. Lowell?"

He sank to his knees before her, clasped her hands in his, and recited the words in the concise manner of a vicar. "Miss Black, I have come to care for you to an exceeding degree. I want to marry you. Will you do me the great honor of becoming my wife?"

Rebecca stared at him with astonishment that turned to consternation. A marriage proposal was the farthest thing from her mind. She suspected he had practiced before his mirror. With a gasp of dismay, Rebecca realized she had to answer. She had not practiced a refusal. Thoughts competed for space in her head. She must not offend him with a paltry excuse. Rather, she must give him a polite, plausible reason. Pulling her hands from his, Rebecca said, "Mr. Lowell, you have taken me quite by surprise. I recognize the honor you do me, yet I must decline. I have no plans for marriage."

"Miss Black, you cannot have considered. All females are on the scramble for a husband."

"No, Mr. Lowell, you are mistaken in your belief," Rebecca replied in a clipped voice. How dare he group all females together as though they were cattle? "I am a business woman. There is no place for marriage in my life."

"I see what it is." Lowell rose to his feet, a smug grin on his face. "As you said, I took you by surprise. You need time to consider the advantages of the married state. I shall give you time to evaluate my offer against any other you might hope to receive. I will offer again. I am confident you will give me a different response when you have considered all I can give you."

Receiving no answer, he continued. "As you already know, I'm employed in a responsible position. Therefore, you need never again lower yourself as you now do. Nor will you find it necessary to rent rooms. Lord Worthington assures me that, as a married man, I will have my own large suite, rather than my present single room, in his home. We will be almost like family. So, your future as my wife is certain to be better than you've ever dreamed possible." He bestowed a quick kiss on the back of her hand and left the room.

Rebecca wiped her hand on her skirt, gazing after him. She didn't know whether to laugh at his smugness or to scream in vexation at his deliberate refusal to accept her answer as final. She was still staring at the door, a bemused expression on her face, when Amelia came in with Louise close on her heels. Rebecca laid her head against the back of the chair. Her burst of laughter was close to hysteria.

"What troubles you, my dear? Why did he want to see you?" Amelia stood beside her chair holding Rebecca's hand until she could answer.

Between gasps for breath, she said, "He asked me to marry him."

"What? Despite the way you play whist?" Louise grinned at her.

"That is enough of your humor, Louise," Amelia admonished with a frown.

Yet the impertinence was just what Rebecca needed. She wiped her eyes. "He failed to mention his magnanimity in that regard, but he did make clear I need to give considerable thought to the advantages of being wedded to him."

"Are you going to do it? Consider his offer, I mean to say."

Rebecca smiled at Louise's anxious question. "No."

Amelia nodded. "I daresay if you should marry him, you would experience more woe than wonder."

"I have never had the opportunity to refuse an offer of marriage." Louise leaned forward in her chair. "Do tell us what you said to him."

"I told him I am a business woman. As such, there is no place in my life for marriage." Business woman, indeed, Rebecca scoffed at herself. All she truly wanted was to be married to the man she loved who also loved her. Shelburne's image skittered across her mental vision.

"I should think your stated reason is as good as any, especially on such short notice besides being completely unexpected," Louise approved. "At least you were polite enough not to laugh in his face, which I fear I would have done."

"The problem is I do enjoy Mr. Lowell's company. I rather think he will prefer to avoid being in my presence once I convince him of my lack of interest in marriage. I believe my refusal may be prophetic. Perhaps I should set aside all thoughts of marriage—be friends with gentlemen, accept their escort, never allowing our relationship to go further."

"Do you truly believe that's best?" Louise's quiet question drew a nod from Amelia.

Rebecca hesitated. Her first thought was on her limited lifespan. Fairness would not allow her to put any gentleman through the despair of her early death. Nor could she now remind her dearest friends of her early demise. "I don't know. I haven't given thought to the possibility, because it just occurred to me when the words slipped out of my mouth of their own volition."

On that admission, the ladies went to their separate bedchambers. Amelia drifted to sleep with fond memories of her less than successful marriage. Louise wondered whether she would ever receive an offer of marriage. Rebecca dreamed of her wedding to Shelburne, whose face changed into Mr. Lowell's immediately after she said "I do."

Chapter 15

Reunion

"Really, Rushton, you cannot prefer the heat in Town to the coolness of Oxfordshire!" Hamilton wiped his face on a large square of immaculate linen. "If I must visit my parents at Long Wittenham, as indeed I must because my progenitor insists, I intend to take a group of congenial people with me."

"Your mother won't appreciate having a crowd of rowdy males setting her household on its ear in the height of summer. You earlier told me that she is already expecting a hunting party in the autumn. Two male parties within months of each other is more than you can ask of her."

"Oh, there won't only be males I assure you. Who could contemplate such a thing?" Hamilton shuddered at the thought of no pretty girls to impress with his strut. "No, no, Rushton. I already have acceptances from Lady Cornelia Branford and her mother as well as the Lunsford girls with both their parents. I expect acceptance from the lovely Alice Drayton-Smythe and Constance Bennett this afternoon. And possibly, just possibly," he cautioned with an admonitory finger, "Lady Margaret Burgess."

Rushton's face lit up at the last-mentioned name, as Hamilton had suspected would happen. Anytime a gentleman could lure Lady Margaret from the side of her ever-vigilant and caustic mama proved to be a delightful interlude.

"Who else are you inviting to keep these lovely ladies suitably entertained?"

"Both Morrison and Jackson accepted. I expect to hear from Sanderson this evening, then there's Blakely who is considering attendance. He believes he can rearrange his engagements. Unfortunately, Shelburne cannot attend. It seems pressing business precludes his acceptance."

Rushton accepted the invitation. A much-relieved Hamilton left his friend's house. Lady Margaret had hinted she would accept his invitation should either Shelburne or Rushton be there. Hamilton knew she would rather have Shelburne, as would any female in her right mind, yet she ought to know his attention was a lost cause. Shelburne could have noticed her anytime these past two years if he had interests in that direction.

Shelburne had no interest in Lady Margaret or any other female since he met those haunting blue eyes outside Hatchard's weeks before. He had declined Hamilton's invitation, which included the hint about Lady Margaret. There was a real possibility he would throttle her if he had to listen to her lisping voice for any length of time. As for her mother, he thought with a shudder, words failed him. Shelburne recognized another problem in the offing. He hoped Oxfordshire was large enough the Abernathys did not hobnob with the Hamiltons because he had not told Hamilton that he, too, would be visiting in Oxfordshire. However, this could prove good news for Colonel Hayes.

As soon as Hamilton departed from Grosvenor Square on his way to see Rushton, Shelburne hurried to Whitehall to warn the colonel of Rushton's probable removal to the country for some days.

"Perfect. This will give us an opportunity to change Wellington's orders and send them on the way. I want to be informed the instant Rushton leaves town," he advised his head clerk.

"Will you need me further at this point, Colonel?" Shelburne asked.

"I don't believe so. Why do you ask?"

"I have planned a couple of weeks in the country with some friends. However, I can postpone the visit if necessary."

The colonel rose to his feet. "Not necessary at all. I'm sure you will find the country air much more salubrious than London's. Let me know when you return, will you?"

That assurance given, Shelburne left the colonel's office striding out to the larger room occupied by the clerks. He glanced around and found Cooper observing him. The clerk ducked his head. Shelburne left the building knowing Cooper's days in Whitehall would soon end, but it was not the earl's place to give out confidential information. With the information leak situation in hand, Shelburne could arrange for his own sojourn in the country.

Mrs. Peters welcomed him into the Harley Street flat. "My lord, may I offer you some tea?"

"Thank you, yes, tea would be most welcome." Glancing at the clock on the mantle, he inquired when she expected Miss Black. "I should have thought to go by Mr. Wright's office to escort her home."

"Mr. Wright is very good about sending her home in his own carriage, my lord. She will arrive within a few minutes, I expect." Mrs. Peters grimaced at voices raised in anger on the street and crossed the room to the windows. "I do dislike closing the windows because of the heat, yet the noise and dust are even more unbearable."

"I agree that London does get quite warm in the summertime although many agree this month has been hotter than any they can recall. Is this your first summer in Town?"

"In the height of summer, yes, my lord. In my youth, I spent two Seasons in town, but we escaped to our country residence as soon as each Season was over. I shall enjoy our sojourn in Oxfordshire and not only the better atmosphere. I truly miss the slower pace. However, I hasten to say I have no desire to rusticate year round."

Before Shelburne could reply, the door opened to admit Rebecca. He rose to his feet and crossed the room, a smile lighting his face. Holding out his hand in welcome, he asked, "Has the excessive heat of the last few days demolished you? Never mind, we shall leave for the country in a few days. You will feel the difference almost as soon as we are outside the congestion of Town."

Rebecca reluctantly withdrew her hand from his and asked, "My lord, have you set the date for us to leave?"

"That is for you ladies to say."

"Louise has arranged to be away from her pupils for a full fortnight. Did you ask Mr. Wright about being away from his office again so soon?" Amelia asked Rebecca.

"Yes, although I felt terrible requesting more time after taking so many days while Miranda was with us. Mr. Wright said I can be gone another fortnight, which leads me to wonder whether I am truly needed in his office."

Shelburne joined the laughter. "Then, with your approval, I will send word to the Abernathys of our expected arrival on Wednesday next for a fortnight visit. The sooner we go the sooner we can enjoy the cooler air of Oxfordshire." With a quick bow, the earl took his leave.

Over dinner the ladies discussed their pending trip, agreeing they would enjoy the cool countryside again.

"Away from the dust and the noise," Rebecca said, waving a fan before her face. "Have you ever been to Oxfordshire, Amelia?"

"I never had that pleasure. My husband often commented some of the best race horses came from Oxfordshire as well as other areas in the southeast." Her tone was bitter. "He never backed any of them."

Rebecca squeezed her hand. "Amelia, we both understand you lived a difficult life for years because of his activities, but just think. If he'd been successful, you would not have been in need of employment, and we would never have met you, which doesn't bear contemplating, as Louise will agree."

"Yes, I do agree, we couldn't get along without you, Amelia." Louise gave her a quick hug. "Now, let us discuss the most important thing about our stay in the country. Clothing."

Rebecca looked wistful. "Do you think we could buy some new ribbons for our gowns? Perhaps a lace fichu? I should think we will need to dress for dinner too. We don't want to appear in the same gown every evening."

Amelia assured both girls, "Yes, we can purchase some gewgaws. Tomorrow is Saturday. Shall we go shopping?"

The girls agreed with enthusiasm.

After lunch the following day, the ladies set out on their shopping expedition. Heat gathering under their parasols failed to depress the ladies' high spirits as they strolled along the street.

At the drapery, they discussed the merits of each purchase managing to stretch their meager funds farther than they had thought possible. They were especially happy to find a large square of figured silk with a stain in the middle which reduced the cost to only a few pennies. Rebecca showed the fabric to Louise. "See, we can cut it into a triangle on each side of the stain. There's still enough fabric to make a shawl for each of us."

"Stu—uh marvelous! We can also purchase some yarn and knot fringes for them too. How elegant we will be!"

Leaving the shops three hours later carrying their precious packages, the three ladies congratulated themselves upon their purchases. With new shawls, ribbons, and fichus, they believed they would be presentable, if not in the height of fashion by London standards.

Amelia reminded them that Amanda Abernathy had been modestly attired, as had Mr. Abernathy.

"I imagine country dress is not as fashionable as in Town," Rebecca noted.

"Not that we know what London fashions are," Louise replied. "So, we will be happy with what we have."

With bonnets and gloves at hand, the ladies were ready to leave early on Wednesday morning when the earl's travel carriage pulled to a stop at their building in Harley Street. With the help of Shelburne's grooms, Morton and Jamison loaded the baggage into the boot. They soon sent the enthusiastic party on its way with promises they would tend to all matters which might occur here.

"Welcome to Abernathy Hall, my lord and ladies." Michael Abernathy greeted his visitors on the steps of a small, red brick Georgian house a few hours later. He led them inside past the waiting butler, who accepted Shelburne's hat, then into the drawing room. Amanda hurried forward to greet them, holding Miranda by the hand. Miranda eyed them closely before recognizing Rebecca then rushing into her arms with a joyous squeal.

Rebecca knelt on the tiled floor to embrace her, pleased that the child remembered her. Holding her close, she said, "Oh, Miranda, I have missed you so." She rose to her feet, holding Miranda's hand. "Do you remember Mrs. Peters and Miss Louise? Lord Shelburne is here too."

Miranda gave the ladies a quick hug, and smiled at the earl.

"Do I not get a hug too?" he asked, opening his arms.

Miranda ran into them for a quick embrace before she returned to Rebecca, clasping her hand. Glancing toward the door, she asked, "Did Mr. and Mrs. Morton not come with you?"

"No, darling, but they said to tell you how much they miss you. Mr. Jamison did, also."

"Miranda, shall we go upstairs now?" Turning to their guests, Amanda continued. "Come, ladies, Miranda and I will show you to your rooms while Michael escorts his lordship. We're pleased all of you were able to visit us. We have planned a variety of entertainments while you're here, isn't that correct, Miranda?"

The child grabbed Rebecca's hand. "We're going for walks and ride horses and have neighbors here for dinner and …"

Miranda stopped chattering only because she ran out of breath.

Leading her guests up the stairs, then down the corridor, Amanda opened a door into a bedchamber sporting two narrow beds, a chest of drawers, and two chairs. A maid was unpacking the girls' trunks.

"Ladies, this is Jean, who will be your maid during your visit with us."

The maid dropped a curtsy, twinkling dark eyes belying her serious mien.

Rebecca and Louise stared at each other. A maid? It had not occurred to Rebecca they would have one. The only time they'd ever had maid service was when the girls at the orphanage practiced on each other. They followed Amanda and Amelia into an adjoining room where they admired Amelia's bedchamber. Amanda introduced Nancy who stood beside Amelia's open trunk.

"Luncheon will be served in half an hour but come down when you are ready. Since her return home, Miranda has hardly talked of anything except her visit with you. Now I must return her to the nursery for her lunch. Come, darling, Nanny will be wondering where you are." Amanda left the room leading her daughter who had danced around the guests, chattering first to one then another.

After a meal of cold chicken, asparagus with a tangy lemon sauce, and a fruit salad, they strolled out to the terrace. Taking a deep breath, Rebecca exclaimed, "How wonderful to be in the country again. I had forgotten how marvelous clean air smells. Our experience in London is that the air is either overwhelmingly hot or so humid our clothing is damp."

With a laugh, the others joined her in a ramble around the grounds. Formal gardens with gravel paths and wrought iron benches surrounded the house. Beyond those, the lawn extended to a small lake in one direction, a stand of birch trees in another. The acreage was not extensive, yet was large enough for a home garden and a succession house for forcing fruit. Even a fair-sized stable block.

"Are you ladies accustomed to horses, or does your busy schedule preclude your riding in London?" Michael asked as he strolled beside Rebecca.

"Oh, yes, Mr. Abernathy, Louise and I both enjoy riding although we have not been able to convince Mrs. Peters to join us."

They had tea on the terrace joined briefly by Miranda who chattered nonstop. By the time they went upstairs to dress for dinner, the feeling of being strangers had disappeared.

When they gathered in the drawing room before dinner, Rebecca realized their gowns were as stylish as Mrs. Abernathy's gown. She relaxed, prepared to enjoy herself for the entire time in Oxfordshire. Hiding her pleasure behind a serene face, Rebecca took her seat next to Shelburne. She had not dared hope for the honor.

Throughout the meal, as a footman served each course, Rebecca rejoiced in eating food she had not even seen, much less had a hand in preparing. She admitted to herself she could become accustomed to this lifestyle.

The ladies returned to the drawing room after dinner, leaving the men to enjoy their port without feminine chatter. Amanda noticed Louise glancing longingly at the piano. "Miss Tracy, would you give us the pleasure of hearing you play the piano while we wait for the gentlemen?"

Louise needed no urging. "I will enjoy that, but please can we be on first name basis?"

Rebecca smiled at Louise's enthusiasm because she knew her closest friend had truly missed having a piano to play at her leisure. Her listeners quickly realized Louise lost herself in the music, her nimble fingers moving from Mozart's concerto-rondo to a Bach fugue then to a sonata by the new German composer, Beethoven. When a footman entered with the tea tray, Mrs. Peters glanced at Rebecca who sat near Louise. With a slight nod, she touched Louise on the shoulder, bringing her back to her present surroundings.

"Please excuse me for monopolizing the evening!" Louise blushed rosily, hurrying to sit beside Rebecca on a small sofa. There she whispered, "Have I been terribly impolite?"

Before Rebecca could reply in the negative, their hostess spoke.

"Oh, Louise, there is no need whatever to apologize. Quite the contrary. You have given us a most enjoyable evening, has she not, dear?" Amanda directed her words to her husband who sat in stunned silence.

"Most assuredly she has. That glorious sound drew us away from our port with promptness. I have never heard a piano played better by anyone, even professionals, Miss Tracy. I never expected to hear such expertise in my drawing room."

"Playing on the piano is something I enjoy, yet I rarely have the opportunity to play for pleasure since I left Hampshire. Your piano produces an exceptionally fine sound, unlike those of my students, whose younger siblings have a tendency to bang."

Turning to their hostess, she said, "Amanda, with this truly superb instrument available, surely you play also. We would enjoy hearing you."

"Compared to you, I am a novice." Amanda turned to Rebecca. "Do you also play the piano?"

Rebecca cast a wry glance at Louise whose lips twitched. "I regret to say I have no musical ability of any sort. The music master's opinion of my efforts on the piano does not bear repeating. As for singing, he mentioned caterwauling when he believed I was not within hearing range."

"Rebecca isn't musical, but she does beautiful needlework, including many items from her own designs," Louise assured their hostess. "Rebecca has embroidered covers for our chairs. Her current endeavor is a wall hanging."

"A wall hanging?" This addition to his love's list of talents impressed Shelburne. "I had no idea you were so accomplished, Miss Black. What is the scene, or can you tell us?"

His words brought a blush to Rebecca's cheeks. "A child in a rose garden with an angel protecting her from the thorns."

"In truth," Louise interjected, "the embroidery is a self-portrait situated in the rose garden at the orphanage. Rebecca spent a considerable amount of time there throughout the years."

Rebecca didn't want to bore their hosts with her childhood trauma, so she turned the conversation onto more general topics until time to retire.

"Ladies," Michael glanced at his guests, "you, too, Lord Shelburne, we're grateful beyond words for your care of our little girl."

He ignored their protestations.

"Yes, I remember that we thanked you in London. However, there is something you do not know which deepens our appreciation." Abernathy cleared his throat reaching for his wife's hand. "Miranda has talked at length about all of you, as well as Mr. and Mrs.

Morton and Mr. Jamison. Yet she never has mentioned the other people."

Amanda took up the story. "We wondered about Miranda's reticence, so we questioned her closely about those people. She answered without hesitation but she never talked about them otherwise. She never had bad dreams, either, which we had expected after her ordeal."

"Therefore," Michael said, "we believe the loving care you gave her has erased the bad times our daughter had with the other people."

Over the hum of murmured replies, Rebecca's steady voice rose. "We appreciate your telling us this, but I can assure you having Miranda with us, even for so short a time, enriched our lives beyond measure."

The others added their assurances. In doing so, the house party ended the evening in a pleasant frame of mind, looking forward to the morrow.

Chapter 16

Country Pursuits

Rebecca woke to quietness the following morning. For a moment, she wondered why there was no shouting from street vendors, no rattle of cart wheels on the way to market. Her eyes popped wide open. With a delighted smile, she reached across the narrow space and shook Louise's shoulder. "Listen!"

Louise raised her head, opening one sleepy eye. "I don't hear anything. What do you hear?"

"Nothing. There is no noise. Is it not wonderful being in the country again?" Rebecca's enthusiasm bubbled over, causing Louise to give up all hope of sleep.

"Since I am awake, much against my will, I might add, shall we go for an early ride?" Louise swung her limbs out of bed.

"I should think riding will be all right," Rebecca replied. "Mr. Abernathy did talk about it with us. I shall just peek in on Amelia to let her know."

Easing open the connecting door, Rebecca heard Amelia's gentle snoring so she closed the door again. After donning their riding habits, the girls descended the stairs hearing only the distant rattle of pots and pans from the kitchen area.

At the stables, they found two geldings already saddled. Stepping inside, they followed the sound of voices to a back stall.

"Good morning, Lord Shelburne. Good morning, Mr. Abernathy." Rebecca's cheerful voice brought their attention around to her.

"Good morning, ladies." The gentlemen spoke in unison, and Mr. Abernathy continued. "Please call me Michael. You're just in time to join us for a ride. What kind of horses would you prefer? We have a wide variety from very mild to practically wild, so there should be one to answer your preferences."

Rebecca chuckled. "Somewhere in the middle of that range would suit us best, sir."

In a few moments, the foursome was riding across the rolling downs. The horses were frisky, so when Abernathy had determined for himself that the ladies could control their mounts, he lengthened the stride of his mount. They soon were galloping toward a distant stand of large oaks. Drawing up in the shade of one, they grinned at each other.

"That was marvelous, sir." Louise was exultant. "I have been longing to gallop like the wind ever since we left Hampshire. We can't ride neck or nothing in London as you know."

Shelburne grinned in appreciation when Louise cast an impish glance toward him.

Rebecca breathed in the morning air. How she had missed early mornings in the country. The chaffinches chattering high in the trees added to the peacefulness. Rebecca smiled at the others. "Louise is right. This is truly marvelous—beyond anything we've experienced since we left Hampshire."

They turned their mounts homeward, chatting until they parted to dress for breakfast.

Over toast, buttered eggs and kippers, Amanda discussed plans for the day. "We want to show you the village this afternoon, but we have no plans for this morning. I understand you had an early ride, so what would you prefer to do now?"

Rebecca didn't hesitate. "Is this a convenient time for me to visit with Miranda? I've missed her so much."

Amanda smiled at her eagerness. "Yes, you may visit with Miranda. I'm sure she will enjoy introducing you to her cat."

"Oh, yes, we must meet Fluffy," Rebecca said. "Miranda didn't speak to us until she inspected Mrs. Morton's kitten informing us it was *not* Fluffy!"

Their mirth filled the room.

"We must not forget Brownie, either," Rebecca said. "I do hope Miranda has not attempted to stand on his back the way John Astley rode his horse."

Michael Abernathy's lips twitched. "So, Astley put the thought in her head at the circus. She didn't tell us where she got the idea. Miranda did inform us she intended to ride her pony like that. When we questioned her, she only told us 'the man' did, and she could too."

"We managed to divert her attention," Amanda said. "I must admit, though, convincing her was not easy. Miranda is a tenacious child, so I imagine she will try before she gets much older."

"Tenacious!" Abernathy bragged. "She never gives up on anything she wants. Heaven help us when her eyes light on men."

Rebecca spent the morning in the nursery where Nanny could not do enough for the lady who had rescued her precious little lamb. "Please sit here, Miss Black," she urged, pulling forth an upholstered chair.

Miranda climbed into Rebecca's lap, commencing a narration of what she had done since returning home. "Fluffy membered me too." She slid from Rebecca's arms, then picked up a small calico that snuggled against her. "See, this is Fluffy. She losted her fluff while I was away, but I still love her." Placing the cat on the floor, Miranda picked up a book. "Will you read me a story, Miss Rebecca?"

"Yes, I will enjoy reading to you. Reading is one of my greatest pleasures." Rebecca cuddled the child in her lap while she read story after story from *Aesop's Fables*, becoming oblivious to her surroundings.

"I dislike interrupting such a pleasant scene, Miss Black. However, Mrs. Abernathy asked me to tell you it's time for luncheon."

The earl's voice brought Rebecca back to her surroundings. She wondered how long he had been standing in the doorway listening to her read. She set Miranda on the floor. "Darling, I must go now, but I promise to visit with you again tomorrow morning."

"I will be here too," Shelburne announced. "The nursery has always been my favorite room."

Nanny glanced at him with surprise. "Will you not be bored, my lord?"

"Bored? Not with Miranda." He confided in a loud whisper, "I intend to beat them to flinders in spillikins."

"It will be the first time, is that not right, Miranda?" Rebecca asked the little girl who giggled.

Shelburne and Rebecca left the nursery on a merry note.

With lunch finished, the ladies donned bonnets and unfurled parasols for a walk to the village. During their pleasant stroll to Letcombe Regis, Abernathy enlightened them on the area.

"There are two Letcombe villages, Regis where we live and Basset which is closer to the Ridgeway."

"What is the Ridgeway, sir?" Rebecca asked.

"It's an ancient track, origins unknown, but local people say the Celtics used the track more than two thousand years ago." Abernathy continued when no more questions were forthcoming.

"A couple of miles from here, nearer Uffington, legend says Celtics carved a horse in the chalk hillside which we will see another day. This is where the village proper begins."

They glanced down a short street with buildings huddled together on both sides. One caught their eyes, which Michael explained.

"That is 'Old House,' built in 1698. Note that the switchback thatched roof is not even. Legend says the then owner laid the thatch to resemble the hillocks and dips of the Ridgeway."

Shelburne voiced his thoughts aloud. "There is a definite resemblance to the hillside in the distance. I wonder whether all the owners since have followed his lead when re-thatching, or if the design has been brought back into use in more recent times."

Abernathy shook his head. "I have never heard anything on that point, even though this is my home area."

Continuing down the street, Amanda became quite animated. "Wait until you see the Church of St. Andrew with a medieval cross guarding the gateway. Some parts of the church date to the twelfth century, but there have been many rooms added through the centuries, so there's something of a hodge-podge of designs now but still beautiful."

They duly admired that antiquity then wandered up the track to Bassett village where they stopped to admire the Church of St. Michael. The low square tower and the barrel-shaped roof crossed by dark oak beams indicated its Norman origins. Inside, the walls were gray stone with brass tablets fixed to them. Sun streamed through the stained-glass windows making patterns of ruby and amber on the uneven flagstones of the floor as well as on the vast pillars of the nave.

Rebecca commented that the people of the two villages were justly proud of their churches.

"Thank you, Rebecca," Amanda said then turned to her husband. "Shall we follow the brook home?"

He smiled at her enthusiasm and led the way. Amanda assured the others this was a most pleasant ramble. The trees offered shade for the tiny flowers nestled among stately ferns. Their footsteps were soundless on the moss-covered lane. As they strolled in comfortable silence, they spotted some inquisitive chipmunks peeking from the safety of fallen logs. They returned to Abernathy Hall accompanied by wrens chattering in the trees.

As they neared the manor, Amanda asked an anxious question. "I do hope you have not been bored with our village history?"

"Oh no," Rebecca was quick to tell her. "History was my favorite subject in school. We never studied anything about this area, so I welcome the opportunity to learn about it."

Reassured, Amanda led the way indoors.

After tea on the terrace, the ladies retired to their rooms to rest before dressing for dinner. Abernathy challenged Shelburne to a game of billiards—soundly defeating him, as Shelburne told the ladies at dinner.

The following morning, Rebecca and Shelburne approached the nursery door after breakfast. She had questioned him as they climbed the stairs to the third floor. "Are you sure about this? Would you not rather spend your time with Mr. Abernathy than with a child?"

Shelburne paused on the top step, forcing her also to stop. He cradled her cheek in his hand, smiling into her anxious eyes. "I want to be with you. If being with you means being in the nursery, that is where I intend to be. Besides, I like Miranda. I've never witnessed her combination of giggles and determination. I find her fascinating."

Miranda met them at the door with the small package of sticks clutched in her hand. "I thinked you would never get here." She plopped herself on the floor, gazing upward at the earl. "Are you sure you will win, sir?"

"I have no doubt on that score," he answered. Half an hour later, he threw up his hands in surrender. "You have been practicing since you came home," he accused her with a grin.

"Admit it, my lord. You have truly met your match," Rebecca informed him.

"Yes, I have," Shelburne agreed, adding, "In more ways than one." He gazed into her eyes for a moment, then rose to his feet. He winked at Nanny as he joined the red-faced Rebecca on a battered old sofa.

Rebecca hurried into speech. "Miranda, you won at spillikins. What will be your reward?"

"A story." Holding *Aesop's Fables,* she settled herself between them. "Read," Miranda said with her enchanting smile.

After the earl had read one story, he handed the picture book to Rebecca. "Your turn." Soon they were both reading the same story, each assuming different voices for the various characters while Miranda glanced from one to the other.

The time passed too quickly for Miranda. "Must you go so soon?"

"Yes, darling, we must." Rebecca gave her a quick hug then set her on her feet.

"Ah, this must be the famous Fluffy." Shelburne glanced down at the kitten slapping at the tassels on his half boots. "You have another friend we have not yet seen. Perhaps we can visit the stable with you this afternoon and meet Brownie." Shelburne gave her a kiss on the tip of her nose, leaving her in giggles before he and Rebecca left the nursery.

"I believe we have time for a stroll in the gardens before luncheon, Miss Black. Shall we?"

"Should we not find our hosts to determine what their plans are?"

A lopsided grin appeared on his face. "We will leave doing the proper thing to Mrs. Peters and Miss Tracy while we escape out the side door."

Rebecca knew manners were more relaxed in the country, but to this degree? Nevertheless, not a bit averse to his suggestion, she followed him outside. They strolled down a gravel path toward the lake and sat on a stone bench in quiet contentment.

"Did you see that, Shelburne?" Rebecca shaded her eyes, staring at a pool of widening ripples. "Something jumped."

"Looked like a perch."

"A perch? Do you mean a fish?"

"Yes, you ninny, a fish," he teased. "Have you never seen fish before?"

"Only when they were ready to cook," Rebecca admitted joining his laughter.

"The Triple D failed in one part of your education. I learned to fish when I was quite small," he boasted.

"Did all the little boys learn to fish, or were you indulged?"

"I would not go so far as to admit indulgence," he answered. "Nanny warmed the seat of my nankeens on a regular basis."

"Undeserved, without doubt."

"Naturally." he assured her. "Except the time I hid her spectacles."

"You hid her spectacles? How could the poor soul see without them?"

"That was the point of my endeavors, she could not, nor did I want her to see," he confessed.

What mischievous behavior would he admit to now? "Dare I ask why?"

"Well," he replied in a near whisper, "it was this way. I was not wearing the clothing she had put on me that morning. If she had seen what I was wearing, she would have asked questions."

"Questions you did not want to answer, I gather," she accused lightly. "Are you going to tell me why you were wearing different clothing, or do you plan to carry the secret to your grave?"

Shelburne considered the matter before asking with a decided twinkle in his eyes, "Promise not to scold me? Receiving her nod, he continued in a whisper. "They were wet."

"Wet? Do you mean …"

"No, no, I don't mean that kind of wet. I had fallen into the stream when I tried to catch the old'un."

"The what?"

"Old'un. I had it on good authority from the stable boy that many people had tried to catch that fish for hundreds of years. I decided I would catch it."

"What were you using for bait? Besides yourself."

"Nothing," he replied in mock astonishment. "You must realize one only uses bait when one uses a fishing rod, which I did not possess."

She eyed him. "Pardon my ignorance, but just how did you plan to catch the fish without a fishing rod?"

"With my hands," he answered.

This time, Rebecca was unable to control her laughter. "Then you did not fall into the stream, you naughty creature."

He shot her a grin. "No."

"How did you get out of that scrape?"

"Oh, my sister, Becca, and some of her friends were there. They interceded on my behalf as they did so many times."

"Is there something wrong, my lord?" Rebecca's concern was genuine. They had been having a pleasant conversation when he frowned at her. She couldn't think of any reason for the change unless she had been too forward in something she said.

"Not wrong," Shelburne replied after a moment. "A thought crossed my mind but disappeared before I could grasp it."

Rebecca breathed a silent sigh of relief. He was not about to send her to Coventry. "I hate when that happens to me too. Was it something important?"

"I have no way of knowing. However, I daresay, the thought will come back to me when I least expect it. That's happened before."

With a distinct twinkle, he continued. "The duchess was derelict in her responsibilities to you. She should have taught you how to fish. However, I will remedy her failure when we go to Shelburne Park."

"Unless you agree to use fishing rods, I will remain ignorant of that particular sport."

Laughing together, they returned to the house for luncheon. Sitting on the terrace in lazy conversation with the rest of the house party, Rebecca inquired at what hour Miranda finished her nap.

Miranda glanced at her in surprise. "She will be awake by three, but you cannot want to have Miranda tagging along after you in the afternoon also."

Before Rebecca could reassure her, Shelburne laughed. "Oh, yes, we do. Miranda truly is a delightful child. I have never seen quite that mixture of amusing mischievousness and beguiling coquetry before. Your daughter is an education in female behavior!"

Rebecca asked Nanny's permission for her darling to ride with them. Miranda was beside herself with joy until she leaned Mrs. Peters was not going with them. She gazed at the lady with consternation.

"Oh, ma'am, you should ride with us. We'll have lots of fun."

"Thank you, dear. I truly appreciate your invitation. However, I prefer not to have a close acquaintance with horses."

"They are big." Miranda chewed the tip of her finger a moment. "You can ride Brownie. He is small enough you won't fall very far."

This generosity earned her a quick hug. "That's nice of you, Miranda. Still, I won't deprive you of your ride. I prefer to remain here for a nice long cose with Nanny."

With that assurance, Miranda skipped out of the nursery, holding Rebecca's hand. Miranda introduced them to Brownie. They were lavish with their praise of his excellence.

The days flew by. Rebecca and Shelburne enjoyed their mornings with Miranda. Shelburne became quite proficient at spillikins, although he never managed to win. Rebecca decided this failure was deliberate after paying close attention to his hands as he flipped the sticks.

They devoted the afternoons to sightseeing. They visited Uffington where they stared in some awe at the White Horse above the track. On another day they visited Wantage where Shelburne proclaimed the chandelier in the Church of St. Peter and St. Paul was magnificent and he had never seen better, much to the Abernathys' gratification.

After their return from visiting Wantage, Rebecca studied the two gowns spread out on her bed. There were to be guests for dinner. Deciding which gown to wear occupied her mind. She chose the midnight blue cambric with her new lace fichu tucked into the already modest décolletage. With a view of learning the style for herself, Rebecca watched as Jean piled her hair on the top of her head, leaving a few tendrils feathering her ears. Satisfied she looked as well as possible, Rebecca joined the others in the drawing room.

There, her host introduced her to the vicar and his wife, John and Carrie Higgins with their son Robert, and Mr. Richard Simpson standing beside his wife, Judith. Rebecca chatted with the vicar's wife, then Mr. Simpson who was the apothecary. Next were Samuel Gasperson with his wife Molly who blushed at the introduction. Rebecca took to her on the instant and attempted to put her at ease. A bluff, red-faced gentleman, who admitted to having three score years in his dish, completed the party.

Throughout the dinner of cold cucumber soup and roast duck with several removes, Rebecca tried in vain to keep her knee out of Samuel Gasperson's reach. She did not want to cause a scene but enough was enough by anybody's standards. Turning toward him, she spoke softly yet with a decidedly martial tone. "Sir, will you please occupy only your allotted space at the table? Or shall I hint to Mr. Abernathy that you are undesirable company in the presence of ladies?"

Rebecca watched him in grim satisfaction as understanding crossed his face. Gasperson dared not risk becoming *persona non gratis* at the Abernathy residence. Without answering, he moved his leg away from hers. Thereafter, she enjoyed her dinner.

Later in the drawing room, Rebecca learned her difficulty with Mr. Gasperson had not gone unobserved. When Shelburne handed her a teacup and sat beside her, she noticed a grim expression in his eyes.

"Is something wrong, my lord?"

"You tell me. Is there?"

"I don't understand."

"You appeared to be having some difficulty with Gasperson at dinner," he said.

"Oh, that. Was it obvious?"

"Only to me."

Rebecca must choose her words with care. She appreciated his concern, yet it would not do to have the earl coming to blows over her. Such a contretemps would spoil the evening for everyone. Besides, Mr. Abernathy might believe she was at fault, might never invite her to visit Miranda again. That did not bear thinking on.

"Mr. Gasperson seemed to have a difficult time exercising control over his limb which persisted in pressing against mine until I pointed out the error of his ways."

The smile hovering at the corners of her mouth reassured him. He chatted for a few minutes before engaging the vicar in a discussion of the local churches.

Later in their bedchamber, Rebecca related the experience to Louise and Amelia, who invariably joined them for a few minutes before seeking her own bed.

"I suppose, if I had not liked his wife so well, I would not have been quite as irritated with him. Molly is meek, hardly spoke above a whisper. She does not deserve a flirt for a husband."

The new day dawned with cloudy skies. Rebecca woke with a nagging headache. Refusing to allow the pain to deter her, she donned her dark blue habit then crept out of the bedchamber, leaving Louise sleeping She stopped by the kitchen for carrot. Her heart leaped when she met the earl on the doorsteps. They walked together to the stables where Rebecca greeted her favorite mount, Miss Lucy, with the carrot while the stable boy saddled Ajax for the earl.

They were the only riders that morning, which was agreeable with her. Reaching the open downs, they released their tight hold on the reins. Leaning low over their horses' flying manes, they soon were galloping the fidgets out of their mounts. Slowing to a canter and then a trot, they rode in companionable silence, exchanging occasional smiles. Reluctantly turning the horses back toward the stables, their conversation was of their stay in Oxfordshire. They had been here a week and agreed their hosts had been all they could have hoped for—more than they had expected.

Unnoticed by the riders, storm clouds had built up. Raindrops began pelting them, at first a light drizzle but then a heavy downpour as they urged their mounts into a gallop. The rain drenched them by the time they reached the stable where they paused long enough to toss the reins into a stable boy's hands before making a dash for the side door of the house.

With a grimace, Rebecca shook her dripping hat before entering. In her bedchamber, Jean gave a horrified gasp and helped her into a warm dressing gown before rushing out to obtain hot water.

By the time breakfast was over, Rebecca felt as though a score of hammers beat against her skull. She met the earl's concerned gaze.

"Did being in the rain cause this? Did I keep you out too long?" Shelburne asked. "Tell me the truth."

"No, my lord. I woke with a nagging headache. Most times, I can depend on headaches easing just by being out of doors." She watched his face relax into an answering smile when she said, "I forgot all about the headache while we were together."

The earl clasped her hand, his suggestion hesitant. "Perhaps you should forego your visit with Miranda this morning."

Rebecca admitted a romp with such an exuberant person was beyond her. "I'll look in on her to explain why I cannot stay, but then I'll return to my bedchamber for a while."

"I recommend a tisane and a lie-down on your bed until you feel better."

Miranda commiserated with Rebecca but she brightened when the earl challenged her to a game of spillikins.

"You go right along to your bed until you feel more the thing, Miss Rebecca. Don't worry about us." Miranda patted her hand. "Lord Shelburne and I will be just fine, won't we, sir?"

"Yes, we will. Now, Miss Rebecca, off you go," he teased.

Returning to her bedchamber, Rebecca found Amelia waiting. She accepted her friend's gentle chiding, then swallowed a few drops of laudanum in water before slipping between the sheets for a nap.

Waking in late afternoon, Rebecca lifted her head from the pillow. Relieved the throbbing pain had disappeared, she was glad to see the rain also had stopped. Hurrying down the stairs, she arrived in the drawing room as the butler announced dinner. Greeting everyone, Rebecca announced her timing was perfect.

However, after sleeping all day Rebecca was unable to settle down for the night. She listened to Louise's even breathing for several minutes, then slipped out of bed and put on her dressing gown and slippers. Closing the door after her, Rebecca crept down the stairs on her way to the library in search of a book. Light from a candelabrum on the center table diffused the shadows of the room, not quite reaching her as she stepped inside. She uttered a soft "Oh" and started to back out the door. The earl sprawled in a large leather chair gazing into a small flame gurgling in the fireplace but rose when he heard her.

"Are you unable to sleep too?" he queried. "Come sit with me awhile."

"I came down for a book." Rebecca clutched her dressing gown and perched on the small sofa opposite his chair. She hesitated to meet his eyes. What would he think of her for coming downstairs without dressing first?

However, she forgot her embarrassment even relaxed against the back of the sofa as he commented about the dinner party. "Robert Higgins seemed quite taken with Miss Tracy, did you notice?"

"I could scarcely help noticing because he made sheep's eyes at her throughout dinner and in the drawing room afterwards. Did you notice how that older gentleman gravitated to Amelia? Our upstairs neighbor in Harley Street is enthralled with her too."

When he didn't answer, she glanced toward him. Meeting his eyes, she thought she would drown in the deep emerald pools. Rebecca never afterwards understood how it happened, yet suddenly they were both on their feet clinging together. Her mouth softened under his. She slipped her arms around his waist, pulling him closer. She clung to him for a long moment but then pulled away.

Gathering her dressing gown closer, Rebecca hurried out the door.

Chapter 17

Vigilance Relaxed

Rebecca sat on a wrought iron bench in the rose garden, drinking in the scented air, enjoying the peacefulness of birds chirping in the distance. Yet the peacefulness was only external, not reaching her agitated mind.

Rebecca felt a deep yearning for her mother such as she had not felt in many years. Would Mama be pleased or horrified at her daughter's behavior with the earl? After a nearly sleepless night, Rebecca had feigned sleep until the others left for their usual early ride. She clenched and unclenched her hands. How could she have behaved so? How could she have been guilty of such wanton behavior? What must Shelburne think of her now? She cringed at the thoughts racing through her mind.

"Can you forgive me?"

Rebecca jumped at the sound of the earl's voice. Feeling a deep flush rising from deep within, she took a steadying breath then forced herself to look toward him. He stood by the bench. She could tell from the dark circles around his eyes that he, too, had passed a sleepless night.

"I was as much at fault as you, my lord," Rebecca assured him in a low tone. She had come to that realization during the long hours she had sat in the window seat of her bedchamber, staring into the moonlit night berating herself for having left the room earlier. "I should not have come downstairs dressed like a wanton."

Shelburne joined her on the bench. "No. You were not at fault, nor were you dressed like a wanton. I had been sitting there thinking of you when you appeared. Your innocence shone from your eyes. I took advantage of you." Shelburne pounded his fist against his right knee. "How could I have betrayed your trust in such a manner?"

Rebecca reached a tentative hand toward him, touching his arm. She could not bear to see his shame. "We should share the blame, since I had come downstairs for a book to stop my thoughts of you."

She met his eyes, watching the dawning hope in them.

"I had planned a special afternoon for us," he said. "If you can tolerate my presence, will you take a boat ride on the lake with me?"

Rebecca breathed a silent sigh of relief. If he didn't think her a wanton, maybe they could be friends again. "I have never been in a boat, but I should enjoy it."

After luncheon, Shelburne and Rebecca wandered away from the others and located the boathouse without difficulty. Finding a rowboat with oars next to the small jetty, they were soon out of sight around a curve.

Rebecca relaxed against the cushions on the stern, a parasol shading her face. She released a deep sigh of contentment. She didn't know what the others were doing that afternoon, nor did she care as long as they were not with her and Shelburne. Rebecca admitted to surprise that Amelia had relaxed her vigilance here in the country.

The lake was as clear as crystal. Rebecca dipped her fingers into the water, enjoying the feel of the current. With an impish grin, she flicked drops of water toward the earl whereupon he pulled in the oars allowing the boat to drift without guidance while they engaged in a water battle. Helpless with laughter, Rebecca admitted defeat.

"Only because your fingers are larger than mine, Shelburne. They hold more droplets than my smaller ones do, so you had the advantage."

"I wish you would call me Edward. Have we not known each other long enough for that?"

Rebecca studied his face, a slight frown marring her own. "I suppose so, except you're a titled gentleman. A nobleman."

"Thank you for telling me."

She ignored the twinkle in his eye. "Addressing you by your given name cannot be proper for an untitled person."

"It is if I ask you to do so."

After giving the matter some thought, she nodded. "All right, Edward, I will call you by your name when we are alone. You may call me Rebecca," she said, almost as an afterthought.

Their gaze held for a long moment before he blinked. Reaching for the oar, Edward said, "We must get back before the others become concerned about our absence."

The others were sitting down to tea when they strolled onto the terrace. Rebecca was thankful the sun was warm enough to have dried her hair and clothing after the water battle.

"Rebecca, you can never guess what our hosts plan for this Saturday evening!" Louise bubbled with happiness.

"Then I won't try, but I am sure you will tell me," Rebecca teased her.

"We are to have a dinner and dance! Is that not simply stupendous?"

Rebecca's eyes sparkled. "Oh, yes, *stupendous*!" She turned to the Abernathys. "We've never attended a dance, you see, although lessons were a part of our schooling."

"I do hope you will not be disappointed. Only our close neighbors will be here, no one of any real importance so the evening cannot compare to a dance in London."

Rebecca answered the uncertainty in Amanda's face. "We like your neighbors, those we have met. A dance is a dance as far as we're concerned. We will thoroughly enjoy ourselves."

Shelburne directed a quizzical glance toward her with a teasing remark about a female with her serious tastes participating in something as frivolous as a dance. What would the habitués of Lady Frederick's literary salon think?

This brought laughter and the conversation drifted toward literary preferences.

After sleeping so little the preceding night, Rebecca stifled yawns after dinner until she could excuse herself. She hoped she would be asleep before Louise joined her because she had not yet decided whether to confide in her about her behavior of the night before. She had never kept secrets from Louise in their years at the orphanage. Was this part of being adults? If so, Rebecca didn't like adulthood. Right now, she was just too sleepy to stay awake long enough to explain. She'd talk to Louise another day, Rebecca decided as she slipped into sleep.

Early the following morning, Rebecca donned her riding habit and hurried to the stables. Perhaps she and Edward could ride out before anyone else came. Entering the stable door, she stopped in her tracks at the sound of Miranda's pleading voice.

"Please, Hutchins, please?"

"Now, Miss Miranda, you know this is too early for you to ride Brownie. You should still be in your cot. Does Nanny know you came out here?"

Rebecca eased into the shadows where she could watch the combatants. Miranda, with her hat on backwards, had buttoned her habit crookedly, but at least she had taken the time to deal with buttons. Rebecca stifled a laugh as Miranda put a finger in her mouth, gazing upward through her lashes.

"Nanny is still asleep. I know you won't tell on me, so won't you please saddle Brownie for me?"

"Now, Miss Miranda, don't try to cut a wheedle with me because it won't fadge. I daresay you can go riding after you break your fast."

"I'm not going riding."

"Then why do you want your pony saddled?"

From her watching place, Rebecca grinned when Miranda danced around in excitement.

"I want to stand in the saddle while you lead Brownie around in the paddock."

"No! I never in all my born days heard anything so harebrained. No one can stand on a moving horse," Hutchins stated. "You would fall, break open your head as sure as anything."

"It can, too, be done," Miranda declared. "A man stood on a horse and rode it around a big tent at the circus in London. I saw him." She laid her small hand on his sleeve. "Please, Hutchins? It will be so much fun," she cajoled with a smile as bright as sunshine.

Rebecca decided she should intervene to save Hutchins from annihilation by the beaming child.

"Good morning, Hutchins," she said, then "Miranda! What are you doing in the stables so early?"

"Tell him, Miss Rebecca. Tell him about the man at the circus who rode standing up on the horse. He doesn't believe me."

Rebecca smiled at the groom. "John Astley did ride his horse standing up, Hutchins. However, little Miss, that does not mean you are to copy him." She ignored Miranda's indignant frown. "Now come, I will take you back to the nursery. Nanny probably has the house in an uproar over your absence."

Miranda's lower lip protruded dangerously, as she dug in her heels. "I will not go. Brownie is my pony. I will ride him. Standing on his back," she declared, stomping her little foot.

The child's recalcitrant behavior stunned Rebecca. She turned with relief when the earl came to her rescue, stepping forth out of the shadows.

"Are we to understand you want Hutchins to lose his job, Miss Abernathy?"

Miranda stood openmouthed. "Sir, you called me Miss Abernathy,"

"Yes, I did. You are a young lady now and should be addressed as such. Providing you behave as a young lady should."

She eyed him. "What does it mean to be a young lady?"

"You must not give orders to people who will lose their jobs if they obey you."

In deep thought, Miranda chewed the tip of her finger. "All right, sir, I will be a young lady." Turning to Hutchins she said, "Hutchins, you may ignore my earlier commands."

"Thank you, Miss Abernathy. You're most kind." The groom controlled a grin with difficulty.

"Now, Miss Abernathy, are you ready to return to the house?" For a moment, Rebecca was not sure the new young lady would deign to answer.

"I do not require an escort, Miss Rebecca," she announced. Then, with a dignity matching that of a matriarch, Miranda left the stables.

Rebecca exchanged smiling glances with Edward and asked the groom to saddle their mounts. By the time he finished, Louise and the Abernathys had joined them for a long ride.

During every spare moment for the rest of the week, the ladies could discuss little except gowns. Did they have anything suitable? Could they change any of theirs to make them appropriate? Ball gowns were not a part of their wardrobe, yet this was not a real ball, they argued between themselves, merely a dinner dance. Something less formal would suffice.

At almost the last minute, Rebecca chose a rose crape with a V-shaped neckline for which she fashioned a rosette from pale pink ribbon. How glad she was she had succumbed to avarice at the drapery. A real rose would wilt in her décolletage from the heat of her body, but she asked permission to cut one from the gardens in the same shade of pink for a hair ornament.

She managed to control her fidgets while Jean arranged her hair in a mass of curls, which she pinned to the top of Rebecca's head, leaving one resting against her left shoulder. The rose nestled just above that curl.

Rebecca studied herself in the long mirror. She approved what she saw and answered the maid's uncertainty with a smile. Picking up her reticule, she hurried from the room. Shelburne stood at the foot of the stairs. After taking a deep breath, Rebecca descended, watching Edward's face which registered stunned disbelief followed by admiration. Meeting him at the foot of the steps, she placed her hand in his.

"Mere words cannot do you justice," he told her. "You are stunning, absolutely beautiful."

"So are you." This was the first time she had seen him in such finery. The green silk coat fit his broad shoulders like a glove while the black trousers emphasized his long, athletic limbs. Emerald thread wound through his satin waistcoat, highlighting the jewel tucked into his starched neck cloth.

"However, you have nine fingers without rings. Furthermore, my lord, where is your quizzing glass?" Rebecca raised gleaming eyes to his and saw the glint of answering humor.

"Nine fingers without rings? My dear Miss Black, you cannot expect a gentleman to wear rings on his thumbs."

"Would you not? Even for me?" she asked, looking at him through her eyelashes.

"No," he answered. "Not even for you!"

She smothered her chuckles as they approached the drawing room to greet the others.

Rebecca floated through the evening, realizing afterwards that she remembered only two things. First, there was the warmth of Shelburne's hands when they met hers during a country dance and clung for a moment before he released her to another partner.

The other memory was a short time on the terrace. Edward led her outside to enjoy the cool evening air after a strenuous reel. Rebecca leaned against the balustrade her gaze fixed on the shimmering stars. An owl hooted in the distance. A slight breeze carried the scent of roses to them. Shelburne turned her face toward him and lightly brushed his lips across hers in a butterfly kiss which deepened when she leaned toward him. After a long moment, he stepped away from her, whispering his love before leading her back to the ballroom.

The next few days passed quickly. They were to return to London on Wednesday. Rebecca dreaded leaving the peaceful gardens and the rolling downs. Would she ever return?

Rebecca's conscience bothered her. She had not spent enough time with the Abernathys. She didn't even know how Louise had passed her time. Rebecca remedied that situation over the next couple of days, which they spent in the grounds. Miranda rode on the earl's shoulders, giggling as she tweaked his ears. Rebecca walked beside them, their togetherness a balm to her fears of losing Shelburne from her life. Oh, if only they could be a family.

On their last morning, Rebecca decided to forego a ride, playing instead with Miranda before leaving the house for one last stroll in the grounds.

The day had dawned with the sort of thin mist that often heralds a beautiful day. The sun was bright when Rebecca left the nursery. Dressed in a pink cambric walking dress, she considered wearing matching slippers before she realized leather half boots would be more serviceable, though less attractive. Deciding a wide brimmed straw bonnet was preferable to carrying a parasol, she strolled through the rose garden, stopping every few steps to sniff the delightful scent so reminiscent of her years at the orphanage.

Wandering without paying attention to direction, Rebecca was not aware she had left the Abernathy grounds until she was on the Ridgeway track. She followed it a short distance then took the trail by the brook that meandered through the villages. Perched on a fallen log, she enjoyed the gurgling brook and chirping birds. Lost in thought she didn't hear hoof beats coming toward her.

"I didn't expect to find a wood nymph waiting for me. How glad I am I lost my way."

Rebecca jumped to her feet when she heard the beguiling voice. She covered her mouth with trembling fingers when she recognized Lord Rushton.

"Well, well, my darling, we meet again."

Rebecca backed away when he swung down from his horse and started toward her. "I was not aware Shelburne had a love nest in Oxfordshire."

"Excuse me, sir, I must return before my friends become concerned for me." Rebecca turned on the path, but he jerked her around. He held her upper arms like a vise. Try though she did, Rebecca was unable to twist free.

"No, no, you won't escape me this time." Rushton tightened his grip to the point of bruising. "I have not forgotten our last meeting. This time I intend to finish what I started."

Rebecca twisted her face in a desperate attempt to avoid his descending lips. Her bonnet scraped against his face.

Rushton freed one hand long enough to jerk off the offending hat. She cried out when the ribbon pressed against her neck before giving way. She became still when Amelia's face appeared in her mind. Her tone brooked no argument. "Turn me loose, now, Rushton, or you will regret it."

Rushton leaned closer.

That was all she needed. Rebecca rammed her fingers into his eyes. When he howled and reared backward, she lifted her skirts and ran in what she thought was the direction of the Abernathy house. Gasping for breath, she rounded a curve running into a pair of arms that held her against a hard body.

"Turn me loose," Rebecca screamed, beating her hands against the hard chest.

"Rebecca! Calm yourself. Tell me what is wrong."

Hearing the familiar voice, Rebecca gulped clinging to Shelburne as if she would never turn loose. Finding her voice again, she tried to tell him. "It was him. He found me at the brook and was going to ravish me."

Shelburne's arms tightened. "Who do you mean? Who tried to ravish you?"

"That man from the park, Lord Rushton. He's back there." She pointed behind her.

"You stay right here, Rebecca. I will take care of him." Shelburne's grim voice promised he would enjoy throttling Rushton. Striding along the path in the direction Rebecca had indicated, he came upon the culprit wiping his streaming eyes with a handkerchief.

"How dare you continue your attempts to molest a lady?" Shelburne swung his right arm forward but stopped when he remembered Rebecca's words. "Vengeance is mine, saith the Lord, I will repay." He lowered his arm. "Leave before I carry out my earlier threat."

"I can't see well enough to ride yet, Shelburne. You don't understand. She jabbed her fingers in my eyes! I could be blinded for life."

"You deserved anything she did to protect herself. Now get on your horse."

Rushton shot him a look of hatred but mounted and turned away.

Shelburne watched the horse until it disappeared around a curve. Retrieving Rebecca's bonnet from the ground, he hurried back to her. "He won't bother you again. I promise."

Rebecca drew her head back from his chest, staring at him in horror. "You didn't murder him, did you? Please tell me you did not!

"No, I promise you I did not murder him, although I admit to the temptation. I remembered just in time violence is never the answer. Tell me something. How did you know how to protect yourself?"

"Amelia told us what to do after my last encounter with him. I doubt I would have thought of it otherwise."

"I'm most grateful to her and shall tell her so at the first opportunity. You must promise me one thing, Rebecca."

"What is that?"

"You must promise me you will not leave your rooms without a male escort. Rushton won't forgive you this insult."

Rebecca nodded as a shudder passed over her body. "Yes, I realize he will not. I can assure you that, after three encounters with him, I will have a male escort every time I leave our rooms."

Satisfied with her answer, Shelburne urged her forward. "Now, let us return. You missed luncheon and will miss tea, also, if we don't hurry."

"I must see to my packing too. Oh, I do hate to leave here. Our stay has been wonderful."

Shelburne gazed deeply into her bewitching blue eyes. "Any place with you is perfect."

Rebecca felt a flush spread up her face as she forced her gaze away.

Late that evening as the house grew quiet around them, Rebecca and Louise settled back against their piled pillows, talking in low voices.

"Your face was shadowed when you returned with Shelburne this afternoon," Louise said. "Can you tell me why?"

Rebecca recounted her meeting with Rushton. "Poking him in the eyes worked, Louise. He turned me loose on the instant."

"I'm so thankful Amelia told us how to protect ourselves because I don't believe I would ever have thought of her solutions. What might have happened otherwise doesn't bear contemplating."

Rebecca admitted she tried not to think of the possible consequences. "Now tell me what you've been doing while I've neglected you."

"I don't consider it neglect because I've used the time becoming acquainted with the Abernathys. I've played the piano to my heart's content too. Oh yes, Robert Higgins, the vicar's son, has paid me marked attention, so you aren't the only one with a beau! He even suggested we should visit the vicarage for an extended stay the next time we come to Oxfordshire."

"Are you considering acceptance?"

"Not in the least." Louise paused a moment. "I do hope I'am not lacking in sensibility. I must admit, though, that I cannot quite see myself having deep feelings toward any man. At least none I have met to date, yet some of them are unexceptional."

Surprised at Louise's outburst, Rebecca tried to reassure her. "Perhaps you haven't met the right man yet. I failed to realize I could become enamored with a pair of green eyes without even knowing their owner's name. Now I'm either euphoric or desolated about a future with Shelburne. Without doubt, I drive you and Amelia insane with my antics."

They continued to murmur until Rebecca said they needed to get some sleep because tomorrow they must return to London.

"I wonder what new adventures waits us there." Louise smothered a yawn as she slid down under her covers.

"Adventures? In London?" Rebecca questioned. "It seems to me our lives there are mundane to the point of boredom."

"Oh, no, not at all. I confess a short period in the country is enjoyable, but I enjoy the hustle and bustle of the City, too, never knowing what new experience each day will bring. I've met people different from any we knew in Hampshire. Do you not enjoy getting a glimpse into lives so unlike your own? I do."

"I had not thought of our circumstances in that way. Although the newness of City life is pleasant, I much prefer country living. There's something else, though. I've found one little girl to help. Perhaps I will find another."

"You've found a gentleman who loves you," Louise reminded.

"Yes." Since she must die young, at least she knew what it was to love and be loved. Rebecca kept her somber thoughts to herself, saying instead, "We do have much to look forward to, do we not?"

Louise's breathing soon eased into sleep, but Rebecca relived this sennight with Shelburne knowing the opportunity might never come again.

Chapter 18

The Military Intervenes

Shelburne stifled a groan when they reached the pall of smoke which hung over London as his party returned from their fortnight stay in the country. Living in the City would be more bearable if burning coal were not a necessity year-round. Meal preparation and bath water were a daily necessity for heat regardless of outside temperatures unless one was agreeable to sitting down in their dirt and eating all meals in a coffee house.

The ladies wafted their fans trying to stir the air. They had debated which was better—have the carriage windows open, thereby letting in the heat and stench, or closed with the air growing stuffier by the minute. Shelburne left the decision to them. After discussing the matter, they chose the closed windows.

At long last, they entered their rose-scented rooms on Harley Street with a sigh of relief. After accepting an invitation to tea later, Shelburne explained he must report to Whitehall. Sketching a quick bow, he left the ladies to their own activities.

He returned to his Grosvenor Square residence only long enough to change his garb and order his curricle. Shelburne had put the army problems out of his mind so he could enjoy being with Rebecca for their stay in the country. However, now Whitehall needed to bring this whole mess to a close. A short time later, he strolled into Colonel Hayes' office where both good and bad news awaited him.

The colonel was confident his dispatches reached their destination since Cooper could not pass along information. However, he conveyed some bad news.

Both of Cooper's predecessors during the time of the known treasonous activity had disappeared without a trace.

"Disappeared? Someone at their lodgings should know of their whereabouts."

Colonel Hayes shook his head in denial. "No. Each disappeared without a word. Their landlords did not miss them until they attempted to collect the rent. They then confiscated all the men's personal effects and rented the rooms to others. My man heard the same story in both places."

"They left all their possessions behind? Perhaps they did not intend to leave."

"I agree. I imagine they are at the bottom of the Thames. No matter what they did, though, they did not deserve such a fate."

"Cooper is sure to go the same route when his usefulness is finished."

The colonel nodded. "Now, what can you tell me about Rushton? Did you have occasion to see him in Oxfordshire?"

"Yes, I saw the scoundrel all right." Shelburne's face hardened as he explained the circumstances of his meeting with the suspected traitor. "Rushton lost his bearings when he wandered too far from Long Wittenham. He made the mistake of approaching Miss Black, who jammed her fingers into his eyes. When I found him, I sent him on his way with some words he won't forget."

"Shelburne, without a doubt, you have made an enemy. Rushton doesn't strike me as a person to ignore such an insult, a painful one at that. Is your lady friend protected from him?"

"I have her promise she won't stir out of her rooms without a male escort. She is terrified of Rushton, so I'm confident of her promise."

"She has good cause to fear him. I would like to meet her sometime." Hayes rose to his feet and shook Shelburne's hand in dismissal.

Over the next two days, Shelburne spent most of his time at Whitehall dealing with other work. They could not proceed with ending the traitorous activities until Rushton returned to town. They had no way of knowing his schedule. However, they did know they must have a quick conclusion before Cooper went the same route as the others.

Shelburne turned his thoughts to Rebecca. Why had he not renewed his offer while they were in Oxfordshire? Perhaps, he admitted to himself, he had not wanted their idyllic country visit marred by her repeated refusal to marry him. After mulling over the situation—would she refuse again and, if she did, must he accept her decision as final? He would face that if he must. First, he would put his fate to the test this very afternoon.

Returning to Harley Street, Shelburne chatted about their stay in the country, expressing a desire to visit there again. When they had finished their tea, he asked, "Mrs. Peters, Miss Tracy, may I speak to Miss Black alone, please?"

Without speaking, they gathered the teacups on the tray and left the room.

"Rebecca, I haven't brought up the subject in several weeks, but after our stay in the country I'm encouraged to try my luck again. I love you far beyond what I ever thought was possible. Will you do me the honor of becoming my wife? My countess?"

A smile settled on Rebecca's face but then faded. "I would like nothing better, Edward, I assure you. Yet I must say no."

Shelburne believed he knew her reason—the problem was getting around it. He could only try. "Your ancestry is of no importance to me because, as far as I'm concerned, Rebecca Black began her existence on the day I first spied her from the steps of Hatchard's Book Store."

"Edward, you truly must accept that my lineage is important to people who matter, not least your family. However, my ancestry doesn't enter into my refusal to accept your offer. I have not given any thought to my identity for weeks."

Shelburne didn't quite believe her. "Neither have I. Perhaps we should just invent some ancestors for you."

Rebecca acknowledged his teasing with a smile. "Such would probably be easier. However, I still can't marry you."

He grew impatient with her. "What kind of talk is this, Rebecca? First, you refused me because you might be baseborn. Now you say otherwise, so what is your reason?"

"I must confess a small part of me is still afraid I will die young. I've tried to overcome the thought, truly I have, but it hasn't gone away."

"*What*?" Shelburne stared in stunned surprise.

"You forget the apparition I saw in Green Park, not once but several times. I studied the situation. I even did an experiment to prove one way or another the apparition is not me. The test convinced me."

"What kind of experiment?"

"I walked through the apparition twice." Rebecca explained about the cold and the warm air. "The apparition is me which means I will die young."

After a moment of charged silence, Shelburne leaned his head against the sofa back shouting with laughter.

"I saw me, Edward. I *saw me* in Green Park on different occasions, whether you believe me or not. In my experiment I was still warm. My early death is the only explanation. You must understand and accept that." Rebecca's desperate tone didn't penetrate his hilarity.

When Shelburne could speak, he said, "You ninny, that was a trick of light."

"No. The apparition was truly there. A trick of light wouldn't produce multiple colours." Rebecca dared him to disagree.

Shelburne flung up his hand. "All right, I concede you believe you saw something there. Nevertheless, whatever you saw could not be you because a person cannot be both alive and an apparition, if such things even exist. I'm far from convinced of that. Therefore, you would have to be dead before becoming an apparition."

A glimmer of light dawned deep in Rebecca's eyes. "Are you sure?"

"Positive."

"Then how do you explain the warm air?"

"I don't. Perhaps those writers never had firsthand experience." Shelburne gathered her in his arms cuddling her against his chest. "Has the possibility of your early death been bothering you all this time?"

Rebecca confessed with a nod. "I couldn't think of any other reason for the apparition. I still cannot. She looks just like me. Truly she does."

"Have I relieved your mind that whatever you saw is not you?"

She nodded. "The solution is so obvious I don't know why I didn't think of it myself. I must be all about in my head as Amelia said."

"We worry about such foolish things, do we not?"

Rebecca relaxed in his arms for a long moment. "It was silly of me, to be sure. Now, I believe we've kept the others out long enough."

"If you insist," he murmured after a quick kiss.

When Rebecca crossed the room to pull the bell rope, she happened to see herself in a mirror. "Just look at me, my hair is a mess, my gown twisted out of all recognition. I can't allow anyone to see me this way."

"Mrs. Peters invited me to dinner," Shelburne told Rebecca when she returned to the drawing room.

Louise explained. "Considering we've spent the last hour in the kitchen while Shelburne pleaded his case with you, the least he can do is eat the food we helped Mrs. Morton prepare."

With a grin, Rebecca asked what she had burned so they could avoid it. Midst the general hilarity, she received only an inelegant sniff in reply.

Amelia assured them that Louise had only set the table.

After dinner, Shelburne asked Rebecca to show him the wall hanging Mrs. Peters had mentioned while they were in Oxfordshire. He bent over the frame, studying the depicted picture.

"You achieved excellent use of color! You made the roses appear real, complete with dew on the petals. Why was the rose garden at the orphanage so important to you?"

"The scent. One of my few memories of being with my mother is of us standing next to a bush with pink roses. There was only the one rose bush, I don't even know where we were, yet I remember the aroma as though these many years were yesterday."

"That's the reason you use rose water as a scent," he commented then nodded toward a small table. "And why you have the bowl of rose potpourri."

"I learned how to prepare the potpourri at the orphanage. Matron said I can go back to collect more rose petals when my supply is gone. I don't want to lose one of my few memories of my mother."

The earl swallowed a lump in his throat at the wistfulness in her voice. "Shelburne Park has a huge rose garden. I promise you will be surrounded by the scent of roses forever. Do you remember anything else about your home? Perhaps the rest of the garden?"

Rebecca didn't comment on a future at Shelburne Park forever. "I am not even sure the rose bush was ours."

Before taking his leave, Shelburne arranged a ride in the park on the following morning.

After the door closed behind his lordship, Rebecca turned to Louise. "It isn't me. The apparition can't be me. Is that not marvelous?"

"Stupendous! I remind you I said, not once but several times, the apparition could not be you."

"Would you care to tell us how you came to your senses over that absurdity?" Amelia inquired.

"Shelburne said one must be dead before one can become an apparition."

"I must admit his logic makes sense," Louise assured her. "Whatever the reason, I'm happy you won't worry about the silliness anymore."

"So am I," Rebecca agreed.

The street noise woke Rebecca the following morning. She lay curled like a kitten as she reviewed the previous day.

Shelburne had said he would learn her ancestry. She must cling to his promise and pray she was legitimate at the very least. Rebecca was waiting for him in the lobby when he arrived astride a roan and leading Lady.

"That is what I like, promptness in a female."

"Promptness in a male doesn't come amiss, either!" Rebecca answered with a pertness which surprised even her. She was speaking to an *earl* after all.

With a groom following at a comfortable distance, they rode toward Hyde Park in silence. Once inside the gate, Rebecca glanced around. Seeing no one on the broad avenue, she urged Lady into a gallop, flinging a saucy grin across her shoulder toward the earl who accepted her challenge. Together, they pulled up at the end of the avenue, their mounts panting for breath and they, themselves, breathing hard.

"I truly do enjoy a good gallop, Edward. Being in Oxfordshire spoiled me."

Hearing Shelburne's name called, they turned to face a man who watched them with amusement from the back of a large bay.

"Colonel Hayes! Good morning, sir." The earl leaned forward to shake the older man's hand.

Without taking his gaze from Rebecca's face, the colonel asked, "Will you introduce the lady?"

"Please excuse my negligence, sir. This is Miss Rebecca Black. Miss Black, may I present Colonel Hayes of Whitehall?"

"Are you related to Charles Blackwell?" The colonel's question was abrupt.

Rebecca glanced at the earl before answering. "I do not know, sir."

"Who is Charles Blackwell, Colonel?" Shelburne's eager question brought the colonel's attention around to him. "You see, Miss Black grew up from age six in an orphanage in Hampshire. We're trying to learn her ancestry."

The colonel nodded his comprehension. "Charles Blackwell was an army major under my command for a brief time some years ago. He and his lady, Louise, were billeted at Folkstone in the late nineties." He again studied Rebecca's countenance. "This young lady is the exact image of Louise as I remember her."

"Can you tell us what became of them, sir? This is of considerable importance to Miss Black as well as to me."

"Not Louise. I know Blackwell was a member of the expeditionary force sent to Holland in ninety-nine. I don't know if he came back. Too many of them did not." The pain in his voice reflected the despair in his eyes.

"Is there any way we can learn whether Blackwell returned?"

Rebecca almost held her breath, waiting for the colonel's answer.

"There should be a record at Whitehall. However, I must warn you, the army failed to keep detailed records in the very early years of our battles with France."

"What can you tell us about Louise?" Shelburne clasped Rebecca's hand in his.

The colonel shook his head. "I'm sorry. Nothing, really, although I do know she was not with him when he boarded the army ship for Holland. However, the backgrounds of the ladies with the army were not a subject for discussion. Louise's gracefulness and speech patterns showed her gentility, though, if that helps."

"I suppose I could have told the duchess my name wrong," Rebecca said in a small voice. "Or perhaps my mother was too weak to pronounce our entire name. It is possible I am Louise's daughter. You see, an elderly gentleman called me by that name several weeks ago at Hatchard's. He seemed to believe he saw me presented at court."

"Why did you not tell me?" Shelburne demanded. "Who was he? Perhaps I can find him."

Rebecca shook her head with infinite regret. To think she might have learned her ancestry all those weeks ago. God had given her an opportunity, but she had failed to recognize His direction. He must consider her a complete dunderhead. "We paid little attention to his words because he was inebriated and we promptly forgot him."

"My darling, do you not see? He thought you were your mother. If she was presented at court, she was of the aristocracy."

The colonel cleared his throat. "If you will both excuse me, I need to report to Whitehall. Will you join me there, Shelburne?"

"Yes, sir, as soon as I have seen Miss Black to her home."

With a sharp salute, the colonel left them. They continued toward Harley Street with hardly a pause in their conversation.

"You must be of the aristocracy, so you cannot find any reason not to marry me." Shelburne's voice rang clear in the morning air.

However, Rebecca ignored him.

"They might not have been married," she said with a tremor in her voice. Before he could expostulate, she continued. "The colonel never said she was Charles Blackwell's wife. He referred to her as this man's lady. He gave the distinct impression she was a camp follower. I think it obvious he did not believe they were married." She took a deep breath. "So, you see, I must be illegitimate—therefore beyond the pale."

"You keep throwing these obstacles in our way." Shelburne pounded his fist against his leg. "I won't permit anything coming between us, do you hear me? I will not."

"I hear you, Edward, but it is you who refuses to understand my position."

He shook his head. "There are shadows in your eyes which I surmise can only be there because of your uncertainty about your identity. I know of nothing else which bothers you. If there is something else on your mind, then tell me now. We'll get to the bottom of the problem together."

Rebecca frowned but had no answer.

"I see I must continue my efforts. However, do assure me nothing else stands between us."

"Nothing else." Rebecca turned toward him, an anxious expression clouding her face, as she tried to explain her continued hesitation. "You see, Edward, difficult though it is, my life could be infinitely worse, and yours, too, if I ever have to wish I had waited, had not rushed headlong into something we both might regret. That possibility far outweighs anything else. Can you not understand that?"

Shelburne nodded. They rode in silence until Rebecca drew Lady to a stop. Turning to Shelburne, she said, "I've grasped the niggling thought that has bothered me since we talked to Colonel Hayes. If Louise was my mother, she might have been a friend of Louise Tracy's mother."

"How do you arrive at a possibility we know the duchess investigated?"

"We have the same names only in different order. I am Rebecca Marie Louise. She is Louise Rebecca Marie. Our names were one reason we became instant friends. If I remember correctly, I mentioned our names to you on your first visit to Harley Street."

Shelburne nodded, a frown on his face. "I asked the duchess if there could have been a connection between you and Miss Tracy, but she knew of none. Something is nagging at me, a thought I simply can't pull out of my brain. I cannot remember ever being this frustrated in my life."

"I've found niggling thoughts become clear if I ignore them. Perhaps that will happen for you too."

"I certainly hope so. Anyway, I will learn whatever I can about Charles Blackwell at Whitehall and go from there. Considering the number of veterans in Town, there surely must be someone who knew him."

Arriving in Harley Street, he clasped her hand. "You shan't discourage me, Rebecca, so cease trying. I vow I will succeed in this."

"I truly hope you will, Edward."

Chapter 19

Caught!

"Colonel, the culprit must be Cooper." Shelburne spoke with conviction in Whitehall a short while after leaving Harley Street. "Let me recapitulate what we know. I've seen Cooper in conversation, not once but twice, with a person who has French ancestry, and who, we have reason to believe, might have French sympathies. One of the other clerks here has seen Cooper listening at keyholes. Another has seen him at the head clerk's desk where all confidential material is. I might add, Cooper has never during his months of employment had any reason to be near the head clerk's desk under any circumstances."

The colonel agreed. "Yes, I see what you mean, Shelburne. Without doubt, Cooper is the person who is giving out confidential information to an enemy agent." Colonel Hayes pounded his fist on the table. "This traitorous activity has gone on too long as it is. I'll call Cooper in at once and confront him with his behavior. He must verify who the enemy agent is. Then we can deal with both traitors."

Outside the door, a white-faced Cooper scurried along the hallway and down the back stairs, thoughts rampaging around in his brain. What did they mean enemy agent? Surely, the colonel and that Shelburne person didn't think he had done anything wrong. They did, though, so he must get away. He must find Major Rushton. Must tell him what the colonel said. Must get the money promised to him, so he could get out of London before the colonel could find him, force him to answer their questions. Major Rushton would need to disappear too.

With his head bent low, Cooper hurried down the street looking neither left nor right.

***

Shelburne stared at the door, waiting. He, Colonel Hayes, Lord Beaufort, and Sir Julian Haverford had gathered in the colonel's office to finalize their plans for putting a period to Rushton's treasonous activities. To accomplish this, they had used the clerk's habit of eavesdropping outside the colonel's door. This time, the colonel used Cooper's eavesdropping tendency to their advantage, not Napoleon's.

"Cooper took the bait, sir!" The head clerk stepped into the colonel's office, announcing their success. From the office across the hall, the clerk had watched Cooper's reaction to the conversation held inside the colonel's office.

"Someone is following him as instructed?"

"Yes, sir. Findley is on the same side of the street and Griggs is across the street keeping pace with Cooper. We can be sure he will go to Rushton, sir," the clerk announced. "Cooper doesn't have any other means of getting away which must be his first consideration."

The colonel grunted his satisfaction, nodding his dismissal. Turning to Shelburne, he said, "All right, thus far everything is going as planned. Our men are watching Rushton, who returned last night. Between the men following him and the ones following Cooper, someone will get close enough to hear their plans."

"If they do not, Cooper may well disappear like the others," Haverford concurred. "We truly must avoid that happening."

"I doubt a peer will hang for treason but what will happen to Cooper when this is all over?" Beaufort inquired. "Will he hang even if Rushton does not? Even though he is surely Rushton's dupe?"

The colonel released a long sigh. "Cooper's future depends on what kind of explanation he gives for his perfidy. He is such a credulous person he might believe anything."

"Could there be an innocent reason, sir?" Beaufort showed his surprise with raised eyebrows

Shelburne answered. "I believe I know Rushton better than any of you—I've been acquainted with him since our years at Eton—so I can vouch for the fact he is a very persuasive person. I could give multiple examples of his leading younger boys into trouble. Who knows what kind of ridiculous tale he spun for Cooper?"

There was a murmur of concurrence before the office fell silent while they waited for Cooper's followers to report to them.

While dodging in and out of the crowd, Griggs never took his eyes off his quarry who almost ran to Rushton's townhouse. There, Griggs joined Findley and watched Cooper speak to someone through the barely open door. After a moment of heated words on Cooper's part, they saw him search in his pockets, then pull out a scrap of paper and pencil. He scribbled a quick note then cast furtive glances from side to side while he waited for a reply which entailed only a few words. Moments later, his watchers heard his mutters as he passed them. Now on the same side of the street as their quarry, they trailed him to a narrow street turning off Piccadilly where he positioned himself to wait.

"One of us must get close enough to hear them," Griggs said. "I doubt Rushton's followers will get close enough to hear their plans if he meets Cooper in the open."

"I can stand inside that shop with the door cracked enough to hear them," Findley said. "You come inside after they meet. Perhaps you can hear their plans as you pass them." Glancing back the way they had come, they saw their quarry approaching in long strides. "Here comes the traitor now, so I will go on inside. Stay alert!"

"Well, Cooper, what do you want?" Rushton's voice was low, menacing. "I told you not to come to my house. Ever."

"I had to this time, Major, I promise I did!" Cooper told of the conversation he had overheard. "What did they mean, enemy agent? You told me that you just wanted to be able to trace the troops' routes on the globe."

Neither of them noticed the man who passed them and glanced into the window for a moment before entering the shop. They also failed to notice the door standing ajar.

"All right, Cooper, calm down. This is all just a misunderstanding. However, since you believe your job is in jeopardy, I will supply you with the funds to leave London for a period. While you're gone, I will explain the situation to the colonel."

"When can I get the money? Where will I go? I don't know anyone anywhere except in London!" A distinct whine entered his voice.

"I said to calm down. You can go to Bath for a few days, or Brighton. You would enjoy either place, I'm sure. Have you ever been to the seaside?"

"No, Major, I haven't." Excitement showed through Cooper's voice.

"Then here is what we will do. I will meet you in the middle of the bridge near Cheapside at ten o'clock tonight and give you the money. Be sure you stand in the middle of the bridge, not at either end because people linger at the ends for their nefarious reasons. I'll be able to find you in the middle despite the fog, which there will surely be."

"Yes, sir, Major, but can you not give funds to me now? The colonel might come looking for me before nightfall."

"I don't carry so much money with me, you numskull. Lose yourself in Seven Dials until after dark." Without further words, and looking neither right nor left, Rushton hurried away.

Through the crack in the door, the followers watched Cooper turn in the opposite direction. Following as closely as they dared, they trailed him to an alley, then watched him enter an unpainted door. Leaving his partner to keep watch, Griggs hurried to Whitehall to report.

"If they're meeting at ten o'clock, we'll be in place not later than nine o'clock," the colonel stated. "Griggs, you keep watch on the house in Seven Dials. Explain our plans to your partner while we make our final plans here."

A few minutes before nine that evening, several masculine shapes slipped into the shadows on each end of the Cheapside Bridge. The damp air soon began to penetrate their clothing, and they restrained themselves from stamping their feet to aid circulation. The watchers easily ascertained that the few people who entered the bridge were about their lawful business.

It seemed an eternity but only some thirty minutes later, they saw Cooper slip onto the bridge and slink to the middle, keeping as much in the shadows as he could. His two followers eased into the shadows across from him thankful for their muffled footsteps.

After several minutes passed without activity, the watchers believed their wait might be in vain. Then they became aware of movement onto the bridge, and felt a stir as a figure passed them in the deepening mist. The newcomer moved with slow yet steady determination to the middle of the bridge. His whispering voice calling Cooper's name identified him as their quarry. The watchers crept forward until they stood in the shadows surrounding Rushton on three sides.

"Did you bring the money, Major?" Cooper's squeaky voice was clear on the quiet air.

"Quiet, Cooper! We don't want anyone to hear this transaction, do we? You could get robbed before you left the bridge."

"Oh, there's no one else here, sir. I arrived nearly an hour ago. Nobody has passed me. I can vouch for that, sir."

"Good. Did you tell anyone where you were going tonight?"

"No, I did just as you told me. I spent the rest of the day in Seven Dials. Never went near my room."

"Good man." The relief in Rushton's voice was palpable to the listeners. "You are so short you need to sit here on the side of the bridge, so I can count the money into your hands."

Cooper eagerly climbed onto the side of the bridge, reaching out his unsuspecting hand for the largesse he expected. Instead, he received a hard right to the jaw, the only sound being the splash as he hit the water.

Pandemonium broke loose. Two men jumped off the bridge to rescue the hapless Cooper while the others surrounded Rushton. He put up a good fight but was no match for his adversaries.

"Your treachery is at an end, Rushton," the colonel said. "You have several questions to answer so come along."

"Who are you? What do you mean, attacking a member of the aristocracy going about his lawful business?" Rushton's blustering voice brought forth some grim laughter.

Shelburne had remained silent as long as he could and he now demanded, "Lawful business, Rushton? Treason is more like it."

"Shelburne, is that you? I might have known you instigated this ridiculous scheme."

Rushton's sneering words were more than Shelburne could or would tolerate. He pushed forward with his fists raised until Haverford's quiet voice stopped him.

"Never fear, Shelburne. We caught Rushton in the act of attempting murder. Neither words nor anything else will help him now."

Shelburne stepped back, relaxing his clenched hands.

"Haverford is right, Shelburne. Now, we must go to Whitehall." Colonel Hayes turned at the sound of hurrying footsteps on the bridge. "Did you get him?"

"Yes, sir, we got him all right." Finley's voice exuded satisfaction. "Cooper was out of it for a minute or two, but we were able to revive him. He missed hitting the buttress. Otherwise, he would be dead. He will hang."

"Not by myself, I won't!" The weak but belligerent voice stated. "The major will hang right beside me," Cooper said.

"Yes, I imagine he will. Bring them along." The colonel had barely spoken when he heard a thump, then a yelp from one of his men followed by a loud splash. "What happened?" he demanded.

"It's Rushton, sir. He jerked free and jumped off the bridge."

Again, pandemonium reigned as three men went over the side in search of Rushton.

Griggs shoved Cooper into the colonel's grasp. "I'm a good swimmer, sir." So saying, he too went over the side.

"Have you found him?" the Colonel yelled after a moment.

"Not yet, sir," Griggs answered.

Minutes later, Griggs shouted, "I found Rushton, Colonel! Meet us at the end of the bridge, sir."

As Griggs hauled Rushton out of the water, he realized the inert man would never move again. "He didn't try to save himself from drowning, sir. Still, there is no reason he would, is there?"

By the light of several lanterns, they inspected the dead man in grim silence. There were no marks on the body, so he had missed the buttress too. The colonel surmised the two missing clerks had not been so fortunate. "Shelburne, go roust the magistrate out of bed. He's more likely to listen to an earl than to any of the rest of us. We can't move the body until he verifies for himself this was not murder, so hurry as best you can."

A long, drawn-out night followed with questions, answers, and explanations. At dawn, an exhausted Shelburne fell onto his bed, having removed only his outerwear and boots. Exhausted though he was, after a mere three hours sleep, he was back at Whitehall where he checked with the colonel, who did not appear to have slept at all. Then with the Rushton problem off his mind, Shelburne went to the record room to learn what he could about Charles Blackwell.

He spent most of the day digging through dusty mildewed files, making notes hardly legible in the dim light from the dirty windows. He should have brought candles. Content he'd found all he could to relieve his love's anxiety, Shelburne stretched the kinks out of his tired shoulders and walked out into the sunlight.

A grimace crossed Shelburne's face when he saw his dusty clothing. Hurrying to Grosvenor Square, he sent a note to Harley Street, then changed, and with his meager information in hand, presented himself in Harley Street for tea.

After eating two large slices of ginger bread, explaining that he had missed luncheon altogether, Shelburne placed his teacup on the small table beside him. He had not told them anything about the Army problem but decided this was the time to reveal the situation, because he needed to reassure Rebecca about Rushton.

They listened in astounded silence, Amelia being the first to speak.

"'Tis probably better he killed himself," she said with prosaic wisdom. "Hanging an aristocrat wouldn't look so good."

"A nine days wonder," Shelburne agreed.

"What about the clerk?" Rebecca wanted to know. "What will happen to him?"

"There was a lot of discussion about Cooper's future. He was appalled when the colonel explained he'd been aiding an enemy agent. The word treason turned him pale as a sheet and he fainted when the colonel told him about the disappearance of his two predecessors. We needed several minutes to revive him."

"Will he be hanged?" Rebecca persisted. "Death does not seem fair to me. As I see the situation, he acted in all innocence."

"I'm afraid apparent innocence gets short shrift in a treasonous matter. However, the colonel agreed the clerk had learned his lesson. They will transfer him to a different clerkship—one that requires less secrecy, if any. We can be sure Cooper will not be so gullible again."

Rebecca spoke in a pensive voice. "I'm happy I will not again be threatened by Lord Rushton, yet his death seems such a waste. In his position, he could have accomplished so much."

"He could have, yes," Shelburne agreed. "We've been acquainted since our days at Eton. I thought I knew him well, yet his treasonous activity caught me by surprise." He shook his head in wonder. "Well, that's enough about Rushton. He's gone and his actions need never concern us again. I have some news for you about Charles Blackwell, Miss Black."

She grew still, her gaze fixed on his face.

"I spent the better part of today in the Whitehall records room. Colonel Hayes was correct. Charles Blackwell was indeed an army major. In ninety-nine, he was part of the contingent that went to Holland in the attempt to free the Low Countries from the French. The records show they landed at the Helder in late August. They then fought their way to Bergen where they stopped briefly in mid-September. The expected Dutch help failed to materialize, and Major Blackwell fell at Castricum in early October. I'm sorry the news of him isn't better."

The room was silent when Shelburne finished speaking. Rebecca had not removed her gaze from his face during the entire recital nor had he deviated from his focus on hers. She forced out the words in an almost inaudible voice. "Did the records contain any information about his family?"

"No, I regret to say the records did not. Blackwell received commendations for bravery, though. That is a good thing to know about your father, my dear, do you not agree?"

Rebecca said in a very small voice, "We still don't know if he was married to my mother."

"Unfortunately, you are correct," the earl admitted. "However, with this much information I can attempt to find some of his comrades in arms. At least one of them must surely have survived their various battles."

Rebecca was unable to utter any words but she managed a small nod.

Rising to leave, Shelburne cradled her hand in his for a moment. "Regardless of whether I find your father's comrades, I still intend to learn more about your mother. Colonel Hayes is convinced she was of gentle birth. I believe him. As surely as I am alive, and no matter how long it takes, I *will* find someone who knows your features. When I do, I will gaze into your beautiful eyes when there are no longer shadows in their depths."

With a light squeeze of her hand and a bow to the other ladies, he left.

Rebecca sat in silence, her hands in a tight grip, ignoring the conversation between her companions. She had not realized there were shadows in her eyes until Shelburne told her. She didn't believe the most recent information would erase them. There was no room for doubt about Charles Blackwell being her father and Louise Somebody being her mother. The colonel had made that clear. Rebecca regretted he had also made clear he did not believe they were married although he was too polite to say so. She was glad to have this much information, but did it make any real difference to her future?

Her mother was probably Charles Blackwell's mistress. She would not have been either the first, or the last, female who followed her lover from place to place.

Chapter 20

The Countess Comes Calling

While Rebecca mulled over her future, Shelburne returned to Grosvenor Square to find the entrance hall crowded with luggage, his house in an uproar with footmen bustling hither and yon. His butler greeted him with a wide smile.

Shelburne glanced about then raised an eyebrow. "Jenkins, may I know which army has invaded?"

"Army, my lord? Oh, no, not an army. Her ladyship has come for a visit."

"Which ladyship, Jenkins? Do you tell me all this luggage is for one person?"

The butler directed a scandalized stare at him. In shocked tones replied, "The countess, my lord!"

"Ah, yes, I do recall that my mother chooses to travel with everything she owns. Where will I find her ladyship?"

"In her usual set of rooms, my lord." The words were matter of fact, yet the tone implied *where else would she be?* "She asked that you join her there as soon as you arrive."

Shelburne climbed the stairs with dire thoughts of old family retainers and their lack of respect toward one whom they had known from the day he had squalled his way into existence. However, he entered his mother's sitting room with a genuine smile lighting his face.

"Mama, you are looking your usual beautiful self. To what do I owe the pleasure of your visit?" The dutiful son raised her hand to his lips, smiling into the shrewd eyes that could see right through him. Retaining her hand in his, he sat beside her on the sofa.

"I came to see for myself if the rumors reaching my ears are true." She tapped her closed fan against his chest. "It appears you're making a cake of yourself over some gel nobody knows. I want to know why. Don't try to bamboozle me, either, for you will never succeed."

"Never could keep a secret from you, Ma'am!" Inwardly Shelburne sighed over interfering gossips while outwardly retaining a smile he knew was false.

"Who is she?" The abrupt question demanded a straight answer. He gave it.

"Her identity is my problem. I do not know!" The countess studied his face as Shelburne told the story of the girl with the haunting blue eyes who had captured his heart.

"It is not like you to make a fool of yourself over any female, much less one you cannot identify. I know you would not consider a *mésalliance* because you know full well what is due your name."

Shelburne ignored her words. Rising to his feet, he strode back and forth like a caged animal. "Mama, I am sure I know her features. Those of her friend, too, yet I am also sure I don't know *them*. Rather I did not know them until some weeks ago. The whole situation is driving me to Bedlam. It doesn't make a particle of sense."

"What are their names again?"

"Rebecca Black and Louise Tracy. They have a chaperone, Mrs. Amelia Peters, the widow of a numskull who lost his money on horse races before succumbing to a fever. He left her destitute as could be expected."

"You say they lived in an orphanage sponsored by the Duchess of Dorchester?"

Shelburne nodded. "I paid the duchess a visit, but she could not enlighten me. She did assure me she tried to find Miss Black's family."

A reminiscent smile lighted the countess's face. "Elizabeth came out the same year as I. We stayed friends during the early years of married life even though she had first set her cap for your father, who, I'm thankful to say, countered her every move with one of his own. She had not yet met the debonair Duke of Dorchester who had all of us girls in alt over him. After his entrance into her life, she had little use for anyone else, especially a man. They were a perfect match for several years until he died from influenza."

"Yes?" her son murmured.

She ignored his interruption. "Elizabeth gave birth to her daughter a few months before Becca was born. Unfortunately, Elizabeth's little girl died at birth. She became a recluse, never leaving her home village in Hampshire. Many years have passed since I saw her, but I remember Elizabeth as being a woman well ahead of her time. I doubt she has changed."

"Yes?" her son murmured again.

"However, that is neither here nor there." The countess paused a moment, seeming to stare into a past he could not share. "Bring the girls here. I might recognize their features. Your obvious interest in them has piqued my curiosity."

"Oh, I could never ask you …" Shelburne's voice trailed off as he caught the sardonic gleam in her eyes. With a sheepish grin he asked, "Would tea tomorrow be convenient?"

Assured on that point, he sent a note to Harley Street.

The ladies were in a quandary. They had answered the earl's note and now were discussing the all-important subject of clothing. What does one wear to take tea with a countess?

"Rebecca is the important one. Just think what can come from the countess' interest in her." Louise smiled in anticipation for her friend.

Rebecca heard her words with anxiety mixed with fear. Did she really want to know who she was? Might her ancestry be even worse than she had imagined? Suddenly, she wanted to stay in Harley Street and hide, or go back to the orphanage. Instead, Rebecca gathered her courage. Tea with a countess would be a new experience, one to savor. After all, why should a *countess* recognize her features? Ordinary people had not.

"I daresay the countess is only concerned about her son's wellbeing. I doubt she would find me acceptable for him, no matter who I might be."

"My dear," Mrs. Peters began, "you're forgetting something again. I suppose your uncertainty arises from the question of your legitimacy, together with your fondness for Lord Shelburne. Still, you must remember God's timing. This could be the occasion He has chosen to answer your questions, so don't doubt Him now."

"I don't doubt Him, Amelia, truly I don't. I'm simply trying not to be disappointed if this is not His time for me to receive answers."

Louise changed the subject. "Amelia, what will you wear?"

"Oh, there is no reason for me to go. You girls can chaperone each other."

Rebecca answered, "We would not dream of going without you to bear us company."

Mrs. Peters was adamant, however. She would not go. She would forget herself, chatter in a rude way, which would never do.

They disagreed but had to accept her dictum.

As they awaited the earl's arrival on the fateful day, Mrs. Peters reassured Rebecca in blue cambric and Louise in amber muslin. "Both you girls are lovely. Now stop worrying about your appearance. Did we not hear that Beau Brummell said a man should not be concerned about his appearance once he was dressed? The same thing must apply to ladies also. It cannot be otherwise."

Shelburne escorted the two ladies to Grosvenor Square in his closed town carriage. Rebecca tried not to gape at the magnificent house as he assisted them from the carriage, then escorted them up the steps to the open door.

"Good afternoon, Jenkins." In surprise, Shelburne got no further as his butler stared, white-faced, at the two girls. "Whatever is the matter, Jenkins? You look as though you have seen a ghost."

The butler swallowed, his gaze moving from one girl to the other. "Perhaps I have, my lord. I had better prepare the countess. This might shock her into a decline." Jenkins stumbled as he crossed the hall to the drawing room.

The three people left standing in the hall stared at each other. Shelburne pounded his right fist into his other hand. "I knew it! Jenkins recognized you, so I was right. I do know your features. I wager my mother does too. She'll solve the mystery of who you are, Rebecca."

The drawing room door reopened, and the butler stood aside for them to enter.

Inside the room, a petite lady with silvery hair sat on a rose silk-covered sofa, her gaze glued to the door.

She released an audible gasp when the girls advanced toward her.

"Miss Black, Miss Tracy, may I introduce my mother, Lady Olivia, Countess of Shelburne?"

The girls curtsied but the countess only nodded, her gaze going from Rebecca's face to Louise's then back to Rebecca.

"They can't be but they obviously are," Lady Olivia murmured.

"You recognize them, too, Mama! Who are they? Where have I seen their features?" Shelburne could hardly contain his excitement. "I knew it, I knew it! I *do* know them from somewhere."

"Jenkins, send for Becca at once. No matter where she is, find her. Tell her to bring Marie."

"Mama, I remind you, Becca went to the country when the Season ended. Besides, why do we need her? You know who the girls are, so tell us."

"Control yourself, Shelburne. Becca and Marie returned to Town this morning. Come, girls, sit here opposite me where I can look at you. This is amazing. I can hardly believe it. The resemblance is uncanny." The countess continued to stare from one to the other. "I know I am right. I could not possibly be mistaken. Becca will confirm my belief."

The door burst open with a bang. Rebecca and Louise turned to see a diminutive, fair-haired lady rushing into the room.

"What's wrong, Mama? Are you ill? I was on my way over here when the footman found me. What has happened?" Becca came to a sudden stop, staring at the two young ladies rising before her. With a hand at her mouth, she walked toward them, tears running down her pale face.

"Louise! Marie! Where have you been all these years? I've missed you so!" Becca stopped short, shaking her head. "No, you are too young to be my dearest friends. You must be their daughters."

The countess agreed. "I'm sure they are, but they don't know they are …"

"Why would they not know …"

"They grew up in an orphanage …"

"Oh, you poor dears …"

"Quiet!" Shelburne had tolerated the babble long enough. When his mother and sister stared at him in surprise, he enunciated each word as if speaking to senseless people. "I want a straight answer. Now. Who are these ladies? Who are the Louise and Marie you mentioned?"

Before either lady could answer, the door burst open again to admit a stylish young lady. "Mama, why am I here? I was having a delightful coze with Susan when the foot …" Her voice died away as she stared at the two strangers.

Rebecca and Louise had been standing in stunned silence, looking first at one speaker, then another, then at each other. Now they looked at the newcomer. They would have known her anywhere as being Lady Olivia's granddaughter and Lady Becca's daughter. The same fair curls, the same cornflower blue eyes.

Her eyes widened. Without moving her gaze from their faces, she asked, "Uncle Edward are these the girls you …"

"Marie, be quiet." Shelburne shoved her into a chair, pointed Rebecca and Louise to the chairs they had just vacated, then stood with his back to the fireplace. His fists parked on his hips, The Tenth Earl of Shelburne directed a fierce glare at his mother. "I repeat, who are they?"

"Edward, you must know them."

"How can you possibly not recognize them?" Becca demanded.

As the babbling began again, Shelburne roared. "I said, quiet! Now, one at a time, if you please!"

Becca gaped at him. "Edward, they are the image of their mothers. Can you not see the resemblance?"

"Wait a moment, Becca. We forget Edward was still a schoolboy. He saw your friends only on rare occasions," the countess began.

Shelburne drew himself up to his full six feet, two inches. How much female babble must a man tolerate in his own home? He had heard enough to last him a lifetime. His voice became dangerously calm.

"Who are they? Can you not see they're sitting there in stunned silence waiting for enlightenment? Miss Black has spent most of her life wondering who she is. I've spent the past several weeks trying to figure out where I've seen their features. I've made a complete fool of myself in front of the *ton*, trying to learn who they are. Both of you recognize them. Even Jenkins recognized them. Before I completely lose my temper, stop your chattering. *Tell us who they are!*"

"We're trying to tell you." the countess said. "Still, I can see the girls are confused, so be quiet and listen."

The countess began. "Becca and her two friends, Louise Carlton and Marie Sanford, were inseparable from early childhood. They spent a great deal of their time at Shelburne Park. Edward, you saw them there, but you are so much younger you didn't know them well. Rebecca is obviously the daughter of Louise, whose parents, the Duke and Duchess of Amesbury, disowned her when she eloped with a military man by name of Charles Blackwell."

Rebecca opened, then closed her mouth without sound. She clasped her hands in her lap and listened.

Becca took up the story. "And it is just as obvious that Louise is the daughter of Marie who eloped with Jonathan Mansfield."

"I know Amesbury," Shelburne said. "By Mansfield, do you mean old Granville's family? I don't believe I even knew he had a son."

The countess nodded. "Granville thought his son had married beneath himself when Jonathan chose to marry the vicar's daughter. Marie had no financial expectations, yet her lineage was above reproach. Granville had his eye on someone else for his heir, a cousin, I believe. He disowned his only child. I don't believe they heard from Jonathan again. I never even heard a whisper if they ever again mentioned his name."

In a rare moment of silence, Louise spoke. "Please excuse me for interrupting. This is interesting, but you must be mistaken about me. I know my parent's names were John and Marie; however, my surname is Tracy, not Mansfield. Or Granville, for that matter."

The countess turned to her. "My dear, all this must confuse you, yet you're so much like your mother there can be no doubt you are her daughter. I imagine your father chose to use only two of his names in his new life. His complete name was Jonathan Augustus Tracy Mansfield. He was heir to the Marquess of Granville. Granville was never happy with anything his son did, primarily because Jonathan had not inherited his own love for the classics. Jonathan preferred horses and spent much of his time in the stables."

Rebecca turned to Louise. "Lady Olivia's words agree with your recollection. You've said many times your father loved horses. And you must have inherited your love for the classics from your grandfather." She turned to the countess, speaking with obvious pride. "Louise is well educated in the classics, my lady. She even speaks and reads Latin and Greek."

Marie, who had been sitting in silence, her eyes moving from one face to another as she took in the story, relieved the tension. "Imagine! Latin and Greek! I can only manage a few words of French."

"This is all very exciting," Rebecca assured them. "However, I'm confused about the names. We all seem to have the same ones."

"I can explain about our names," Becca assured them.

"We were ten years old …"

Bright sunshine had found its way through the barred windows, and reflecting on the tousled curls of the three young misses sitting on the window seat.

Becca, the pampered daughter of the earl who owned this estate, held sway over her two visitors, Louise the raven-haired only child of a duke, and Marie the auburn-haired offspring of a vicar.

Suddenly, Becca bounced to her feet and whirled around the room. "I have the most wonderful idea! When we grow up, we will each have a daughter and give her all three of our names. They will be best friends just as we are."

"Will the names not be confusing? I mean, with mother and daughter having the same name?"

"No, Marie. We will give our daughters our own names as their third name."

Becca's joyous laughter filled the room. "It's a matter of wonder our husbands did not object to our childish whim." She turned to her daughter. "So, Marie, your name is Marie Louise Rebecca. Louise is obviously the daughter of Marie, so, of necessity, her name is Louise Rebecca Marie. Rebecca, you are the daughter of Louise therefore your name is Rebecca Marie Louise. See how simple all this is?"

Perhaps simple to Becca, but the rest of them needed time to digest what she had said. In the following silence, Marie inquired why Rebecca used only the name Black instead of Blackwell.

Shelburne answered. "Perhaps she was too upset to say her full surname to the duchess, or her mother was too weak to speak clearly to the vicar. I suppose we will never know, but her name doesn't matter."

Louise grinned at Lord Shelburne. "Your niece is the third girl the ladies in the confectionary mentioned all those weeks ago."

"Why did you not tell me your niece had the same names as we do?" Rebecca so far forgot herself as to shake a finger at him. "We suspected there might be such a person, even talked about finding her. We didn't know how."

"I suppose I did know all Marie's names. If so, I have long since forgotten them. Perhaps that's what has been niggling at my brain." Shelburne shook his head in wonder. "Just think how close I have been to the answer all along."

"Edward, you ninny. You know all Marie's names," Becca said. "You were present when I convinced Julian that I must have the privilege of naming our daughter."

Rebecca spoke in a low voice. "Am I legitimate?"

"I just told you that Amesbury disowned Louise because she and Charles eloped."

"Am I legitimate?" Rebecca insisted.

Becca turned her puzzled gaze toward Shelburne who said, "She wants to be sure they did, indeed, wed. However, I have told her she is going to marry me regardless."

"Not unless I'm legitimate." Rebecca reached a hand toward him before dropping it back into her lap. "I will not, I cannot, allow you to be disowned for marrying beneath you, Shelburne. Do you understand me? *I will not!*"

"Rebecca, my love, you are not beneath me. In fact, a duke might well look higher than a mere earl for his granddaughter."

"Only if I am legitimate, Shelburne. Can you not see the distinction?"

The countess forgot her earlier concern about a *mésalliance*. "My dear child, there is no question of being disowned. Shelburne may marry whom he pleases, no one will say him nay. Becca can tell you about your parents' wedding. Also, the wedding of Louise's parents."

"I should say I can. I helped them elope and was present at the double wedding, for which Papa sent me to Shelburne Park in disgrace. I missed the rest of the Season while the ruckus died down." Becca's voice dropped almost to a whisper. "I believe the worst thing about being banished to the country for helping them elope was that I could not stay in touch with them. If I had, you girls would not have grown up in an orphanage. You can be sure that I would not have permitted either of you to live outside my reach."

Rebecca smiled at her vehemence. "Louise and I know living with a loving family would be better than otherwise." She continued as an impish grin crossed her face. "However, I must admit to some hesitation about our belief considering what we just heard about our ancestry. All the children at the orphanage talked about family endlessly, yet we were not unhappy were we, Louise?"

Louise clasped the hand extended to her. "No, we were not because we always had each other."

Shelburne broke the silence that followed their touching words. "I wonder why your mothers failed to stay in contact."

"I can only surmise one thing," Becca commented. "Charles Blackwell was possessive about Louise, even objected to Marie and Jonathan sharing their wedding, so he might have refused Louise permission to correspond with Marie."

"Rebecca, do you remember your father at all?" The countess inquired.

"I regret I do not, my lady." She spoke slowly, working her way through a nebulous thought. "If our mothers were so close, and my father was dead, would not my mother turn to her old friend? Maybe this is the reason no one knew me in Hampshire. I did not belong there."

"So perhaps your mother and mine did stay in touch with each other," Louise told her.

"Why would your mother not come to me, Rebecca?" Becca demanded.

"She might have felt she could not without encountering her family. I imagine she had too much pride to risk them knowing her situation. She wouldn't have wanted to hear anyone say 'I told you so'. I wouldn't want to hear that."

Shelburne considered what might have happened if Rebecca's mother had swallowed her pride. He would have met Rebecca earlier, watched her grow up as Marie's friend. Would he have appreciated her, learned to love her? She wouldn't have been the person she turned out to be, so the possibility was doubtful. She probably would have been just another young miss gracing the marriage mart, although undoubtedly more appealing.

"Oh!" Louise turned to the countess. "Something just occurred to me. If Rebecca is the granddaughter of a duke and I'm the granddaughter of a Marquess, does that mean we have titles?"

"Not in an official way, but you have the honorary title of Lady. You will be addressed as Lady Rebecca and Lady Louise."

They stared at her then each other. Rebecca spoke. "We have gone from no name females to Ladies in the space of an hour. Too many changes in too short a time. We will never become accustomed. Do you agree, Louise?"

Louise mouthed her title and name. "Never. I am not at all sure I want to be called by a title. I'm happy with Miss Tracy, if people must be formal. I don't believe formality is necessary either."

"You would not be Miss Tracy in any event because your correct family name is Mansfield," Shelburne told her. "Rebecca, you are properly titled Lady through your mother."

"Titles are too complicated as well as being unnecessary. I have done nothing to earn the respect inherent in being titled, but then, because titles are inherited, I daresay the current holders have done nothing to earn them either."

Rebecca broke the silence that followed Louise's protestation. "Do you know if my parents ever visited Green Park?"

Becca shot a mischievous glance at her mother. "Oh yes, Green Park was their favorite trysting place. The number of times I was less than truthful about Louise's whereabouts is far beyond my recollection. Why do you ask?"

Rebecca gave Shelburne a sidelong glance. "It occurs to me the apparitions I've seen there several times might be my parents. The woman looked like me except her curls, and the man was in regimentals. They always appeared so happy together, unaware of their surroundings."

"They were blissfully happy, I promise. I envied both of my friends for finding their happiness in their first Season. I had to wait another year for mine."

Rebecca nodded. "And you were truly present at their wedding ceremony?"

Becca reassured her. "I was present and envious, as I said."

"Then you know where to find the marriage registry? I want to see the evidence of my legitimacy for myself," Rebecca confessed. "No, I truly *need* to see the official record."

"Oh, yes, a vicar in Kensington performed the double ceremony. We were in a constant state of apprehension during the three weeks he read the banns. Even though the chapel location is out of the way, you can find the records easily enough."

Shelburne smiled as he saw the dawning hope in his loved one's face. "Now, will you agree to marry me? You can have no further objection." With his arms outstretched, he took an impetuous step toward Rebecca who rose to meet him.

"No!" The countess stopped him in his tracks.

Rebecca dropped back into her chair. Her eyes were wide, her hands gripped together.

"What do you mean 'No'?" Shelburne roared.

"I mean she must have a Season first. Then if she still wants to marry you, she can."

"Oh, yes, Mama, I can see it now—Rebecca, Louise, and my Marie together. They will set the *ton* on its ear just as their mothers did. Who would have believed our daughters would look so much like us? Oh, what fun a Season will be!"

"No!"

No one paid the least attention to Shelburne's objections.

Marie managed to get in a word when her mother paused for breath. "Has anyone considered their own families might have something to say about all this? They might have different ideas."

Her words brought an instant of silence before the countess spoke. "You're right, Marie. We will contact their grandparents. Perhaps invite them to Shelburne Park for a visit."

Rebecca interrupted without compunction. "I would rather have my parents' blessing."

Only perplexed stares met her soft statement until Shelburne inquired how she proposed to obtain their blessing.

"They live in Green Park," she replied. "I'll go there and ask them. Besides, now that I know they're my parents, I would like to see them again, up close, perhaps feel Mama's love once more."

Shelburne doubted there was a dry eye in the room as he cleared the huskiness from his voice. "My love, I will personally escort you to the park and stand by while you converse with them to your heart's content. Perhaps they will give me their blessing too. However, I believe you need more earthly influence regarding our future."

"Considering my grandparents' behavior toward my parents, I don't care to see them." Rebecca's face settled into stubborn determination which would have earned Matron's disapproval.

"Those are my sentiments exactly." Louise agreed.

"Nevertheless, I fear meeting them is necessary, girls." The countess gave them a sympathetic smile. "Since your grandparents have avoided Society for many years, I imagine they will let us share in the girls' Season."

"I don't want to wait until after the Season to marry Rebecca," Shelburne complained. "That's almost a year! She might give her heart to someone else."

Rebecca, responding to the anguish in his voice, hurried to him. With a light shining from the depths of her eyes, she slipped her arms around his waist, raising her gaze to meet his. In a voice meant only for him, she asked, "How can I give my heart to someone else when it has been in your keeping from the first day I saw you at Hatchard's?"

Ignoring the others and with a feeling of triumph, the Earl of Shelburne wrapped his arms around the girl with the haunting blue eyes, all the shadows now gone.

Her uncertain heart now at ease, and with a deep sigh of contentment, Rebecca nestled her head against Shelburne's broad shoulder.

Home at last.